Sofia
Waves of
Change

By

Terry Biggar

Terry Biggar

Dedication

With immense love and gratitude, I dedicate these books to my beloved husband and cherished family. Your unwavering support and encouragement have been my anchor, propelling me through every challenge until the very end.

To my readers, I extend my heartfelt thanks for not only delving into each book but also patiently awaiting the release of the next. Your enthusiasm and anticipation have been the driving force behind my creative journey, and for that, I am truly thankful.

Acknowledgment

I extend my heartfelt gratitude to all my friends and family for their unwavering patience and steadfast support throughout the journey of completing this book series. Your encouragement has been my source of inspiration, and I am truly grateful for the understanding and encouragement you have generously showered upon me.

Thank you for being the pillars of strength that fueled my creative endeavor.

Table of Contents

Dedication iii

Acknowledgment iv

About the Author vi

SOFIA WAVES OF CHANGE .... **Error! Bookmark not defined.**

About the Author

As an author, I find inspiration in the simple joys of life. My wonderful husband and our adorable Yorkie are my constant companions on spontaneous adventures, particularly our love for impromptu cruises.

With a vivid imagination and a passion for writing, I've crafted a trilogy that begins with "Sofia Above the Clouds," inviting readers into a world where simplicity meets imagination. This book is 2nd in the trilogy. I hope you pick up the first one first.

Stay tuned, as the third installment is nearing completion. Join me on this literary journey of love, simplicity, and unexpected escapades.

SOFIA WAVES OF CHANGE

The phone rang; it was Ashton. "Good morning," He said cheerfully.

"Good morning," Sofia responded with excitement.

"We're on our way to get you. Are you ready yet?" Ashton asked.

Sofia replied quickly, "Oh yes."

"Great, we'll be there in a few minutes."

They hung up, and she gathered her suitcases and headed down to meet them.

Moments later... the black limo pulled up. Paul jumped out and opened the door for her.

He took her luggage and placed them in the back.

Ashton handed her a coffee once she was settled.

"Awe.... you read my mind, LOL. I only had one this morning! I was just so excited, I guess." Sofia adoringly said.

Ashton smiled. "Well.... Save your energy until we board. It's really another kind of adventure!"

Sofia sipped her drink and said, "I'm soo happy the flight is short, and the time is the same as here. It does get difficult when you leave in the morning...then arrive in the evening, LOL."

"I know what you mean. It screws up your system."
Ashton laughed.

They were not flying Exotic this trip...but for the first
time in Sofia's life, she was flying first class!

Just the first of many new experiences.

They soon arrived and went through security. Then they
found their gate.

There was a gigantic window, and Sofia wanted to sit
close to watch the planes as they took off.

That always fascinated her!

Soon they boarded… and were on their way.

Sofia had the window seat. She stared out, looking at the
clouds.

Thoughts of everything that's happened were playing
out in her mind.

The clouds seemed to soothe the moment.

The Hostess offered drinks and nice snacks. They had
their own bathroom.

Only the First class could use it.

Their seats were three times the size and went almost
flat back.

"This is a real treat!" she exclaimed to Ashton.

"Yes, it is. It's a lot roomier and more
comfortable,"Ashton replied.

"Lay back and close your eyes. The short trip will be over in a blink," he chuckled.

"I have a feeling you'll be awake till very late tonight. LOL," Ashton teased.

"OK," Sofia agreed. "Maybe I will."

Ashton leaned back in his seat and did the same.

They both awoke to the sound of the captain announcing that they were now

making their descent. He gave the weather report and mentioned a few highlighted

attractions in the area.

The seatbelt signs lit up.

Sofia shifted in her seat and gave her head a quick shake… to wake herself up.

"Wow... that was fast," she muttered.

Ashton just grinned. "I told you, " he replied.

She gazed out the window…and down on the sparkling water.

There were a lot of low clouds to pass through before they touched down.

Then… finally, the runway came into sight.

The plane, full of passengers, all applauded as the tires hit the tarmac.

Ashton pointed out to Sofia… the direction where they could already

see the cruise ships. "Oh, Yaa. I see them!   That's close!" Sofia exclaimed with excitement.

They were the first to leave the plane. The Airport was very busy.

They passed through security and out the main doors.

There was a shuttle there, waiting.

The trip to the ships was only 5 minutes.

They were dropped off at the main entrance and preceded to check-in.

There was such an air of excitement and anticipation.

People were dressed in all kinds of colorful travel clothing.

Big hats… and tropical shirts. It seemed appropriate!

They were guided to a waiting area… and had the option of having their picture taken as they entered. They thought it would be fun.

Since they were very early… they were allowed to board but couldn't go to their cabins for an hour or so.

Ashton knew there was a pizza place…where they could have a bite… and sit watching everyone else.

Enter the amazing ship.

Sofia's mouth dropped to the ground... as she walked through the opening.

No words...just an expression of disbelief! Sofia exclaimed, utterly impressed by the sheer grandeur.

Ashton put his arm around her and turned her towards the pizzeria. They found a table... and he went up and chose a couple of slices that were just prepared.

It looked delicious......and tasted even better! Then he went back to get them a drink.

"I thought we could just hang out here for now. We can watch people."

Sofia took a bite of her pizza." Mmm," she nodded. "It's delicious!"

"I know…. They always are." Ashton replied while adorably looking at Sofia.

"This place is so full of energy," she said. "The lights, the beautiful décor!" she continued praising the vibe.

"Well… This is just the beginning," said Ashton. "We've only stepped inside the door! Lol." He added.

More and more people entered the ship, most with the same reactions as Sofia.

"Pictures just cannot describe this," she retorted.

"Come on," Ashton said with enthusiasm as he stood up. "Let's start making our way to the elevators. They are a work of art as well!"

As they walked towards the elevators, Ashton explained, "You have a choice of regular or scenic elevators. The scenic ones are circular and made of glass. You can see each level as you move."

Sofia grinned and said confidently, "I'll choose scenic. I'm not afraid, LOL."

They rode up to the 12th floor, where their cabins were. The crew was just finishing up with their cleaning and allowed them to go in.

"Thank You," Ashton said to the crew. "We'll just wait outside on the balcony."

"Ok ... This is your cabin. Mine is the same, just next door." Ashton told Sofia.

"Oh wow.... this is gorgeous," she exclaimed.

Sofia went directly out to check out the view. There wasn't any yet.

The ship was still docked.

"You'll be staring out over the crystal blue waters very soon," Ashton assured her.

Ashton informed her that their luggage wouldn't arrive for probably another hour or so.

"That's okay," she shrugged.

And... he said, "We'll have to go down for a quick muster meeting."

"Everyone must go," He also explained it was a safety information session but will only take

half an hour or maybe less

"No problem," Sofia replied with a smile.

"This cabin is so nice!" she exclaimed once again.

She said while exploring the rest of the room, "A king-size bed too! This is perfect! There's lots of storage, I see. And look… A dressing table. Love it!"

They went next door to check out Ashton's cabin.

It was just the same.

"Perfect!" Sofia exclaimed, pleased with the setup of the room.

"They'll make an announcement when it's time for the muster meeting. Let's take a stroll outside." Ashton suggested.

They headed to the elevators and found where to go to get out.

"5th deck…that's it. There's a door." Sofia pointed toward the deck's door.

There was a gentle breeze as they found a spot to watch the other ships in the port.

They could hear talking over intercoms by crew members.

Soon, they heard the call for everyone to go to the muster areas.

No one is exempt!

They went back in and were shown where they should go.

The different decks had different areas.

They took a seat and listened to the captain's announcements.

Sofia was just so fascinated with the scenery, and watching the other guests,

she barely heard anything that he said, as there was so much to take in.

The captain was done speaking in no time and wished everyone a fabulous cruise.

"Ok....," Ashton turned to Sofia, "We are officially on Vacation!"

Everyone started getting up and leaving the area.

They decided to just sit and wait for it to clear out a bit.

"How about... we get ourselves a wine... or coffee... and go back to our cabins?" Ashton suggested.

"Our luggage should be there... and then we'll sit on the balcony... and watch as we pull away from the dock. It's cool to see..." Ashton told her. "It will be a while... so we can relax and decide what to do first."

"That sounds good to me!" Sofia replied.

"You know about cruising?" Ashton asked her.

"I don't, lol. I'm just going to follow your lead!" Sofia replied.

Just as Ashton thought… their luggage was at their doors.

"Ok… I'll just bring mine in…and then come join you." Ashton said to Sofia.

"We'll sit on your balcony and have our drinks," Ashton said with a smile.

"Sure…" Sofia agreed.

He opened her door for her and let her in, then went to his cabin.

Sofia was pleasantly surprised by how nice her cabin was.

It had everything she could possibly need.

There was even a king-size bed! Yes…...

There was also a nice dressing table where she could sit and do her hair and makeup.

That was perfect.

She set her luggage down and went out to the balcony.

There were about 4 other ships at the dock.

In the water, there were some small little boats that were the border security. They seemed to be putting on a bit of a water show.

That reminded her of Miami Vice!

She let Ashton in…and they sat at the table.

He explained what was happening and said it was cool watching each ship leave.

They were the largest ship. So, they would be leaving last.

"Ok…That's neat… We'll see the others leave," Sofia smiled.

"I'm already getting excited," Sofia added.

"By the time we set sail, we'll be getting hungry," Ashton commented.

"There's a quiet restaurant in the ship's park," Ashton suggested. "I thought it would be a nice spot to dine."

"Park? What park?" Sofia asked, amused. "Are we getting off the ship?"

"Nooo…The ship has a park of its own." Ashton exclaimed.

"Oh wow! She replied, "You never mentioned that before!"

Well…. there's a lot I haven't mentioned...I want you to be surprised! Lol.

They sat enjoying their wine… as they watched the action on the water.

After some time, the ships started to leave port.

One by one, with some having to do a big circle to turn in the right direction.

Once the others had left… it was then their turn.

Sofia barely even noticed any movement.

They stood at the railing and watched as they pulled away from the dock.

There was a large stream of people along the shore waiving and cheering them on!

"How exciting…..," Sofia thought to herself.

They waived back at the crowd.

Slowly… they approached the opening to the open seas!

"Cheers! We are officially on our Cruise!" Ashton yelled in excitement.

"Cheers!" Sofia rang out.

They tapped glasses. They could see the silhouettes of the other ships….as they all turned In the direction towards their destinations.

In the setting sun… it seemed almost mysterious. She took out her phone… and began taking pictures.

"Soo…. Are you getting hungry?" Ashton asked.

"Yes. …. I am very hungry! Lol," Sofia exclaimed.

"Ok then…let's say half an hour? That should be enough time to freshen up and change." Ashton asked.

"Perfect!" Sofia answered, "I'll meet you outside my door."

They both had their showers and put on something nice. Sofia tried out the dressing table. It was great.

She fluffed her hair... and a spritz of perfume.

And ready to go!

Ashton stepped out his door almost at the same time.

They headed to the elevators and picked a glass one.

She watched as they passed each deck.

When the elevator stopped.... They got off and went through a set of doors.

There.... they entered the Park!

"Oh wow!" Sofia lit up. "This is so beautiful! Look at all the flowers and greenery!" She added.

"Yes," said Ashton, "And they are all real!"

Sofia took in all the beauty and mentioned, "There must be a million plants in here! Lol."

"Well, not quite.... But there are a lot," he responded.

"Oh... there's our restaurant." Ashton continued.

Just down the pathway was a cozy Italian-style eatery.

The aroma was intoxicating the closer they got.

There was a handsome young man at the entrance, and he beckoned them inside.

He sat them at a table, looking out to the park. They ordered a wine each… and were given menus. Everything looked delicious.

Sofia ordered the Ravioli and Ashton the Linguini and meatballs.

They each shared a sample of each other's.

"Wow… I don't know which I like more!" Sofia said.

"You're right. I agree. Both are just awesome! Real Italian!" Ashton replied in awe of the food.

They finished their wine and headed out.

"So, I thought we could go down to the promenade," Ashton suggested.

"We can take a stroll and check out the stores and shops. Maybe not tonight… But most evenings, they have all these specials out right down the middle. Clothing, gadgets, souvenirs, etc. It's just a fun time. The place gets so lively." Ashton continued explaining.

"Oh, sounds fun to me!" Sofia laughed.

They reached the 5th deck…...and got off.

Most people were having dinner currently, but there was still enough around to make it feel like a shopping mall. Sofia liked that.

She was completely fascinated with the décor… and the whole ambiance of this ship!

"Everything is so gorgeous." Sofia praised the view.

They walked by the Barber Shop, and next was an English Pub, then a Camera store.

Sofia's eyes just kept moving!

They came upon a nice place…which was like a variety type store.

They had most there at the store if you forgot to pack your toothbrush… or any toiletries.

"That was great," she thought.

There were a ton of other products as well. They made a quick pass-through.

They spotted a café just ahead and stopped for a coffee. They were getting a bit weary.

After a long day, Sofia suggested they bring their coffee and a few pastries back to her balcony so that they could listen to the waves. Ashton thought that was a great Idea.

They entered Sofia's cabin…and went straight out to the table and chairs on the balcony.

"Wow…. listen to those waves…. I'll be sleeping like a baby tonight with this. I'll just leave my door open!" Sofia exclaimed.

"Great idea, I might do the same, lol," Ashton replied.

"That meal tonight was delicious…. We'll have to go back another time." Sofia commented.

"Yeah, I just loved my Linguini! It was perfect! Cooked al dente and so much flavor! But…there are so many places to try. You wait and see! Ashton excitedly told her.

Ashton also mentioned that most of their dinners would be in the grand Dining Room.

The other meals…they can spread themselves around! They finished their coffees and decided to call it a night. Tomorrow's another day. Soo much more to explore!

"Text me when you wake up," Ashton told Sofia.

They can decide where to have breakfast then.

Ashton kissed her good night and went to his cabin.

It didn't take long for those Caribbean Sea waves to take effect on both.

The next morning brought clear skies… warm breezes…and beautiful sunshine! Sofia awoke feeling refreshed and excited. She jumped up and went out to the balcony.

"What a calming view." She thought to herself, appreciating the soothing view.

The water glistened with the sunlight, which created sparkles in the waves.

Something she's never been able to see from 30 thousand feet!

She only touched the small waves of blue waters…while in Jamaica… but that wasn't quite adventurous.

The same as being out in the open seas.

She took her phone... and sent Ashton a text.

"I'm up! And I will be ready to go in 20 minutes! Meet you outside my door."

She ran… and got dressed. She put on her new pink shorts and top set that she had purchased in Italy.

It fit her perfectly. Then... her white running shoes.

She had also bought a sweet sun hat that went perfectly with everything.

Sofia picked up her sunglasses and purse…checked her phone….and headed out the door.

A minute later, Ashton appeared to join her.

"Morning!" He greeted her with a smile a mile wide!

"I take it you slept well?" He added, seeing Sofia in full form.

"OMG………..Just like I thought! Like a baby." Sofia laughed.

"Yeah, I never woke up once," Ashton added.

"Now I'm starving!" So, I thought we would go up to the Windjammer! That's the huge Buffett! You'll have so much to choose from, as much or as little as you'd like. We'll try and get a seat by the windows." Ashton suggested a rich and royal buffet breakfast.

"Sure…" Sofia spoke up. "Right now, I could eat everything I see, LOL!"

"Ok… The Windjammer it is!" Ashton said.

They hop on the elevator and stop at Deck 11.

A lot of people were in the area, all heading the same way.

"That's ok… there's lots of room." Ashton scanned the place to sit.

They entered the dining area. Sofia's eyes lit up.

"Wow, this is huge! Where do we begin? Soo many choices!" Sofia exclaimed.

Ashton smiled and said, "Just wander around and see what they have in each area. Then decide what you want. You can take a little of everything if you like."

"I'm so hungry… I just might do that! LOL." Sofia replied.

"I know what I want…so I'll go and get us some juice to start. I'll get a couple of different kinds." Ashton suggested.

"Sounds good." Sofia went off to explore.

Ashton found a table…and set some Juice down to reserve it. He knew what he wanted and headed straight there.

In moments, Sofia was back with her food.

"Mmmmm! Smells so good," she said as she sat down.

She had a variety of Bacon and eggs… Cottage cheese…and Crepes!

"I guess you are really hungry! LOL," Ashton commented.

Sofia asked between bites …" What plans do we have for today?"

"Well… I'm giving you the full tour!" Ashton replied.

"We are at sea today….and tomorrow we'll be docking at Cozumel." He continued explaining his plans.

"You'll want to get off, I'm sure! Not to shop or anything! LOL…." Ashton teased Sofia.

"Nooo, not to shop," Sofia laughed aloud.

"It's a good thing you're having a good breakfast! There's a lot to see!" Ashton continued talking.

"I would love to enjoy a nice hot tub later too!" Ashton said excitedly.

"I'm ready when you are," Sofia nodded.

"Let's go! We'll start at the Top!" Ashton said as they got on the elevator.

"This is where there are sports activities." Ashton showed Sofia around.

They walked around, following the running track, which he pointed out to her.

"It's so cool up here," she commented.

"Look, there's a mini-putt! Oh, I love those! Lol," Sofia said while admiring the mini-putt.

Next...they stopped and watched a couple of athletic young guys riding the wave machine.

"THAT! That was kind of funny," They both ended up tossed all over!

Carrying on...they came to a building-like structure, where they peaked inside and spotted the Bumper Cars!

"OMG," Sofia shrieked!

No way! I only went to one carnival in my life. I was about 7. All the kids were going crazy to ride them. They looked like soo much fun! I was never allowed on any rides at all." Sofia frowned.

Well.... We will go on all the rides you want! As many times as you want! We're just doing a quick tour for now.... But then you can choose whatever you like and enjoy all you want! We can come back all you want! I promise you." Ashton said to her, seeing all her sentiments flowing like a river.

Sofia nodded.... "Sounds great!"

"I'm very excited .....," she kissed his cheek.

"Ok.... let's keep going," Ashton replied, sensing her excitement.

They strolled along the running lanes to another area, where they could see someone floating in midair!

"Wow.... That's a SKY DIVING machine! Now.... That's awesome!" Sofia exclaimed.

"Yaa…that would be a great experience, I think." Ashton nodded.

"Most people could never skydive for real," Ashton said to Sofia.

"That's for sure!" Sofia agreed.

They stood for a few minutes and watched.

Just down away from there…. they came upon a HOT DOG CART!

They could smell them being prepared!

"Mmmm … Let's try one," Sofia nudged Ashton.

"Sure! I'm game." Ashton replied.

"Who says you have to be hungry, to eat a hot dog?.......NO ONE! LOL," Sofia retorted.

"It was soo good!" They both said it aloud, together.

It had been a while since either of them had one.

"Ok…Let's head down to the pool area…and have a tropical drink. It's getting very warm out here!" Ashton suggested.

"Yaa, you're right…...it is getting hot! To the elevator!!!!!" Sofia agreed.

There were lots of activities going on around one of the main pools.

Island-style Music was playing…people were dancing.

It was a competition for prizes. Lots of fun and sun!

They chose to sit in the shade and where they could feel the warm breezes of the sea.

Ashton went up to the bar…and ordered the drink of the day.

He came back with two large Bahama Mamas.

"Ohhhhh, I love those," Sofia said, picking up her drink.

"'Thank You…Looks awesome!" Sofia said to Ashton.

What a gorgeous day…. blue skies…and bright sun.

There was just soo much more to see.

Ashton suggested they take their drinks and carry on with the tour.

They headed straight down the path they were on…which took them into a huge Solarium.

It was massive, filled with plants, trees, and a Rain Forest-like feel. It was breathtaking.

You could lay in the sun…but without the heavy heat.

The solarium is climate controlled.

There were hot tubs…and a water fountain-style pool.

Right in the middle was a Healthy Eating restaurant.

Sofia and Ashton passed through, taking in the ambiance.

On the other side of the ship now…...they came across another pool.

This was a fantasy playland area for kids.

Fountains and wading pools. Even a hot tub.

They saw a lineup….and noticed there was an ice cream station!

Of course…they have to have one!

Perfect to cool down with.

"Ok…,"Ashton spoke up. "Enough walking."

"Time to take a break! Let's go change and hit the pool." Ashton suggested another fun activity to beat the heat.

They turned and went up to their cabins to change into their bathing suits.

Sofia put on her favorite two-piece suit.

It looked very nautical…. Navy and white, with a little pink.

She had a matching hand and cover-up.

Ashton wore a stunning black suit with a hint of silver and turquoise.

He had such a sporty look. Almost like a model!

They decided to go for that hot tub he was looking forward to.

Afterward, they would cool in the pool.

They picked up another tropical drink on the way.

"Awe…...now this is what it's all about," Ashton exhaled!

They sat quietly…letting the heat and bubbles work their magic!

Next…. the pool.

They swam for about 30 minutes, then relaxed in the shade.

As they enjoyed the view…watching all the excitement around, Ashton got a text from a friend.

It was Robin, who is the Cruise director on the Ship.

"Hey, Ashton! I just heard you were here! We must get together…. I would like to take you to dinner if I can. Let me know." Robin suggested a night out.

"OH wow!" Ashton smiled!

"What?" Sofia turned to him.

A good friend of mine is working on this ship! She must have transferred when they came out with this one.

"You would love her! She wanted to take us for dinner." Ashton told Sofia.

"Sure…. That sounds fine with me," Sofia responded.

Ashton sent a text back… "Sounds great! Where and when?"

"So… how did you meet Robin?" Sofia quizzed.

"Oh, we went to school together. We were in the drama club in the last year of high school. We kind of lost touch after that. You know…everyone tends to go their own ways with work and moving around. It was a lot of fun, though. She had such a friendly and cheerful personality. I'm sure that helped her to decide on being a Cruise director." Ashton told Sofia about Robin.

Ashton received another text from Robin, "I'll meet you at the Sand and Sea Restaurant…...6.00 PM."

"Perfect," Ashton replied. "See you there."

"Ok, so we have about 2 hours before dinner. I think I'll go up and relax a bit before getting ready. How about you?" He asked Sofia.

"Yaa… I could stretch out a bit…. Before I get ready." Sofia replied.

"Ok, let's go," Ashton said.

Sofia wanted to pick the right outfit to wear to meet Ashton's friend.

She brought a pretty pink dress…from Italy.

"Hmmm, I think this is perfect," She thought to herself.

She would pair that with her white pumps and a white beaded necklace, which also had hints of pink through it.

After a brief rest… she jumped in the shower, then did her hair and makeup.

It was nice to wash the chlorine from the pool out of her hair.

She wanted to wait till the last minute to get dressed.

She reached for a cold beverage from the bar fridge and sat on the balcony in her robe.

The sounds of the waves were mesmerizing.

Just then…. Ashton peaked around the corner.

"Hey…. You look refreshing!" Ashton commented.

Their balconies were attached.

"Oh... Hi! Come on over," Sofia snapped out of her thoughts.

She opened the door for him, and they went back to the balcony.

"Yes... I am doing great! A little rest…and ready to go."

"Me too. I'm excited to meet up with Robin…It's been a while! I know you two will get along great!"

"Well, she sounds very nice," Sofia responded.

They sat for a little longer; then, it was time to get ready.

Sofia changed into her outfit…It was very comfortable.

A light splash of perfume, and she was done.

She met Ashton in the hall, and they headed to the restaurant.

When they arrived, Robin was already there. She was talking to another young guy and a girl.

"Oh, there they are," she said, introducing them to Robert and Deny.

They are my Tour Guides. We dock tomorrow....so we're just comparing notes.

"Ok......so we're all set.... I'll see you in the morning." Robin said to the tour guides.

The two left.

"Come on... let's go in." Robin took the lead.

There was a beautiful table set up waiting.

There were appetizers… fresh bread…and a bottle of wine.

"Oh…. wow.... this looks awesome," Sofia commented.

They took their seats.

"Yes, it does!" Ashton said.

What a beautiful Restaurant!

"I know, Eh!" Robin replied. "I just love it. Wait till you try the food!"

They each had a menu…and looked it over. They all wanted the same.

The Seafood Platter! That was the most popular dish.

It has Lobster…Crab Legs…Mussels…and served with either Steak or Linguini.

Shrimp Cocktails to start.

"Now I'm hungry," Ashton laughed.

They all agreed.

"Soo Robin...How have you been? We lost touch after high school." Ashton started the conversation.

"Yaa, I know. I was very busy trying to find what and where I wanted to be in life! LOL," Robin replied.

"Well…. you know where I went, lol. It was exactly where I wanted to be." Ashton added.

"And… Sofia? Were you the same? Wanting to work for the airlines?" Robia quizzed Sofia.

"Yes…I have always wanted to be a Hostess since I was around 7, maybe 8. I only had a few short trips on a plane… but it left a major impression, I guess. It's wonderful being able to travel around now." Sofia smiled.

"Well, guys………Cheers to new and fond friends!" Robin yelled in excitement.

"CHEERS!" They all held up their glasses.

They each had a sip of wine.

"So we'll stop in Grand Cayman tomorrow! Are you two going to take a tour?" Robin asked the two.

"I know where you can find one, lol," Robin laughed.

"Oh… I'm not sure yet." Ashton looked at Sofia.

"We haven't thought about it. I'm still trying to give Sofia the Grand Tour!" Ashton replied after pondering over it for a bit.

Robin looked at Sofia, "What do you think of our newest Gem so far?"

Sofia rolled her eyes, "I'm completely in awe!"

"There are no pictures or words to describe this ship!" Sofia exclaimed in admiration.

"Well, you haven't seen it all," Ashton added.

"Oh…. Guess who the captain is?" Robin changed the subject.

"Victor Michela. He signed on the right from day one! We also have Riley Donavan as Head of the Medical crew. I've worked with them before. Also, Zachary Hayden is now Customer Service Special Guest Manager. He's always had such a pleasant calm demeanor, perfect for dealing with the public! Robin introduced the main people on the ship.

"It's nice knowing some of the crew ahead of time," Robin commented. "It makes adjusting a lot easier with these larger and grander ships."

They finished dinner and ordered the drink of the day.

A light, refreshing juice with rum and sparkling water.

The perfect way to end a meal.

"I think that was one of the best Seafood dinners I've ever had," stated Sofia. "Thank you for inviting us!"

"Yaa, I'm impressed too," Ashton added.

"I'm so glad you contacted me. It's really nice seeing you again!" Robin replied.

"Yet, the Head office notified me that you would be coming aboard. I told them I'd be happy to take care of you. LOL," Robin told them.

Sofia turned and looked puzzled at Ashton.

"That almost sounds like you are Royalty or something! LOL," Sofia teased.

Robin jumped in…. "He is almost here and one of our favorites! They sent a separate sheet of all the top shareholders when they brought me over. This company is soo much more active with its guests! They really like to show their appreciation. " Robin explained.

"Oh…and by the way, if you stay on for the second week….We have a suite reserved for you. You'll love it!" Robin welcomed them in for another week.

"A suite? Sofia inquired…" That sounds cool."

"Yes…. two bedrooms…. private hot tub… a huge deck…and it overlooks both the sea and the boardwalk." Robin sounded excited.

"Boardwalk? We haven't seen that yet!" Her eyes open wide!

"No, we haven't explored that area yet," Ashton stated.

"There's a lot you haven't seen," Robin answered.

"Ok. So, I'm beginning to see why the two-week cruise." Ashton exclaimed.

"Well…this has been great! Thank You again," Robin.

"Yes, Sofia added. "It's been very nice meeting you!"

"Same here, and it's been great to catch up with you, Ashton," Robin smiled. "We'll definitely get together again."

"Now…I think we should walk off our meals. We can go down to the Promenade and shop around." Sofia suggested.

"Sounds good to me. I'm stuffed. LOL," Ashton replied.

"And……I should go check on the staff and game plan for tomorrow. Let me know if you decide to take any tours or activities on the Island. Here's my card, with how to reach me." Robin handed over his card.

"Great Thanks," Ashton put it in his pocket.

They get up and head out the door.

"Ok, guys…enjoy your cruise. I'll be in touch soon." Robin waved.

"Yes… I hope so," Ashton waved back and went their separate ways.

"She seems so nice," Sofia commented.

When they reached the Promenade…Sofia got all excited.

There were pop-up booths lined up all down the center.

There were tee Shirts, watches, jewelry, cameras, gold by the inch…etc.

There was a gathering around each booth and lots of excitement!

All the other shops were open as well.

"Come on! Sofia pulled on Ashton's arm! "Let's each one of us get a gold chain."

"That's my kind of Souvenir!" Sofia exclaimed.

"They have Silver too. I think I want that instead." Ashton followed.

There were a lot of sizes and styles to choose from. They decided to get matching silver chains. They strolled along and stopped in a few places. Sofia picked up a bunch of hats for her friends. They both chose tee Shirts for themselves. One booth had the most beautiful bathing suit cover-ups. Sofia quickly chose a few.

She was all excited! And Ashton just stood back and laughed.

"This is fun," she shrieked!

They decided to take a coffee and relax on the balcony.

While they sat with their coffees... they also decided to take an early morning tour of Grand Cayman.

Ashton sent a text to Robin. She replied, "She'll have tickets sent to their rooms In the morning."

"What a beautiful evening, Sofia said, as she looked out over the dark waters.

There were just hints of water seen in the lights of the ship.

****

There was just a gentle breeze keeping them comfortable.

"Ok …, I think I'll call it a night." Ashton yawned as he stood up.

"We can have an early breakfast and go down for our tour." Ashton suggested.

Sofia nodded, "Yaa, that sounds good to me."

They said good night….and Ashton went back to his cabin.

The next morning, Sofia awoke and ordered coffee at her cabin.

She sent a text to Ashton to come over. It was early, but she took a chance. In case he was awake and he was.

She ordered enough for both of them. She also ordered some croissants and pastries, and bagels with cream cheese.

On a separate plate, she had soft-boiled eggs with slices of ham. They both loved their eggs that way.

Ashton arrived just as she finished laying it all out on the center table.

"Mmm, what have you done?" He asked.

Sofia smiled, "Do you like my little array of goodies?"

"Oh, yeah...this is nice! All our favorites!" Ashton licked his lips.

"I'm hungry! Now we don't have to rush... or wait at all. We're at dock... but it's nice we face the water ,"Sofia said.

"It's such a great feeling out here. Let's dig in! Smells wonderful! Sofia poured the coffee. Strong as she asked for.

"Mmm...I'm impressed! You outdid yourself!" Ashton started in on a bagel with ham and cheese.

Sofia went for the eggs and ham on a croissant.

"This is so much more relaxing and private," Ashton remarked.

"Yaa... I thought you might enjoy this." Sofia wiped the egg off her chin. "Besides... I make a mess when I eat, LOL, no one can see me here! LOL, I should have ordered some bibs."

"I could use one, too," Ashton laughed.

"So, we'll take a tour of Grand Cayman.... Then how about some shopping?" Ashton asked, Sofia's eyes light up!

"Yes.... I was hoping you'd be game for that." Sofia replied in excitement.

"Of course .... I'm always good at shopping too!" Ashton answered.

"Great.... I've become quite a shopaholic, LOL," Sofia chuckled.

"Yes, you are," Ashton laughs. "I'm guilty of that also."

"Later…I'll show you a really fun spot on the ship. We have so much more to see. And we're halfway through the cruise already!" Ashton said.

"Great, I can't wait! I just love it here. I don't want to think of leaving yet. I'm just in awe of this ship! The décor, the luxurious features…and all the activities. We haven't even tried out any of them yet. I'd like to try sky diving… and of course the bumper cars...and that huge water slide!" Sofia exclaimed.

"Well… we have a few more days…and then, if you want to stay. we will shift over to a suite. Then you'll be even more impressed! We'll have the chance to explore even more. "Ashton suggested.

"Ok…It's time to head down. I have our tickets. They actually came last night. Robin does her job well!" Ashton said.

"I really like her," Sofia said. "She's a lot like me."

"Hey... wait! Before we go, let's take some selfies. Let's stand by the railing, so the water shows. I want to send some to Maina! She'll be happy to see where we are. She can send them on to the others. I'll go through some of our other pix as well." Sofia said.

They posed in a variety of ways…and then headed down to the dock.

The tour guides were all there, holding up signs for the different activities.

Their guide was at the end of the long dock.

When everyone was present and accounted for...they then boarded the shuttle.

It was getting hot already, but the vehicle had great air conditioning.

The seats were comfortable too.

The tour lasted about 3 hours. There were a number of stops along the way, and Sofia made sure she picked up some cute little items for her friends.

The island was just gorgeous!

There are a number of beaches and places to see, but they decided to just do the tour and go back to the ship.

There was so much for them to do aboard.

Ashton suggested that they put their bathing suits on under their shorts, that way they could take a dip in the pool as well.

"I'm taking you down to the boardwalk today," Ashton told her. "I think you'll enjoy that!"

"Oh, great!" Sofia lit up. "Sounds fun to me!"

"We'll grab a snack while we're there. I'm getting a bit hungry." Ashton said to her.

"Yaa… I am too. We did eat a bit early." Sofia replied.

The elevator opened…and just around the corner they reached the Boardwalk.

Sofia's eyes opened wide!

"Oh…Wow!" She shrieked! "This is awesome!"

"Look…... A Merry Go round! I don't believe this!" She ran over and touched it.

"This is soo cool!" She said in amazement. "Let's get on!"

Ashton laughed, "Ok, let's go!"

He helped Sofia up and onto a horse.

It's not as easy as when we were younger! But…Ashton struggled, to got up and on. "Ok…… let's go."

The ride was funny to them. They felt a bit out of place.

Sofia looked at Ashton and broke out laughing, "Ok…, I feel like a kid again."

Soon they got off and stretched themselves out.

"That was fun…but maybe we should stay on the ground! LOL," They both chuckled.

"Oh…. what is that?" Sofia spied a little shop. "Is that a candy store?"

She turned and headed for the door.

"Mmmmmmmmmmmmmm! Now… this is for me! LOL, I love my candy! Come on… let's check it out!" Sofia simmered in the mesmerizing sweet smell of candies.

Ashton followed her in.

There had to be a thousand different types of goodies.

There were rows and rows of clear tubes filled with all sorts of colorful treats.

"I'm in heaven," Sofia's eyes circled the room. "Let's fill some bags! Lol."

They moved up and down the aisles, gathering everything they could.

When their arms were full …. they headed out.

"I've never bought so much candy in my life! LOL. This was so much fun!" Sofia jumped in excitement.

Just as they were leaving the candy store…. Ashton received a text message. It was his father. The look on his face told Sofia that something was very wrong. She watched as tears slowly filled his eyes. Ashton put his phone away after responding to his message.

"Can we go up to our cabin? I'm suddenly not in the mood for fun." Ashton said with tears in his eyes.

"Yes, of course," Sofia said to him.

"I'll explain when we get there. Let's get a coffee." Ashton replied, seeing the tension on Sofia's face.

They rode the elevator in silence.

They brought their coffees out on Sofia's balcony.

The tears came even more now.

Ashton struggled to speak without breaking down.

"That was my father. He said my mother had taken a turn for the worst," More tears ran down his face.

"Oh… I'm so sorry, Hun… I didn't know she was sick. You never mentioned your mother to me at all." Sofia replied in sympathy and confusion.

"Yaa… I'm sorry… she's been in remission for quite a while now. She has cancer." Ashton replied, crying immensely.

"Oh … that's too bad," Sofia wiped his eyes.

"Yes," Ashton sniffled. "She's still very young! Why her?" He shook his head.

He told Sofia that the message sounded like, "She is not very good at all! It's too soon!... "Ashton breaks down. "Too Soon! We were so close all my life. My father idealized her. What is he going to do?"

Sofia lost her composure. She was in tears and put her arms around him, and they both cried.

"You have to go to her," Sofia said with a firm tone.

"You have to be with her and give your father support. They need you now!" Sofia retorted.

Ashton looked at Sofia, "But…what about you? There are still 4 days left."

"I'm fine…. I'll go with you," Sofia replied.

Ashton stared at the ground, lost in thought.

"No…. This is something I must do myself. You are staying here. I'll have Robin take good care of you.

We have 3 hours... before sailing out. I don't want this to spoil your trip." Ashton said.

"OMG.... you're not!... but I understand. We could both leave... but I'll just go home?" Sofia suggested.

"No.... You stay and meet me in a few days. Right now... I need to concentrate on my mother." Ashton told her.

"Ok...," Sofia agreed, with tears streaming down her face.

Ashton called up to Robin. He told her he had to get off.

She was shocked... and said she'd be glad to check on the first flight out.

"Thank You," Ashton tried not to cry.

Robin informed the front desk and asked Zachary to find a flight.

There was one leaving first thing in the morning.

Ashton would have to leave the ship and get a hotel, so they made the arrangements.

"I'm so sorry, Ashton!" Robin said as she gave him the information.

"Thanks...can you please take care of Sofia for me? I don't want her to leave." Ashton humbly requested Robin.

"Oh, of course, I will! I'll seat her at a table with other people. I'll do whatever I can. Don't worry about anything." Robin replied in a comforting tone.

"Thank You, Hun. I appreciate all your help, and thanks for making the arrangements." Ashton thanked Robin before leaving.

"No problem…you just go and be with your mother. She needs you now." Robin replied.

When they hung up…. Ashton hugged Sofia…like never before. He broke down again.

Soon… he was running out of tears.

"I'm sorry he said. I never cry like this. Never!" Ashton said, wiping off his tears.

Sofia dried his face. Here sit and finish your coffee.

"Don't worry about me at all. I'll be just fine. I'll be back in four days. And if you're up to it, you can call me. You just take care of what is needed. My heart will be with you. I'll miss you." Sofia comforted him.

"Thank You…,"he attempted to smile. They both made an effort.

"So…. They have a flight for you. That's good. One less thing to think about. You'd better go and pack! You'll be pulling out soon!" Sofia said to him.

With that… Ashton slowly got up and headed to the door.

He hugged Sofia again…and said he'd stop and say goodbye before he left.

"I'll be here," she responded with a nod.

Sofia went back to the balcony where she sat staring out to sea. Her mind was reeling with thoughts. Her heart was breaking for Ashton.

Ten minutes later, Ashton was at the door. His face was solemn.

"I guess I'll see you in a few days…," he said as he left.

"I'll feel bad leaving you. Are you sure you're ok with this?" Ashton asked in a concerned tone.

"Yes…. Really. I have so much exploring to do. I'll keep myself busy. 'Sofia assured him.

Ashton hugged and kissed Sofia, "You're so understanding! How do I deserve you?"

"Just go and take care of your mom," Sofia told him.

"I'll text you when I'm home. Ok?" Ashton replied.

"Yaa…you better! I'll need your smile." Sofia answered.

They hugged again… and he turned and walked away.

Sofia knew he needed time alone. She felt so helpless. Maybe things will work out, and she'll be ok.

She decided to jump in the shower. Her face was streaky with all the tears. She'll just stay in now.

She felt a bit better after her shower. She went out to clear her mind.

The air was warm, but there was a gentle breeze. She closed her eyes and let the sea air steal her thoughts. There was a knock at her door. It was Robin.

"Hi … I hope I didn't disturb you?" Robin asked Sofia.

"No, come in," Sofia invited her. "Ashton left a while ago," Sofia told her.

"Yes …We were lucky to find a flight tomorrow," Robin told her.

They are usually filled by this time.

"I'm glad, too," Sofia commented. "He needs to be home. He must be on his way home now."

"Well…that's why I'm here. When Ashton told me you were staying on alone. He arranged for me to spend time with you." Robin informed Sofia.

"Is that ok?" Robin asked.

"Sure! That would be nice. Thank You." Sofia was grateful for Robin's gesture.

"So, I thought we could have breakfast together tomorrow, and Ashton thought you would love a real tour of the ship. A behind-the-scenes tour. How does that sound?" Robin asks.

"Oh…great! I'd love that. I don't want to put anyone out though," Sofia responds. "I'm okay alone too."

"Oh, I know…. I'll just be here to help guide you around and show you the ropes. We can have breakfasts together, and if you choose to get off, I can accompany you. Then, I'll go back and check on my department, and you can have any time you like for yourself."

Frank was very grateful when Ashton told him that you encouraged him to go home. He just wants you to enjoy the few days left.

"So… I'm at your disposal. Also, I added you to a table of 5 people for the dining room. That's if you don't mind. That way you are not sitting alone."

"No, that's fine," Sofia agrees. "I love meeting new people. Thank you."

"Okay…How about 8:00 AM. We'll go to the main dining room. The people at the table we sit at will also be there at the dinner as well. That way, you'll get to meet them beforehand."

"Sounds good," Sofia agrees. "I'll meet you there at 8:00 AM."

"Okay, good night, Robin. …. good night."

The next morning, Sofia was awoken by her phone. It was Ashton.

"Morning, Hun…Did I wake you?"

"That's OK, I have to get up now anyway for breakfast with Robin."

"I'm glad you called," Sofia yawned.

"Yaa… I miss you too."

"Well… I'm just glad Robin is there for you. She will take good care of you."

"Thanks, Ash…. I'll be fine."

"I'm more concerned about you!"

"You can call me anytime. I'm here for you, remember."

"Thanks … I need that."

"My flight leaves in a couple of hours. I just wanted to say thanks again. I needed to hear your voice."

"I know it's going to be hard on you," Sofia responds. "I feel so helpless. I wish there was something I could do!"

"I know. You have such a big heart. That's what attracted me to you."

"Well… remember… anytime you need a shoulder, I'm always here."

"I will."

"I'll let you go….and please enjoy the last few days. It will go by fast."

"I will, Hun. You take care …. We'll talk soon. Have a safe flight."

"Thanks," Ashton replies… "Talk soon."

They hung up, and Sofia got ready. She had time to have a coffee out on the balcony. This is a ritual she's been enjoying immensely. Her thoughts were with Ashton.

She met up with Robin outside the dining room and found their table. There were three people there. The other two decided to go to the buffet. Robin introduced Sofia, and they were happy for her to join them. Walter, Julia, and David were from Florida.

The man sitting next to Sofia, Walter, was around 55 years old. The others were about 60. They were all very friendly, cheerful, and welcoming. Robin briefly explained why they were there. She knew they would be the perfect people for her to meet. They were seasoned cruise ship travelers. They knew all the ins and outs of the ship. If Sofia had any questions, they could answer.

The conversations were light. Walter commented that they were all retired and spent three-quarters of the year on cruises.

"That's awesome," Sofia replied. "This is my first cruise… and I'm in love! I could live on this ship any day!" The group all laughed.

Robin got a text. "I'm sorry," she said and politely excused herself. She told Sofia if she needed anything, just to text her.

"Thanks," she replied…. "But I'll be fine. I'll talk to you later." Robin said goodbye to the table… and disappeared.

In one of the conversations, Walter mentioned how he rescues animals. Sofia seemed very interested. He told her a story about finding a poor puppy…abandoned in the cold. Mia…he called her, was starving and in bad shape. It looked like she was abused. As he was telling the story, he noticed tears in Sofia's eyes.

"Oh… I'm sorry, my dear…I didn't mean to upset you."

"It's OK! I still have her. She's a beautiful girl, and super spoiled LOL," Sofia wiped her tears and smiled. "That's great," she said. "I see you are a huge animal lover," Walter placed his hand on her arm. "That means you have a big heart."

Sofia said, "Well, I can't even watch those commercials about abused animals. I just end up crying."

"You sound like a wonderful human being!" Walter nods. "Well… you'll be happy to hear, that I have a huge property…and I take in any animal that needs any help. I give them the life they deserve. I work with lots of shelters, and rescue groups. They know where to find help."

"Oh… That's great," Sofia cheered up. "We need more heroes like you!"

Julia jumped in and said that help out with the pick-ups. She and David were Walter's neighbors. They were always close, from before his wife died. Suddenly Walter felt he had no purpose. We suggested that he followed his other true love. ANIMALS!

"It's been a godsend for him. Now he's very fulfilled."

"Yes, I am. I love life again!"

"Wow," Sofia shook her head. "You guys are awesome! Too bad, everyone wasn't like you."

"So...to change the subject, what are your plans today, Sofia?" Walter lifts the mood. "Anything in particular?"

"No... I thought I'd stroll around, get some exercise, then lay in the sun for a while. Later...Robin will be giving me a tour, behind the scenes."

"Oh great!" Walter says. "You'll love that."

"Yaa... now I think I should go walk off this breakfast, LOL," Sofia chuckled.

"Well... you enjoy. We'll be here for dinner. Hopefully, you'll join us," Robin said.

"Thank You. I think I will," Sofia replied.

"Great... We'll see you then!" Robin responded.

Sofia stood and wished them a great day, then headed out.

She went to the pool area and found a lounge chair. Her bathing suit was under her clothes, so she just removed her shorts and top and dove into the water. After swimming for a short time, she decided to soak in the hot tub. That... she found so relaxing. Now, she thought she'd just lounge in the sun. She needed some color.

Sofia half-drifted off and half went into thoughts of Ashton. How was he doing?... Was his mother okay? She wished she knew. Her heart felt so heavy. She picked up her phone... no messages. She laid it down.

It was really starting to get hot... so after an hour or so, she went back to her cabin. The air conditioning felt wonderful. Then… it was a quick cool shower, and into her lounge clothes. She ordered some light snacks and a pot of coffee. There was a beautiful breeze enticing her onto the balcony.

She had just sat down, with her snacks, when a text came through. She grabbed her phone. It was Ashton. It was a long message.

"Hi Sofia. Sorry again for just taking off. I'll make it up to you. I hope you're having fun, and Robin is taking good care of you. It's not very good here. I've never seen my father so sad and quiet. My mother is in bad condition and can barely speak. I feel so helpless. Really missing your smile right now. It's pouring rain here… sort of fits the mood. I'm soo glad I have you as my sunshine. That's what I think about. Anyway, you'll be back in a couple of days. There are so many people around, but I feel so alone. Enjoy the rest of the cruise, and I'll see you soon! I have to go now. Thinking of you…… XOXOX," Ashton's message read.

Sofia was in tears. She replied, "Soo sorry, Hun…. I am thinking of you. Can't wait to see you……… XOXOX."

She put her phone down. She felt the pain he was in. Her heart felt heavy. She shook it off and headed out. She'll have more time later to try and cheer him up.

The flight home was smooth. It was quicker as well, due to tailwinds. There was a text from Ashton. "I tracked your flight…. Paul is waiting for you outside. Welcome Home!"

"Oh…. Great! lol…. I was just going to call a taxi!" She collected her suitcases and went out the door. Sure enough…

there was Paul! She waved. He pulled up to the curb… and got out. "Welcome home, Sofia! You look wonderful! The Sea Breezes were good for you."

"Thanks, Paul…. I'm glad to be home. How is Ashton? Is he OK?"

"Very sad, Hun…. It doesn't look good for his mom."

"Yaa… that's why I'm glad to be here."

"That's nice of you, dear… he'll need you. I haven't seen him since I dropped him off at home."

"Yaa… I've only talked to him a few times. He's soo down. I'll be hearing from him in a while. Thank You for picking me up, Paul. I appreciate this."

"No problem, my dear…. I love seeing you." Paul helped her in with her luggage. "Just let me know if you need me. I'll be here."

"Thanks…. You're the best! See you soon…… take care."

"Bye."

Sofia dropped her luggage in her bedroom. She then showered and changed into her lounge clothes to settle in for the rest of the day. She put on half a pot of coffee and toasted a bagel. It was beautiful outside, so she brought her lunch onto the balcony. The view sure wasn't what she had been enjoying the last week but she was home.

With her feet up, she let the nice breeze wash over her. Ashton was on her mind. She didn't want to bother him, but was hoping he would text. After eating her bagel… she laid her head back and closed her eyes. She wanted to clear her mind and get some rest. With the comfortable chairs and soft wind, she was out like a light.

About an hour later, she was woken up by her phone. It was Ashton. "Hey Ashton…. How are you?" She asked cautiously.

"Oh… OK," he replied solemnly. "My mother has gotten worse, and it's just killing me."

"I'm sorry, Hun… I know it's hard."

"I miss you," he said.

"Yaa…. I miss you too. But you must be there for her. We'll get together soon," Sofia said with tears in her eyes. "I'm always here if you need me, OK?"

"Thanks …. I'm glad you stayed on and finished the cruise, but I'm glad you're home now. We will take another cruise, I promise!" Ashton stated.

"Yes, that would be great! I really loved it! Oh, and Thanks for the tour of the bridge… That was amazing! I met the captain too."

"Good," Ashton responded. "I was hoping he was available for you."

"Well… I'd better get back. I'll keep in touch. I'm not sure when They'll call me back to work. But I'll try and find out. Hopefully not for a few days. I don't want to leave you yet."

"Hmm, Yaa…... Let me take care of that," Ashton said. "I do have connections LOL!"

"Oh, Yaa… I wasn't thinking LOL," Sofia felt dumb. "I rather have you here," Ashton stated.

"OK… just let me know, so I know whether to pack again."

"I will. I'll get back to you later. I should go…. We'll keep in touch, O K?"

"Yes," Sofia agreed. "You take care, Hun…. We'll talk soon." They hung up.

Now that she was wide awake, she decided to make some popcorn and put on a movie. She needed something to take her mind off the somber mood and heartbreak.

"Oh… I should call Maina! She doesn't know I'm back yet." She picked up her phone and called. "Hey……Sofia! Where are you? Are you still on the ship?"

"No, I'm home," Sofia replied. She then told Maina all about what happened.

"OMG…. You are kidding! That's too bad." Maina replied.

"So sorry! I hope Ashton is okay." Maina felt bad for Ashton.

"He's not that good. I just talked to him. He is just so close to his mother. All I can do is listen and try to make him feel he's not alone." Sofia explained Ashton's situation to Maina.

51

"Hey.... are you working tomorrow? Why don't you come for breakfast? We can catch up more then." Maina inquired.

"I'm off for the next three days," Sofia replied.

Maina replied, "What time?"

"Let's say 9.00....is that OK?" Sofia suggested a time.

"Sure.... I'll be there," Maina said.

"Ok.... See you then," Sofia said.

"Talk to you later," Maina replied.

They hung up.

Sofia went back to her movie but found it hard to stay interested.

Her mind and heart were with Ashton.

She laid back and closed her eyes. Soon, she was off to sleep.

The next morning, she awoke to a text from Maina, "On my way....,"

She jumped up into the shower, dressed, and then started breakfast.

The smell of bacon filled her apartment.

The coffee was almost ready, and bagels and cream cheese as well.

Maina arrived just moments later.

"Morning! Morning!" Maina happily greeted Sofia.

"I'm sorry to hear about Ashton's mother. That must be very hard for such a young guy. Maybe she will be okay," Maina said hopefully.

"Yaa...," Sofia responded. "I hope so, too."

"Soo...what now? Do you have to go back to work? That's going to be hard, to be cheery and sweet to people when clearly, this is weighing on you." Maina suggested.

"I know. We'll see .... I haven't heard yet." Sofia replied, feeling exhausted from all the tension.

"Let's eat now! I'm starving!" Maina tittered.

"Me too!... smell delicious. Mmmmmm bagels!" Sofia revered.

The two ate enough for an army. It was so good.

They took their coffees out on the balcony.

They could feel a fall in the air, but it was refreshing.

"How are the guys doing?" Sofia asked.

"I haven't talked to them yet. I've been in a non-talk mood since I've been home." Maina replied.

"I have no answers, so I'm just waiting. Maybe I'll hear something today. Hopefully, something positive." Sofia said, looking at her phone and waiting for a text from Ashton.

"I think this calls for a shopping trip," Maina stated.

"Just to try and lighten the mood for a while. How does that sound?" Maina suggested.

Sofia bit her lip, "I don't know Maina….,"

"Just for an hour," she added, "Just, a quick break."

"Hmmm… Okay." Sofia agreed.

They cleaned up the kitchen and grabbed their purses. Then, out to the mall. Sofia wasn't in the mood but picked up a new purse.

After about an hour and a half, they headed back. Sofia kept looking at her phone.

She thought she might have heard from Ashton by this time, but nothing!

****

Sofia was unaware…. that his mother had been rushed to the hospital earlier that morning.

Ashton was now sitting by her side in a private room.

After spending a few hours with his wife, Frank left Ashton to be alone with his mother. He knew he needed that.

The doctors had worked extensively on her… but there was nothing more they could do.

Ashton knew her time was coming. He sat close, holding her hand.

His head was bent down, and the tears were flowing.

He listened to her shallow breathing. She was very pale-looking.

Her body was weak, and her face was sunken in.

This wasn't the mother he had seen just a week ago.

He whispered softly to her, not knowing if she could hear him.

"I wish you wouldn't leave me, Mom, but I understand. I don't want you to suffer anymore. I don't want you to be in pain. I love you so much! You're still so young! This shouldn't be happening to you. I need you," Ashton broke down in tears and squeezed his mother's hand.

"You'll always be in my heart, forever!" He cried again.

Her breathing seemed even more shallow.

"I promise to be the man you taught me to be. I'll remember everything you instilled in me. And…. I'll always take care of dad. Thank You for being my mom." Ashton cried heavily.

Ashton's tears were uncontrollable now. He knew the end was near.

He looked at his mother's face …. there was no sign of life. Her hand fell limp. She was gone.

Ashton sat for the next few moments, taking in his last glimpses of his mother's face.

He kissed her forehead and told her he loved her.

He then turned and walked away.

Frank was in the hall when he came out.

Ashton broke down in his arms.

Frank also broke into tears.

"Sorry, son.... we did everything we could. It was just her time." Frank tried to calm him.

"I know," Ashton sniffled, "I know she's at peace now. We'll meet up again one day."

Frank put his arm around Ashton. He held him close, "Come on.... there's nothing more for us here. Let's go home."

The two walked down the long hallway to the front of the hospital.

With their heads down and tears flowing, they never looked back.

When Paul met them at the curb, he knew it was over.

No one spoke.

They drove back to their home in silence.

Ashton went up to his room. He needed time alone.

He hadn't thought a lot about how things would be without his mom.

She had been doing so well. It just wasn't expected so soon.

He felt soo alone.

With a dull kind of headache... the kind you get from crying so much, he lay on his bed.

A million thoughts took over. He closed his eyes and fell into a deep sleep.

Downstairs, Frank was on the phone making the arrangements. He was able to keep composed enough to do so. His thoughts were now on Ashton. His heart ached, "He's going to need some time to absorb this."

No one was really prepared.

He was glad Ashton had found someone special, 'Sofia.'

Frank picked up the phone and called the office. Kyle answered.

He told Kyle what had happened and asked him to work around Ashton and Sofia for the next month.

He wanted Ashton to feel comfortable returning, which would take time. Sofia would help a lot.

Kyle gave his condolences and agreed with Frank. He knew how close Ashton was to his mother.

"Just leave it with me," he said, "I'll take care of everything for you."

Frank thanked him.

He sat back in his chair... in deep thought. He went over the events of the past week or so.

It just hit him.... That now, he was alone as well.

The tears came back. He cried.

A couple of hours later, Ashton came down the stairs.

"Are you okay, Dad?" He inquired.

"Yes, son…. And we'll be just fine. How are you?" Frank answered.

"I'm Okay," Ashton sighed, "I just took some aspirin, and I feel a lot better."

"Yes… we'll be just fine. We'll have a private service…as your mother requested. Then… we'll go out and have a wonderful dinner. It's arranged for Tuesday." His Dad walked him through the schedule.

"Ok," Ashton's sad eyes teared up.

"Hey…… How about we order a giant pizza and have a father-and-son night?" Frank tried hard to smile.

"Sounds good, Dad…... I think I'll have a shower. Just order whatever you like." Ashton tried to gather himself for his Dad.

"Ok……," and Frank picked up the phone.

After ordering the Pizza, Frank called the cruise line and arranged for Ashton and Sofia to spend two weeks in the best suite on the ship.

He wanted them to have the cruise they missed out on together.

Sofia was alone most of the week. They could carry on where they left off.

Hopefully, this will help Ashton's spirits.

When Ashton came back down... Frank mentioned what he had planned.

He managed to get a slight smile from his son.

"But.......," Ashton said.

"I'm willing to go, only if you join us! There's no way I'm leaving you here alone. Not so soon." Ashton demanded.

Frank was thrown off. He thought for a moment, then said, "You know?... Maybe I will. It's been a long time since I've gotten away. Maybe we should talk to Sofia too! We shouldn't assume anything without asking her. Maybe she has other plans!"

"You're right …. I'll call her after dinner," Ashton agreed.

The two of them enjoyed their pizza and remembered happy times.

They both knew they had to accept what happened and carry on.

When they were both full…. Frank said he was going to head to his room and watch a movie as it was a long day.

Ashton said, "Yaa...," and he would call Sofia.

"Ok…See you in the morning," They hugged.

Ashton poured a glass of water and stepped outside for fresh air.

He wasn't sure how to put it all into words…. But he made the call.

Sofia answered, "Hi, Ashton! I was hoping to hear from you! How are you?"

Well…he fought back the tears…. then explained what had happened.

"Ohh,, I'm soooo sorry, Hun," Sofia fought back her own tears.

"Are you Ok?" She asked anxiously.

"I'm Ok," Ashton sniffled.

"Are you free for breakfast tomorrow?" He asked.

"Of course!" Sofia replied.

"How about we go out? I'll pick you up around 8.00."Ashton inquired.

"That sounds great!" Sofia replied.

"I also have something to run past you. I'll call when I'm on my way." Ashton said.

"Ok, great," Sofia perked up, "It's great to hear from you."

"Yaa, I'm so glad to hear your voice, too," Ashton sighed.

"I really miss you. I'll see you tomorrow. I'll be ready." Sofia snickered a bit.

The two hung up. The butterflies returned, and Sofia felt better.

This was the first night she could sleep without such worry about Ashton. She needed to hear from him. She slept much better.

Morning came, and Sofia jumped into the shower.

She was excited to see Ashton again. She put on her favorite outfit and, of course, her favorite perfume.

She put her hair up with a beret... with the sides down. A little make-up and she was ready.

The coffee was ready, and she poured a cup. The apartment smelled so good.

It reminded her of the French café they enjoyed each day in France.

Soon, Ashton would be there, and she could hold him again.

Their time apart.... had enhanced her feeling to a new level. She couldn't help but smile as she sipped her coffee.

Suddenly she was snapped out of her thoughts by her phone.

Ashton was on his way! She put her cup in the sink and headed outside.

The air was crisp, and it was overcast. Winter was on its way.

Then……. the limo came into view. She could see Paul behind the wheel.

They pulled up to the curb, and Ashton jumped out and gave her the biggest hug yet!

She was filled with excitement! She gave him a giant kiss.

Ashton squeezed her hand, and they headed to a beautiful Restaurant.

They were both famished.

The waiter seated them, and they ordered their breakfast.

And coffee came first.

"I felt just awful hearing about your mom,"…. Sofia said, "How are you doing?"

Ashton just shrugged, "It was very hard to take," He responded, "I feel worse for my dad…. Now he's all alone. But…. We'll get through it."

"I wish I could help … you know I'm always here for you," Sofia tried to calm him down.

"I know you are, and that's all I need. You always make me feel good. So…. I have something to ask you. Well……... My father thinks I should take some time to get over our loss. He thought you and I could go back and take that cruise again! Would you be interested?" Ashton opened up to her about his Dad's suggestion.

"Ohhhh, I'd love to...but I think I have to get back to Exotic! It's been awhile now. I'd hate to get fired!" Sofia exclaimed.

Ashton paused, "What if I told you my father had taken care of that? He's arranged for you to be off for the next month, with pay, of course."

"Really...... Are you serious?" Sofia looked shocked.

"Yes," Ashton replied.

"This was all his idea. Now...I told him that he must come as well, though. There is no way I'm leaving him home all alone at this time. It's too soon. It was my mother's love of the sea and cruising that he invested soo much in stocks. He went a bit crazy, LOL. They also have been on about 100 times, maybe more." Ashton told Sofia how much her Dad adored his mother.

"For a while there, I thought they were going to live on board. Anyway..........Would that be ok with you?" Ashton asked for Sofia's decision.

"OMG... Sounds awesome, Hun! This will definitely help you feel better. I would have stayed for the second week if you were with me. So... to answer your question?......YES!" Sofia replied excitedly.

"Great," Ashton smiled, "I think it's time for new beginnings."

Their breakfast came just as they toasted their trip. Both were starving now.

"This is fabulous!" Sofia raved, "Best food... Best company!"

"Ohhhh, Yaa......I'm stuffed," said Ashton.

"Your coffee is better, though." Ashton liked her coffee more.

"OK...how about I make you some? We can go over the trip at my place," Sofia suggested.

"Sure .... Let's go!" Ashton replied.

They finished and headed back to Sofia's.

They ran into Lenora in the hall.

Sofia introduced Ashton.

"I promise I'll have you over for coffee this week," Sofia apologized, "It's been a crazy time lately."

"No problem," Lenora replied, "I know you're busy."

Ashton got a text message. It was his dad.

"Excuse me, Ladies....," and he entered Sofia's apartment.

Sofia then entered as well.

"My dad just texted me.... the funeral is on Wednesday. She just wanted a short, simple, private service. Will you come with me?" Ashton's eyes teared as he sat down, "I know you didn't know her....but It would make me feel better."

"Of course, I'll be there for you. This cruise…. I'm a little nervous about going with my boss, LOL. Maybe he'll get sick of me and let me go!" Sofia expressed her nervousness.

"Nah…... he won't be with us much," Ashton laughed, "He knows almost everyone and will visit the departments with the business heads. He'll let us know the details soon." Ashton tried to relax her.

"Ok…I'll make coffee. I'm just happy to see you and spend some time together! We'll get through this. I promise," Sofia gave him a kiss, then a big hug.

"I have an idea…...," Sofia hesitated.

"If there's time, between the funeral and the cruise…. How about we get together with the group? It's been a while since we've seen them. Ricky called yesterday and said we are overdue for a night out. He sends their condolences." Sofia explained the plan.

"That may help take your mind off what's happening. How would you feel about that?" Sofia asked him again.

"Actually…. I think that would be great!" Ashton perked up, "I really want to get to know your friends as much as I can. I want them to know me better as well."

"Great….I'll call them as soon as we get the details from your Dad," Sofia replied.

"MMM, this coffee is delicious!" Ashton commented.

Just then… his phone rang. It was his dad.

"OK…. As I said, the funeral is Wednesday." His father said.

"A week Friday, the cruise. Two weeks. I booked two suites… You and Sofia have two bedrooms with a large balcony and hot tub. I have my own." His father explained the plan and bookings.

"Wow," Ashton responded.

"That sounds great! Sofia will love that! Thanks a lot, dad…... You're the best!" Ashton jumped in excitement.

"I'm just happy to hear you excited," Frank replied, "Talk to you soon."

Ashton filled Sofia in. She was shocked!

"That sounds Fabulous! I'll call Maina….and have her organize a night when everyone can make it. We'll go to Alexanders!" Sofia replied.

"OK, Great!" Ashton smiled. He gave Sofia a kiss and said, "Thank You."

"For what?" Sofia looked puzzled.

"For being here… for being you." Ashton replied.

They embraced.

"If you don't mind… I think I should spend a couple of days with my dad.

I know he's very heartbroken. He needs me." Ashton asked Sofia.

"Oh, of course! You should be with each other right now. You can text me as much as you want." Sofia replied, sensing Ashton being worried.

"Thanks for understanding, Hun. Let me know about the get-together! I can't wait," Ashton gave Sofia a long kiss.

He turned and headed for the door.

"Talk soon!" Ashton waved at her.

"Yes…. I'll text you the night when I hear. Give my condolences to your father." Sofia replied.

Sofia poured another coffee. She grabbed her phone and called Maina.

There was a big yawn… as she answered.

"Morning Sofia…. How are you?" Maina asked.

"Oh… I'm sorry, did I wake you up?" Sofia replied.

"No, Hun, I woke up 5 minutes ago. I worked till 3 AM. There was a big accident. Luckily only one fatality. It could have been worse." Maina explained what happened.

"Oh wow…," Sofia said, "That's horrible!"

"Ya… I never get used to these things. Anyway…. How's it going with Ashton? I feel so bad for him. His mother was still very young!" Maina inquired about Ashton.

"I know… he's taken it hard. But…. We'll work through it. I'll be there for him." Sofia replied.

"You're always so helpful, Sofia. Everyone knows they can count on you." Maina replied.

"Well…they can. I love people." Sofia said.

"What else is new? We've both been busy." Maina asked.

"Yaa… I know," Sofia replied, "Ashton and I would like to get together with everyone. It's been so long. Can you call the gang and find a night? As long as you have the time." Sofia asked for Maina's assistance.

"Oh … certainly! I love our group get-togethers! YAY!!!!" Maina replied excitedly.

Sofia laughed, "Geez... how did I know this? That's great, thanks. We have a lot to catch up on."

"Yes, we do….I'll get to it this afternoon." Maina replied.

"It has to be between this Friday….and next Wednesday," Sofia told her, "The funeral is on Wednesday…and I'll explain the rest later."

"Ok…," Maina sounded curious, " I won't ask! LOL."

After a brief conversation, Sofia let Maina get back to her day.

This seemed as good as any to invite Lenora over.

She went a couple of apartments down and knocked on the door.

Lenora answered with a smile.

"Hey…Hi Lenora…. I have some time if you want to come by!" Sofia asked.

"Hi, Sofia... sure... I'll be right there." Lenora replied.

Sofia made a fresh pot of coffee.

Lenora was there in no time. She was carrying a small pet carrier.

"I hope you don't mind.... but I brought my puppy MIA." Lenora said.

"OMG.... She's beautiful!" Sofia squealed!

"I love her coloring too. Can I hold her?" Sofia asked.

"Sure...," Lenora replied.

Sofia picked her up out of the carrier.

"Aw... she is such a cuddly puppy. Look.... she kissed me!" Sofia fell in love.

"I would love one of these, but I'm always on the go. My heart just melts." Sofia held the puppy close while they got more acquainted with each other.

She learned that Lenora was a widow... she had quite a bit of money, her husband was a veterinarian, and she loved to travel.

Sofia had great vibes from her. She is sweet and caring. Just a wonderful person and a new friend.

Sofia gave her a brief rundown of her life, too.

Lenora said she loved to fly, cruise, and shop!

Sofia laughed.... "That sounds like my life, LOL,"

Lenora also wanted to be an Airline hostess… but when she got married, it kind of got lost in the mix.

Her husband came first…. And, of course, their pets. They were both huge animal lovers and made huge donations to Shelters and Rescues!

"That's awesome," Sofia hugged Mia.

"I would love to open a rescue….and help all those poor animals. My heart breaks when the commercials come on. I have to look away. It kills me to see abused animals. I cry!" Sofia became very emotional.

"Yaa… Me too," sighed Lenora, "My husband was the same. He gave and gave to any shelter he saw."

"What a great man!" Sofia told her, "No wonder you loved him sooo much!"

"Oh, by the way," Lenora changed the subject.

"Your friend Ashton…... He's a real cutey! He seemed very pleasant. Are you very close?" Lenora inquired.

"Yes…," Sofia responded, "I care about him a lot!"

"Well… you look like a beautiful couple!" Lenora adored them.

"Yes… I'm so lucky to have found him." Sofia blushed.

"Hey…..My friends are getting together soon. Would you like to join us? They are all very professional, decent, fun, and loyal. No wild and crazy parties or heavy drinking. I think you'd fit in well with us. You'd love them!" Sofia invited Lenora to the dinner.

"Oh… I don't want to impose," Lenora replied.

"Noooo really…. You come out once…. you'll be hooked on us all LOLOL," Sofia chuckled.

They both laughed!

"Well... OK. Let me know when," Lenora agreed.

"I will…… we do have fun. And it's better than sitting alone. Oh… My friends Ricky and Fred also have a Yorkie. Her name is Moka. She's such a sweetheart; maybe Mia will like a friend!" Sofia suggested.

Lenora laughed…., "Yaa… maybe she would!"

"More coffee," Sofia offered.

"Ok… just half a cup. I have to leave soon for the groomers. Mia really needs her nails trimmed and a good bath. I love it when she comes out! She smells like a baby!" Lenora laughed in awe.

"Awe………," Sofia sighed.

"Well…. It was about time we met formally," Sofia stated.

"I'm so glad I had the time. I'll be leaving again soon," Sofia added.

"Yes," Lenora nodded, "I'm glad we had this chance,"

"And…... Please bring MIA over whenever you come. I'm in love now. She's always welcome," Sofia said.

"Thank You," Lenora smiled, "She's really my only family now,"

"Awe…... maybe we'll be like family to you soon. That's how we all feel about each other. Everyone needs close friends in life. You don't have to be alone," Sofia exclaimed.

"Sofia…. you really are a wonderful person. You have a heart of gold. I think we WILL! Become great friends," Lenora stated.

"I'm sorry to leave… but I'd better get to the groomers. This was great…. Just let me know when your get-together is. Maybe it's just what I need," Lenora added.

"I will……take care…and I want to see MIA when she's all beautiful and fluffy, too, LOL," Sofia replied.

Lenora laughed, "OK…. Talk later"

After Lenora left, Sofia cleaned the kitchen and then went to start packing.

The cruise was in a week and a half. She also wanted to make sure she brought some really nice, dressy clothes as well.

Frank Davis was going to be there. Who knows what he might plan?

She'd better prepare for everything.

There were two beautiful outfits she bought in France. She pulled them out.

They were perfect for any elegant dinners or events.

Channel #5….and Y'satis will be her perfumes. They are her favorites.

Sofia picked up her phone and made an early morning appointment.

With the hairdressers. Monday...8.30 am.

She wants to look good for the cruise and Frank.

She never dreamt she'd be going on a vacation with her boss.

Ashton may have also been a factor as well.

Sofia's phone rang. It is Maina.

"Hey...how about Tuesday? Everyone is good that day," Maina inquired.

"Ohhh ...great! That's just perfect!" Sofia replied.

Sofia called Ashton......and Lenora. She was thrilled everyone could make it.

Her friends were very important to her. They were her only family.

She felt so fortunate to have found such decent people.

The next couple of days... Sofia went through her wardrobe and finished choosing what she wanted.

She also picked an outfit for the funeral.

The next day was Wednesday. She knew Ashton would be needing her.

She'd never been to a funeral before. That made her nervous.

Ashton called and said that he would pick her up around 9.30.

Service was at 10.00 am. It was being held at the church they belonged to and with only a small group of friends.

Afterward…a celebration of life at her favorite restaurant.

"I'll be ready," she replied.

The next morning, Paul showed up right on time. Ashton and Frank were in the Limo. Ashton met her at her door and hugged her tight. Tears were in his eyes. She wiped them away.

"It will be Ok," she said.

They reached the church and went in.

The ashes of his mother were there, encircled by the most exotic flowers.

Ashton whispered to Sofia that her wishes were not to be buried and instructed Frank to keep her and place her someplace peaceful and beautiful.

Sofia thought that was so sweet.

She stared at the flowers throughout the whole service.

It wasn't too long…and they were off to the restaurant.

There was an elegant spread of seafood and salads and fancy desserts.

Frank mentioned to Sofia that it was her love of the sea that he chose the menu.

It was his wife that started him into cruising, and that's what gave him the Idea of buying so much in stocks.

"She was very smart!" He stated.

"Ohh... So that's how Ashton got to take so many cruises! Now I see," Lenora teased her.

"Well...that was a great choice. I fell in love after just one cruise. I'm so excited about next week," Sofia blushed.

"I am, too," Frank nodded, "I think Ashton and I are overdue for a nice getaway....and not for business."

"We need to just relax and enjoy ourselves. Are you sure you want me on this trip, Frank? Maybe you'd rather have some father-and-son time?" Sofia suggested.

"Oh no, dear.... If anyone can cheer Ashton up and get him over his sadness, it's you. He needs someone his own age. I'm so glad he has someone like you in his life." Frank trusted Sofia.

"Well...thanks...I'll try my best. I think the world of him. We have a great time together." Sofia agreed.

Strange to say....the celebration was beautiful.

The food...the people... the music.

Ashton seemed to lighten up, and maybe it was just the closer.

His mother was at peace now... and maybe he can slowly feel better and carry on.

While Frank and Ashton spoke with some of the guests….Sofia went over all the nice comments.

She heard Frank talking to someone about his wife's love for cruising. The sea was her favorite place.

The sounds of the waves and salt air gave her peace. Ashton came over and gave Sofia a kiss.

To her surprise…. he smiled.

"Sorry if I've left you alone too much," he apologized.

"Oh no… I'm just fine," Sofia replied.

He took her hand, and they went over to where his mother's urn sat amidst the array of flowers.

They stood in silence.

They turned and headed to the refreshments, where they poured two coffees.

They took a seat at one of the tables. Frank came over and joined them. Suddenly, Sofia turned and looked at Frank.

"I have a great Idea, Frank! Maybe it's not my place….and maybe you have other plans, but……. What if we bring the ashes on the cruise? You and Ashton can sprinkle them into the sea. I heard you say that's where she always felt at peace," Sofia suggested.

Frank sat for a moment…. Ashton turned and looked at him.

Neither one spoke.

Then....

"You know.... I think that's a wonderful idea! She would have loved that!" Frank agreed.

Frank turned to Ashton. I think you have a very smart girlfriend.

"Why didn't I think of that? Thank You, Sofia.... That's what we'll do." Frank said to Sofia.

The celebration was coming to an end now.

Frank excused himself and went to say his goodbyes to his friends as they were leaving.

When everyone was gone.... They, too, left for home.

The ride was quiet until Frank spoke out.

"You know Sofia... the more I think about your Idea.... The more I love it! Thank You for that." Frank appreciated Sofia's thoughtfulness.

"Well... I kept hearing how much she loved the sea. It only makes sense. That's where she'll be happy!" Sofia replied empathically.

"Yes,.... Very true!" Frank nodded.

They reached Sofia's apartment. They said their goodbyes.

Ashton and Sofia stepped out, and Ashton closed the door.

He gave her a huge hug and kiss, "Thank You,"

"For what," Sofia asked.

"Thank You for being here today. It really helped me a lot. And… I think my father thinks a lot of you too! We're going to have a great trip together," Ashton thanked Sofia.

"I think so too now. I was worried a bit… but I'm OK. Call me later Ashton… when you're free. Now… I'm looking forward to our get-together," Sofia replied.

"Oh, Yaa, me too," Ashton smiled.

"Spend tonight with your dad. Everything will be OK." Sofia advised him.

"You're the best, hun! You have a good night, too. I'll call to say good night," Ashton replied.

They hugged again, then the limo drove off.

Sofia headed to her apartment. It was quite a day for her. She jumped in the shower and into comfortable clothes.

She was so glad it was over. Now, check in with her friends.

Sofia called Ricky and Fred…...she just felt the need to talk to those guys. She needed their warm and caring hearts and the security she always felt with them.

Fred answered, "Hello?"

"Hi, sweety…. How are you guys?"Sofia answered.

"Oh hi, my love… We are good! We are looking forward to seeing you. You've been so busy." Fred asked concerningly.

"Yes.... Sorry. It's been a bit of a trying time. Hopefully, things will get back to normal soon." Sofia replied.

"Hey....," Fred said, "We reserved our favorite corner at Alexanders,"

"Oh that's great! I never even thought of that! And.... We have one more guest. My new neighbor, Lenora, is coming. She's alone, and I thought she could use some time with some great people," Sofia said excitedly.

"You're such a kind soul, Sofia.... always looking out for people in need," Fred replied.

"Maybe that's why we love you so much!" He added.

"Awe... thanks Hun...It just comes naturally to me. I love helping anyone when I can," She said.

Sofia also told him about MIA.

"I think you two should get your puppies together for a play date. We'll have them meet one day soon," Sofia said.

"Anyway... I think you'll really like Lenora! She loves wine, too. Ricky will love that, LOL," Sofia chuckled.

"So..... I'm glad everyone can make it Tuesday. I'm excited even more now that the funeral is over.

Give Ricky my love... and we'll see you then," Sofia said.

"Yes....and again, give our condolences to Ashton. We'll do our best to cheer him up," Fred replied.

"Ohh I know you will," Sofia agreed, "You always cheer me up! Talk later……Bye."

Sofia ordered Chinese food from her favorite place.

3 Egg rolls….Beef Chow Mein and Honey Garlic Ribs.

She loved Ribs. She put on an old comedy and waited.

Angel called, and she invited her over.

Sure… but just for an hour or so.

"I must go take an exam this evening. I hate it when they do this at night! My brain shuts off at 7.00 PM, LOL," Angel said frustratedly.

"Oh well… I'll be there in a few minutes. I'm not far from you," Sofia tried to calm her down.

Sofia put on the coffee, a strong coffee.

"It's great to see Angel," she thought.

She had missed a couple of get-togethers because of Dental school. Soon, she'll be a full-fledged Dentist. That will be wonderful for her. She can open her own practice and make her own hours," Sofia thought.

Angel showed up, and the two of them hugged!

"I'm so glad you can make it on Tuesday …... We're going to have fun," Sofia jumped.

"Yes," Angel agreed excitedly!

"I'm looking forward to seeing the gang. I miss everyone," She said.

They quickly caught up and relaxed with their coffee.

"Mumm this is just what I need tonight, Sofia!" Angel gasped in awe.

Strong coffee and a moment of peace and quietness.

"I'm so sick of this heavy traffic. It takes so long now to get anywhere. It's loud and nerve-racking," She closed her eyes and sighed, "Maybe I'll just stay here, LOL,"

"Sure, anytime," Sofia offered, "But get your degree first!"

"OK…. With that… I think I'll leave now. I don't want to be late," Angel headed for the door.

The buzzer rang.

"Ohhh there's my food! I'm starving!" Sofia said excitedly.

"Oh, Yaa… just because I'm leaving! Thanks! LOL," Angel teased.

"I'll let him in on my way out," Sofia replied.

They hugged goodbye… and Angel left.

"GOOD LUCK….," Sofia yelled down the hall.

"THANKS, HUN….," Then she was gone.

The food was at her door.

Sofia ate as much as she could eat…then put the leftovers in the fridge.

"Wow…that was good," she thought to herself!

"Now… I'm done for the night. It's been an emotional day," She curled up with a good book and fell asleep.

The next thing she knew….it was morning.

It seemed a little extra bright for the time, though.

She jumped out of bed to find snow on the ground!

"Oh…...cool," she thought. It looked so pretty. Now she had an excuse for shopping! Not that she really needed one. She needed a new pair of boots.

The ones she had were more for fall, and her other boots were worn out.

She made the coffee and got dressed. At least there were only a couple of inches. Her shoes would be just fine.

She made her way to the mall and right to her favorite shoe store.

After exploring all the choices, she chose a dressy pair and a casual one; her favorite ones were the little shoe boots with fur trim.

As she wandered around in other stores, her phone rang.

It was Ashton.

"Hi, sweety…. what are you doing?" She answered.

That morning, he responded, "I'm just having my coffee."

"Well…. I'm at the mall. With all that's been going on, I forgot winter was coming, and I needed some new boots.

It's actually beautiful outside. Not too cold. It's rather nice out for November.

It looks like all the stores are getting ready for Christmas now! I love it!"

"LOL…,"Ashton laughed, "You're just like a kid! It's so refreshing."

"Yaa… I know," She replied.

"So, we have received the brochures on the ship. Are you going to be home soon?" Ashton asked.

"I'm just leaving now," Sofia answered.

"Great! How would you like some company? You can see the cabin we're staying in. It's the same ship we were on, too!" Ashton replied.

"Oh…. Awesome! Maybe we'll see Robin again! I loved her," Sofia assumed.

"Yaa... we might," Ashton responded.

"OK… I'll be there in an hour," Ashton said.

"I'll see you then," Sofia replied.

They hung up. There was a note of excitement in his voice that made Sofia feel good about it.

Perhaps this could be the start of a new chapter in their lives. She'd concentrate on keeping Ashton feeling positive and happy.

As soon as she got home…. She put some coffee on and freshened up.

The new boots she bought were just adorable. She put them in her closet.

She called Yvonne and made arrangements for her to look after her place again, and Yvonne agreed.

"Thank You," Sofia said gratefully, "sorry to bother you so much."

"Oh, no problem, Hun. You know I'm here anytime." Yvonne replied.

"Well… as long as I don't become a pain for you, LOL. I really appreciate it. Maybe I should switch to artificial plants! LOL," Sofia chuckled.

Yvonne laughed.

****

Ashton was at her door. Sofia greeted him with a big hug.

"Hey…. come in! The coffee is ready." Sofia invited him inside.

"I can smell that European aroma!" Ashton smiled.

We'll have to go back to France and Italy to restock soon, LOL." Ashton teased.

"Oh…That would be awesome," Sofia's eyes lit up.

"Soo…. I have our itinerary here." Ashton laid out the papers.

"It looks great! Two weeks and 6 Islands." Ashton explained the plan.

"Wow…," Sofia looked up.

"That sounds perfect! Maybe we'll get some color? That also sounds like a big shopping spree! LOL," Sofa jumped in excitement.

Ashton laughed, "I'm sure it will!"

"Maybe we should have Paul meet us halfway and pick up what you purchase until then, LOL," Ashton teased her again.

"Funny…. I'm not that bad….Am I? LOL," Sofia asked.

Ashton looked down to avoid answering, "What? Did you say something?"

"You heard me," Sofia giggled, "Never mind,"

"Anyway, this trip sounds like heaven. My father is even excited. And…Thank You for that suggestion about spreading my mother's ashes in the sea. That was perfect." Ashton praised her.

"So… look at these pictures. This is our suite! It's so big! Two bedrooms and a personal hot tub. It's like a small apartment!" Ashton gave her a virtual tour of the suite.

"Oh…that looks beautiful, Hun! Look how big our balcony is! We may never want to leave! LOL," Sofia laughed.

"Don't laugh…. we could stay forever, LOL," Ashton smiled.

"Anyway, I'm looking forward to our get-together, and then the trip. I need this right now." Ashton was ready for the fun.

"Well… We're going to have a great time and enjoy the adventure!" Sofia replied.

The two of them went through all the details and then sat back with their coffee.

"It's so nice to see you smile again, Ashton. That makes me happy." Sofia contentedly said.

"Yaa… I've decided to accept what's happened and go on. My mother wouldn't want me to be depressed for too long. She'll always be in my heart." Ashton became emotional.

"That's right," Sofia hugged him, "I'm here for you as well."

"Yes… You are! I'm so grateful for that." Ashton replied.

"So… what time are we meeting on Tuesday?" Ashton asked.

"I think 6.00 PM," Sofia replied. We can go a bit early if you want; our table is reserved. We love that back corner with the fireplace." Sofia told him.

"Perfect!" Ashton nodded.

"Don't tell the others, but I'd like to pick up the tab for everyone," Ashton said.

"Oh…Hun…you don't need to do that?" Sofia murmured softly.

"I know, but I want to. They are your family." Ashton replied with affection.

"What am I going to do with you? Sofia shook her head, a fond smile creeping onto her lips.

"You do too much!" Sofia exclaimed, her tone a mix of gratitude and amusement.

"Nah…You're worth it," Ashton warmly replied.

Sofia shook her head again," Maybe one day I will find a way to reciprocate!"

"Noooo… just be you! That's enough," Ashton said while adoring her.

"Hey… would you like to go to a show tonight?" Ashton inquired.

"That sounds good," Sofia said.

"OK… I'll check to see what's playing," Ashton googled the theaters.

"Well, there are a couple of good movies; I'll let you decide. They start at 7.00 Pm. How about we grab a hamburger before we go?" Ashton suggested while scrolling through his phone.

"Sounds good," Sofia answered.

"OK….I'll go home and change, then come back to pick you up. How about 6.00?" Ashton asked.

"Great," Sofia nodded, "I'll be ready!"

The limo pulled up right on time, as usual.

Sofia ran out, and as Ashton got out to greet her, she grabbed him and gave him a big kiss!

"Wow...what was that for? LOL," Ashton chuckled.

"Ohhh… I'm just feeling excited about everything now. The trip… the get-together…and seeing you looking after yourself. I'm just feeling grateful." Sofia admired the fact that Ashton was back to normal or at least trying.

Ashton took her hand and squeezed it gently.

They looked at each other and smiled.

They stopped at a gourmet hamburger place and enjoyed their meal.

Sofia chose a romance-type movie, and they snuggled into each other as they sat with their popcorn.

Nothing like movie theater popcorn! Of course, they made a mess.

"Oh well… some hit our mouths! Lol," They both laughed.

They picked up as much as they could.

After the movie, they decided to take a nice drive.

Paul took them downtown to where the action was.

The lights… the people…the excitement.

New York was just bursting with life.

It was beginning to snow, and that made everything even more prettier.

"Hey… let's get out and go for a walk," Ashton suggested.

"Ok…. I'd love to," Sofia replied.

Paul found a spot to pull over, and the two got out.

"Give us an hour…and we'll meet back here," Ashton instructed Paul.

"You got it," he responded.

The two turned and, hand in hand, strolled down the street.

Ashton stopped suddenly and looked at Sofia.

"My mother would have loved you…," His words sounded a little shaky.

"I know she would have," He repeated his words again.

Sofia looked at him and said, "I'm sure I would have loved her too."

They smiled and continued on.

"Come on… let's get back. It's getting kind of cold," Ashton said.

Sofia agreed.

They sent a text to Paul.

"This was a fun night," Sofia said, and Ashton agreed.

They pulled up to Sofia's apartment. Ashton stepped out.

Sofia got out, and they stood quietly for a moment.

"Will I see you tomorrow?" Ashton asked.

"That would be great," Sofia replied.

"Call me when you wake up. I'll bring pastries!" Ashton exclaimed with a playful tone.

Sofia said, "Awesome! You know what I like." her voice filled with anticipation.

"Ok…. Talk to you then. Good night." Ashton said warmly.

"Good night," Sofia responded softly.

Ashton watched Sofia disappeared into her building.

The limo drove away.

As she entered her apartment…she yawned. It was a bit chilly

So she turned up the heater.

Winter is here!

Sofia chose her warmer winter pajamas and climbed into bed.

What a wonderful day…and night.

She laid there with all sorts of thoughts running through her head.

It seemed so long since she worked!

She was not used to that. She had always been a hard-working employee.

Now.... she was getting ready for another vacation! Two weeks!

She had to adjust to some big changes in her life.

Soon, her thoughts faded, and she drifted off to sleep. It seemed like only minutes when her phone rang.

Ashton was on his way!

"OMG.... It's 9.00 Am!" She jumped into the shower quickly....

Sofia dressed and made the coffee.

"Whew...I must have been in a deep sleep! I made it though, lol," She chuckled.

Just in time...she greeted Ashton at the door.

His hands were full, with two boxes. One had with croissants...

The other with little breakfast sandwiches. He carried them to the kitchen.

They smelled heavenly.

"Awe... my favorites! I'm going to get fat, you know?" Sofia exclaimed in excitement.

Ashton laughed, " Nah…you're too active. Besides… I wouldn't care If you did,"

"Well… I would…," Sofia stated, "I love my clothes, and I don't want to have to replace them! LOL,"

They sat at the table and devoured quite a bit of the succulent treats. Then... they laughed at themselves for having no control!

"OK," Sofia blurted, "I'm making breakfast from now on! Look...Look how much we just ate! LOL,"

Ashton's phone rang. It was Frank.

He told him that he would be out of town until tomorrow.

There were some business meetings he should attend.

"Sure," Ashton replied, "I'll see you when you get back. Talk to you then,"

They hung up.

"So…. I guess I'm on my own for the night!" Ashton announced.

He filled Sofia in on what was said.

We'll be leaving in a few days… so he should touch base with business. It's good for him, too, to keep busy right now.

"Yaa…," Sofia agreed.

"How about we go and spend some time at the gym? You can come as my guest. I'd love to do some swimming. They have a great heated pool and hot tub." Sofia suggested.

"Sounds like a good plan," Ashton nodded, "We can stop and pick up my bathing suit and gym clothes."

"Great... Let's finish our coffee first." Sofia replied.

"Mmm...This is the best coffee in town!" Ashton commented.

"We may have to make a trip back to France and re-stock!" Ashton teased again.

Sofia laughed, "Yaa...I think so! Well... maybe we can find some on our travels. But... I don't think any can compare. We just may have to go back! LOL

They finished and headed out. First, they went to pick up Ashton's clothes and then to the gym.

It was snowing pretty hard now. The driving was treacherous!

Even the limo had trouble staying straight.

They made it to the gym safely, but it was a bit nerve-racking.

There weren't many cars in the parking lot. The weather has deterred many; it appeared like that.

"Looks like the place is empty, Hun! No waiting for machines!" Sofia confusingly said.

"Yaa... the pool is empty, too. YAY!" Ashton jumped.

Sofia signed them both in, and they split up to their changing rooms.

"I'll meet you in the hot tub," Sofia told Ashton.

"Ok," Ashton nodded.

A handful of people were around, but not what it should be.

Most of the lockers were free. Sofia was waiting in the hot tub when Ashton came out.

"Wow…. how did you beat me?"' He yelled.

"Women always take longer than men for everything, LOL" He teased.

Sofia laughed, "Shut up and get in."

"I already had my bathing suit on, under my clothes! LOL," Sofia chuckled.

"Awe…you cheated," Ashton conceded.

"The water is so warm! Look… We can watch the snow coming. Down from here! I love it!" Sofia asked him to jump in.

One whole wall was glass. They could see out…. but no one could see in. That was nice.

They decided to go for a swim. The pool was empty. That water was warm as well. They did laps for a while, then just floated around.

All the time, they kept their eyes on the snow.

It was really starting to come down heavy, and they wondered.

If maybe, they should leave.

Ashton suggested they call Paul and get a weather report. He went to the changing room and picked up his phone. Sofia followed and stood outside the door.

Just then, it rang, "Oh good... I hoped you'd answer." It was Paul.

He told them, "The weather is getting bad now...they are calling. For a big storm! How long do you want to stay?

Ashton looked at Sofia.

"I think we should leave now," he told Paul.

"Good answer...I'll be there as soon as I can," Paul replied.

The two got dressed and waited by the entrance. The wind had picked up, and it was very hard to see out. There was a feeling of stress in the air.

"I hope he doesn't have an accident," Sofia said worriedly.

"He'll be ok," Ashton assured her.

It seemed like an eternity, waiting. It was getting worse out.

Now... even Ashton was starting to worry.

He called Paul. Paul answered.

"I'm just around the corner," he said.

With a sigh of relief, Ashton said," Great! We were worried,"

"Yaa… well, it has been testy out here," Paul answered.

A few minutes later, the limo pulled up to the door. Ashton and Sofia could breathe again! The wind almost blew them away as they ran out.

"Wow!... It's even worse than it looks! If we would have known, we wouldn't have gone!"They said as they got into the car.

"Yaa… It came up unexpectedly!" Paul answered.

Paul has always been good with tracking weather, but this was not predicted. Something to do with the Lakes.

As they entered the highway…the traffic came to a stop.

Paul turned around and said, "OK…. this could be a long drive home, guys."

They started to roll ahead slowly. Paul could sense how Icey the roads had become. There wasn't much traction, even with the weight of the limo.

Tension filled the air as they inched along so slowly.

Visibility was even more difficult as time went on.

Paul concentrated hard and kept his eyes on what was going on behind him.

He was getting very worried but tried not to let on.

The traffic seemed to be moving along a little faster now. Paul kept up with the flow without getting too close.

Just as he thought, they would be making some progress....

There was a loud bang! The limo slid sideways and was hit by

the car behind! They started to spin uncontrollably!

Again, they were hit and pushed into the ditch! Sofia and Ashton were thrown around like dice.

Paul managed to bring the limo to a stop.

Ashton looked over to find Sofia unconscious.

She had hit the window pretty hard!

"OMG.... Sofia! Sofia!!!! Wake up!" Ashton was panicked.

"Nooooo, Don't leave me!" He sobbed, "Sofia!!!!!!"

"Call 911," Ashton yelled, "Sofia!!!!!!!"

She lay bent over in his arms. No response.

"Wake Up!!!!! Sofia!!!!!!!" Ashton cried!

Paul jumped out and opened the door where the two sat. He took Sofia in his arms and checked for her breathing.

Ashton was white with fear, devastated!

Paul looked for obvious signs of wounds. There was a trickle of blood that ran down her hair.

He quickly grabbed his scarf and wrapped it around her head.

She still had a pulse.

"She's going to be OK! She's breathing!" Paul tried to calm Ashton down. He was in tears.

"Where's the ambulance?" Ashton cried.

"What's taking so long?" He was trembling.

Paul rocked Sofia, and Ashton kept watching.

Soon… they saw the lights of the ambulance! Ashton was shaking, "Sofia! Wake up!"

The emergency attendants opened the door and quickly took charge.

"Is anyone else hurt?" One of them asked.

"No… we're ok," They replied.

"Great!" The man replied.

He asked a bunch of questions regarding Sofia as another was checking her out.

Just as Ashton began to cry out loud…. Sofia seemed to be awakening.

"Sofia…..," the man called her name, "Sofia…. wake up, sweety! Sofia?"

There was a soft moan.

The attendant cleaned her head and said they were taking her to the hospital for a more extensive check.

Ashton nodded, "Please make her well. I love her!"

He broke into tears.

"We'll do our best. She'll be in good hands." They tried to calm him down.

"I love her," Ashton repeated.

There were a number of tow trucks now. Paul hoped they could be out of there soon.

The lights and the sirens of the ambulance made Ashton feel even worse.

"Are you Ok, Paul?" He inquired.

"Yes.... Are You?" Paul asked.

"I'm ok," Ashton replied.

Paul told him Sofia would be ok. It didn't seem to help, though.

Ashton had his head in his hands.

Eventually....they were pulled to a body shop and called for a ride home.

No one spoke.

As soon as Ashton got in the house, he called the hospital.

A nurse informed him it was too early. They were taking X-rays and doing a ton of other tests.

She did say...that Sofia was awake and not in pain.

Ashton sighed in huge relief!

"When can I see or talk to her?" Ashton asked.

The nurse said to call back in a few hours.

The waiting was horrible! Not knowing what was happening was killing him.

Ashton paced and paced. He kept staring at his phone, wanting to call.

Time dragged on and on.

Finally …he called back. He was so nervous.

The head nurse answered, and he asked about Sofia.

He was informed that everything was going to be all right. She was resting comfortably.

The head nurse told him, "She is able to have visitors."

"That's great," Ashton perked up, "I'll be there as soon as I can."

The weather was clearing up a bit. Maybe he could get another limo.

He called Paul.

"I'm at the airport, inquiring about that now," he said.

"I had to put in a report and do all kinds of paperwork, but that's just routine. Give me some time," Paul informed him.

"Ok," Ashton replied and told him the good news.

Paul was so relieved.

Ashton jumped into the shower and put some fresh clothes on.

He prayed that they found no further problems with Sofia.

He did feel excited to see her, though.

Things could have been a lot worse. He ended that thought there.

As soon as Ashton was ready, he called for a taxi. He didn't want to bother Paul. He had enough of a tiring day.

He reached the hospital in no time. The roads were sanded and somewhat cleared. That was a relief. He didn't need another episode with traffic.

He entered the emergency doors and went to the admin desk.

"Hi….," he said politely, "Can I see Sofia Di Carlo?"

"Sure… let me check where she is. Just one moment." The receptionist replied.

Ashton waited patiently while the woman made a call.

When she hung up, she gave him the room number.

"OK…She's in room 1127. Just go around the corner, and she's 5 rooms down," She guided him.

Ashton thanked her and then followed her directions.

He wasn't sure what to expect. He was a bit worried.

101

Slowly, he approached her room. He paused, then walked in.

Sofia was lying there in bed. Her eyes closed.

He didn't know if she was sleeping or what. He stood still.

"Maybe I shouldn't disturb her," he thought.

His excitement left his body.

He just watched her and checked for her breathing.

"Thank God, she is breathing normally," Ashton thought.

There was a chair by her bed... and Ashton sat down. He took Sofia's hand and held it tight.

Suddenly, he had flashbacks of what he had just gone through with his mother.

Tears began to flow.

"Please... not again?" He cried.

Just then... his phone rang. He jumped up and stepped outside the room.

Frank was calling to tell him that he'd be home around 9:00 PM.

Ashton filled him in on what was happening.

"OMG...Is she OK? Are you OK?" Frank sounded panicked.

"Yes... I think she is OK. I'm just waiting to talk to her," Ashton answered.

"Let me know later how she is, and you stay positive, ok?" Frank said.

"She'll be just fine," he tried to assure Ashton.

"Yaa... I'll let you know when I know more. Talk to you soon," Ashton replied.

They hung up.

Ashton stepped back into the room to find Sofia awake and sitting up.

"Ohh, Hi!...," he shouted, "Did I disturb your rest?"

"I was so worried! How are you feeling? Are you OK?" Ashton bombarded her with questions.

Sofia smiled, "I'm just fine. They said I can get out tomorrow. They're just keeping me for observation.

They did a ton of tests…and were very nice. They don't think there are any other problems. I've just

got a head wound. They said I'll be fine," Sofia gave him the details.

Ashton gave her a big hug and kiss. He suddenly filled with excitement.

"That's so great to hear. OMG… you scared me!" Ashton felt better.

"I'm sorry, Hun…I don't even know what happened! I'm glad you're alright. What about Paul?" She asked nervously.

"He's perfect," Ashton found it hard to hide his happiness.

"Did they say what time you can get out? I'll be here to pick you up," Ashton inquired.

Sofia shrugged, "I'll let you know when I know."

Ashton squeezed her hand, " I'm so thankful you're OK."

He filled her in on the accident.

"Ohh… wow," she looked shocked.

"That must have been scary! Glad I was out of it! LOL," Sofia chuckled.

Ashton laughed, "Yaa…it was very scary."

They sat and talked for a while…. Then the Doctor came in.

"How are you feeling, young lady? You have quite the bump on your head!" Doctor examined her.

"I'm Ok," she answered, "A little sore…. But I'll live! Won't I, LOL."

Even the Doctor laughed, "Yes, you will."

"We'll just make sure for the night…and I'll discharge you for 9.00 am. Is that Ok?" Doctor inquired.

"That's awesome," she answered.

"Thank You," Doctor Drake

"Yes…Thank You," Ashton added.

The Doctor left… and the two of them talked for another hour.

Then… Ashton said he was going home and would call in the morning.

He wanted her to rest as much as she could. She agreed. He kissed her and left the room. He was on Cloud 9. He called for a taxi again and headed home.

"Wait! Stop….," Ashton had the driver pull over.

"I'll be right back! Wait for me," He told the driver.

There was a flower shop, and he thought he'd pick out a beautiful bouquet of fresh flowers.

He chose the prettiest pink and white roses he'd ever seen.

Baby's Breath was intertwined throughout.

"Sofia will love these," he thought to himself! "She loves fresh flowers."

"They look so perfect! They smell so wonderful!" He smiled.

He took 2 dozen. He climbed back into the taxi.

"Thank You! I'm sorry for yelling." He excused.

"No problem," The driver responded.

"Looks like you have someone very special!" The driver inquired, "Two dozen. Wow."

"Yes….," Ashton smiled. He would bring them when he would pick her up.

"Ok… Take me home," Ashton said.

Ashton gave the Taxi driver a huge tip. Then he went into the house.

He knew he had some nice vases to choose from because his mother was always picking them from her garden.

He found a very unique white one. It was also large enough to hold.

Two dozen roses.

He smiled and felt excitement with each rose he placed in the vase.

His mother would have loved to have him use the vase for Sofia.

He felt her presence as he arranged the flowers.

He knew she was at peace. He also felt at peace with what happened. She was not suffering anymore.

Ashton stood back and admired his work. Watching his mother over the years has paid off. They looked beautiful! Just like Sofia.

He grabbed his phone and sat in the chair in front of the garden window.

He called his dad while looking out over the yard. Frank was glad to hear from him.

"How is Sofia," he asked?

"She's going to be great," he answered, "I would pick her up in the morning."

"OH…. I'm so glad to hear that. I've been thinking about her. I'll be home in a couple of hours." Frank informed.

"OK…. I'll order some Chinese food. I'll see you then." Ashton replied.

Ashton was starting to really feel good about himself and Sofia.

It's a good thing she gets out tomorrow morning! Their get-together is tomorrow night!

Hopefully, Sofia will feel up to going. He'll find out soon enough.

Ashton had a short nap… then picked out the menu for dinner.

He called and ordered it to be delivered about an hour after his father came home.

The rest did him good. He felt a little more energetic.

When his father arrived, they hugged and then sat at the table.

Frank told him again how thrilled he was that Sofia was Ok!

Then…he noticed the Roses.

"Wow….I think you really have some strong feelings for her! Does she know it? LOL," Frank teased him.

Ashton rolled his eyes, "Not yet… maybe…a little," he stumbled with his words, "LOL…...Soon.

We decided to take it slow."

"Great Idea, son! That's the best way. You'll know when it's time." Frank advised him.

They started talking about the cruise. Ashton told him that Sofia was amazed when she saw their suite. She's getting very excited!

Ashton mentioned their get-together and told him a bit about his new friends.

Frank thought they all sounded wonderful.

"It's hard to find good friends," he said, "And so many are just amazing."

"Yaa… well, Sofia is amazing too." Frank continued.

Their food arrived, and the two enjoyed every bite.

"Maybe we should go jogging and wear this off, LOL," Ashton suggested.

Frank just nodded, "I hear ya!"

Ashton's phone rang… it was Paul.

"Hey guy… I'm back in business, LOL. They replaced the limo. I'm at your disposal," Paul answered.

"Oh great! I'm picking up Sofia in the morning," Ashton replied.

"OK…Just call when you're ready." Paul said.

"Thanks, Paul." They hung up. Ashton was glad to hear that.

"Well… I think I'll go and unpack," Frank said.

"Then I have some calls to make. We'll leave in a few days." Frank added.

"I'd like to go away and be caught up," Frank said with a satisfied smile, "Dinner was fabulous. Great choice!"

"Yaa. I think I'll go for a walk, then call it a night." Ashton replied.

"I can't wait till tomorrow," Ashton anticipated for the next day.

"I'll have the coffee ready for you in the morning," Ashton added.

"Thanks," Frank said and headed up to his room.

He stopped on the stairs…., "Oh! if I don't see you…. Have fun!" They both laughed.

Ashton grabbed his jacket and stepped out the door.

There was light snow coming down. It wasn't cold, though.

He headed down to the parking area at the end of the street.

As he casually strolled on the walking path, the events lately filled his head.

He felt excitement for what was to come.

In a way…he felt guilty about feeling so good so soon, but that's the way Sofia affected him.

She has that way of making everyone feel good.

I'm so in love with her, he thought.

After about an hour, Ashton turned and followed the path back home.

The sooner he went to sleep…. the sooner tomorrow would come.

The next thing he knew…he was off in La La Land. The fresh air knocked him out, and he slept like a baby. Just as he thought… the morning came in a flash.

He jumped out of bed, hit the shower, and dressed in his favorite jeans and a sweater.

Oh, and a spritz of enticing cologne to finish.

The coffee was almost ready, and he made himself some toast.

Frank came down the stairs.

"Oh… I wasn't sure I'd see you today," he said.

"I know," stated Ashton, "I'm up early."

"How come you're up so early?" Frank inquired.

"I just got a text... They want me at the airline to sign some papers. Then...I think I'll do a bit of shopping." Ashton replied.

"Our cruise is in a couple of days," Ashton added.

"Good idea, Dad...you're due for some updates in your wardrobe," Ashton said to his Dad.

"Oh...Thanks a lot, kid! Just for that, I might just pick something out to embarrass you, LOL."Frank answered.

"You'd better not!" Ashton laughed and rolled his eyes.

They sat and enjoyed their coffee for a bit.

"I assume you won't be home for dinner?" Frank smiled.

"No.... We have our get-together at 6.00 PM." Ashton replied.

"Sorry.... You'll have to eat alone." Ashton apologized to his dad as he grabbed his coat and headed for the door.

Frank nodded, "That's Ok. I might just have a bite at the mall."

Ashton sent a text to Sofia, " Are you awake? Give me a call."

It was starting to snow again and was a little overcast.

It was very pretty out, like a postcard. He waited for her response with another coffee.

Sofia woke up and saw the snow.

The nurse came in with her breakfast.

"Good morning, young lady!" She pulled the curtain open around her bed, "How are you feeling?"

Sofia yawned, "I feel ok so far. I didn't get much sleep, though. Too much on my mind, I guess."

"That sounds good. You should be able to leave then. You'll sleep better in your own bed tonight." The nurse sounded reassuring.

"It's a beautiful day," The nurse remarked with a warm smile, looking out the window at the clear blue sky.

Sofia sat up. She gazed out the window. It did look nice out.

Of course, Ashton was in her thoughts now that she was more awake.

There was a tray with some scrambled eggs, toast and a Cup of fruit beside her bed. Also, a cup of coffee.

She had a few bites, then chose the coffee.

"UGHHHHH.... Dishwater," she thought, "Now I do have to go home LOL."

She reached for her phone. There was a message from Ashton. Quickly, she called him.

"Morning!" Ashton answered, "How are you feeling?"

"I didn't want to call and wake you." He added.

"Morning! I'm feeling OK. The nurse just brought in breakfast."

In a very soft voice…she whispered, "Coffee sucks! LOL."

Ashton broke out laughing.

"I'm sure it does!" He replied.

"Well, when I pick you up…. I'll bring you a good one." He said.

"Ohhh … Thank You!"She chuckled.

"I think the Doctor said 9.00 AM." She informed.

"OK… well, I'm heading over in about 20 minutes. That will be close." Ashton replied.

"Great," Sofia said excitedly! "I'll get dressed and ready."

"OK…see you then." They hung up.

The Doctor soon appeared in her room and asked her a series of questions. Mainly how she felt at that time and if she felt any other soreness.

Sofia shook her head….and said, "I'm ready to go!"

The Doctor laughed and said, "So, you are! That's a good sign."

"Okay, I'll sign you out," the doctor continued, "but if you find you get any other symptoms, I want you to come straight back. Okay?"

Sofia promised him she would and said, "'Thank You!"

Ashton showed up with the gorgeous flowers he had picked out.

The vase he chose was just what they needed.

"Ohh… WOW!" Sofia lit up.

"Are they for me?" She ran over and smelled them.

"Mmmm…these are beautiful! You shouldn't have!" She blushed.

Ashton held them while she put her coat on.

"I'll carry them," he said, they are a bit heavy.

"I guess so," Sofia remarked, "Look how many there are!"

Everyone they passed seemed to look and want to smell the roses. They were heavenly.

When they reached the front door…. Paul was waiting and took the flowers from Ashton so he could secure them in the back.

They drove off to Sofia's.

Ashton told Sofia that he was going to take care of her today.

He brought a change of clothes for going out that night.

"Oh, you are …. are you? And what makes me deserve such attention?" She asked.

"Just being you," he responded.

Sofia smiled, "Thanks, Hun...you don't have to do that."

"I know, but I want to!" He squeezed her hand.

"How are you doing, Paul? Any aches or pains?" Sofia inquired about Paul.

"Just a few bruises. Nothing to mention." Paul replied.

"That's good," Sofia said, "It could have been worse!"

"Yes," Paul looked back through the mirror... there were quite a few ambulances from what I could see. Hopefully, no one was really hurt badly.

They reached Sofia's apartment and thanked Paul.

"We'll see you around 5.45," Ashton instructed.

"I'll be waiting outside when you want me," Paul agreed.

"Great...Catch you later." Ashton replied.

Paul drove off, and the two entered her apartment. Ashton put the flowers down in front of the window in the kitchen.

Mumm, he took a deep breath, "These really do smell awesome!"

Sofia agreed. The fragrance filled the room.

"So...How about you make the coffee, and I'll jump in the shower," Sofia suggested.

"No problem! I can do that," Ashton nodded.

115

"Great," She turned toward the bathroom.

"I think I'll wear one of my cute outfits from Italy. I haven't had a chance," She raised her voice.

"Oh, Yaa … I love those. The one with a sweater, now that it's getting so cold. Look!... It's snowing again!" Ashton replied.

"I'm looking forward to tonight!... I guess we have a lot to talk about." Sofia said excitedly.

Sofia came out of the bathroom, dressed in a comfy sweatshirt.

She was drying her hair with a towel.

"Mmm… That coffee smells fabulous!" She poured a cup.

They sat at the table. Ashton reminded her that he was picking up the tab for everyone that evening.

"That's too nice of you," Sofia responded, "You really don't have to."

"Yeah, I know…but I'm just feeling so fortunate and want to share my good luck," Sofia sighed.

"Well… you're the best," She gave him a big kiss, "That's very nice of you."

"I was thinking," Sofia paused, "Since your mother died, your secret is out on who you are!

Now…everyone knows you're Frank Davis's son!"

"Yaa… I thought of that, too. I kept that hidden for so long," Ashton nodded.

"I'm not sure how they will take to that. I'm no longer just a regular staff member/co-worker." Sofia got a little tense.

"Hmmm…It will be uncomfortable, I think. Who knows! I guess I'll find out when we get back to normal." Ashton tried to lighten up the moment.

Sofia nodded in deep thought, "It seemed so long since we were at work! LOL."

"I hope we can stick together!" She added.

"Ohh… I'll be checking in with Kyle. He's my buddy! I'll have him take care of that for us. LOL, I think he's due for a raise! LOL," Ashton said teasingly.

Sofia looked up and laughed, "That's one way."

"Ohhh… I'd better call Lenora! She's coming with us tonight! You don't mind, do you?" Sofia inquired.

"No, of course not," Ashton replied.

"She's always alone, and I thought she would appreciate a night out. She seems so nice." Sofia said.

"She can drive with us," He added.

"Oh, that's great! She'll feel special," Sofia smiled.

"Lenora was thrilled at the plans. She thanked them for thinking of her. Now I don't have to go out and clean off my car." She chuckled.

"It's probably frozen over. Just text me when you're about to leave. I'll be ready." She said to Sofia.

"Ok," Sofia replied, " See you then."

They hung up.

"You're always thinking of other people," Sofia.

"You're always trying to make others feel special!" She praised her.

"Well… I never really had a close relationship with anyone."Sofia replied.

"I was always passed around from home to home when I was growing up…. I know what it's like to be alone." She added.

"It's not that much fun. We all need friends," She exclaimed.

Ashton just gazed at her and felt a sense of sadness in her words.

His heart melted. He fought back tears.

"Well… That's not going to happen anymore. You have me and a lot of great friends now. We're your family!" Ashton comforted her with his words and a warm hug.

"Awe…. Thanks, Hun!" Sofia gave him a kiss.

"Ok… now…Let's find a good movie and make some popcorn. We'll just relax until we go out." Ashton suggested.

"That sounds good to me," Ashton agreed, "It's so cold out there,"

They chose a comedy romance. It was very good.

When the movie ended…. they took turns getting ready in the bathroom.

Of course…Ashton was a lot quicker. He does, however, spend a lot of time on his hair. He cares how he looks.

Sofia sent a text to Lenora, saying they would be leaving in half an hour. Lenora sent a thumbs-up.

They sat for a few minutes chatting, then did a final check on their looks.

"I think we look awesome!" Ashton said, turning in the mirror.

Sofia laughed, "Yes, You do! LOL,"

"My turn… Oh yes…... I'm not bad, either! LOL," She looked at herself in the mirror.

"OK…. let's go!" Paul is out front.

Lenora was in the hall waiting.

"Hey, Lenora!"

"You've met Ashton? Haven't you?" Sofia asked.

"I think briefly in the hall one day," She replied.

"Yes... I think so, too. I love your outfit, and your hair looks gorgeous!" Sofia liked her look.

"Thank You," she smiled shyly, "You two, look adorable."

"Great…I guess we're ready to go! LOL," They all laughed.

They stepped out the door, and Paul was there.

"Is that limo for us?" Lenora looked surprised.

"Yes…he's my driver," Ashton told her.

"Oh… Nice… we'll arrive in style! Now I feel like a movie star, LOL," She chuckled.

Ashton and Sofia laughed as they climbed in.

"To Alexanders… my friend!" Paul tipped his hat.

"This is just lovely," Lenora commented, "It's been a long time, since I rode in one of these."

"My husband used to use them all the time. He hated to drive. Plus…he was always dealing with top executives from big companies," she told them.

"Ohh….," Ashton said, "What did he do for a living?"

"He owned a huge imported furniture business, but he also spent a lot of time entertaining possible donors for his animal shelters," She replied.

"Oh…Wow," Sofia perked up, "That's awesome!"

"I love Animals...They're sooo innocent. I wish I could save them all." Sofia adorably said.

"OK! …," Ashton broke in, "We'd better change the subject before the tears start to fly, LOL,"

"Good Idea," Sofia agreed, "I'm just too sensitive."

"Now…. Let's go have some fun!" They all chuckled.

As they pulled up in front of the restaurant…. They saw Ricky and Fred were about to go in. They stopped and waited.

"Hey…. There's my girl!" Ricky blurted, "Glad to see you; looking good! How are you feeling?"

"I'm good, guys…. I'll be fine."

They all hugged and greeted each other.

They went inside and found their reserved corner.

"Looks like we're the first here... Let's get a drink." They laughed.

Sofia, Ashton, Lenora and Ricky ordered a wine. Fred had his sparkling water with a twist of lemon. Sofia introduced Lenora to the guys as they got settled.

In moments, the others appeared. Maina, Kaylee, and Angel.

They were brushing the snow off themselves.

"It looks so pretty out… but the driving is getting treacherous. I hope they clear the roads soon." One of them said.

"Don't worry," Fred said, "We saw them on our way here. You know, New York is usually pretty good at this. They have to be, with all the traffic."

"Yes," Maina agreed.

"Soo.... everyone! what's new and exciting?" Sofia raised Her voice.

Their server came over and took the rest of the orders.

Ashton got up and excused himself. He slipped over to their server and told him he was taking care of everything.

He then ordered a variety of appetizers and returned to the table.

Ricky started off by mentioning his new commercial.

He's been semi-retired but still loved to do a little TV.

Then... Kaylee informed them she passed an exam. It was an important one.

Soon, she can go for her full nursing.

Everyone congratulated her.

Maina just shrugged her shoulders; nothing really was new with her.

Sofia spoke up, "Well.... Ashton and I are leaving in two days!"

She added, "His father arranged for us to return on the cruise, but he had to leave.

Ashton didn't want to leave his father alone so soon, so he's making him come with us.

I thought that was really thoughtful of him. Frank needs the distraction now as well."

She told her friends, "We will also bring Ashton's mother's ashes to sprinkle into the Sea. She had always loved cruising and found peace in the waters. It was her happy place."

"Oh…That sounds beautiful," Fred added, "What a lovely gesture! Great idea!"

"Soo…. We're sorry to leave you guys in this beautiful snow…. but…we'll be back in time for more." Sofia excused.

"Christmas is coming up soon….does anyone have plans yet?" Sofia changed the subject.

"Well, you know, we are on our own," Ricky responded.

"Our families have never accepted our relationship,"

Angel added that she was going to Florida for a few days.

That's where her family is. Kaylee would be here and have dinner with her parents.

Maina, too, would be here. Lenora is alone and had no plans. She didn't have any kids,

And her husband's kids really never bothered with her.

"Well….," Sofia spoke up.

Sofia, being her thoughtful self, said, "How about … sometime just before…. we have our own Christmas Party. We can put our names in a jar….and pick one each for a gift. We're like family, right…We must always stick together and do what all families do! No one will be alone!"

"There she goes again," Ashton replied, "Always thinking of everyone! You really have a big heart!"

"Well…," Maina spoke up, "I think that is an awesome idea! Let's do that!"

"Cheers…...," Ashton raised his glass, "We're having our own Christmas!"

"CHEERS!" Everyone raised their glasses and took a sip.

"When we get back," Sofia spoke, "we'll get together and pick our names. We can set a price limit. We'll find a time that is good for everyone."

"Sounds great," Kaylee added.

Just then…an array of food came to their table.

"Oh…. we haven't ordered yet! LOL," Maina looked surprised.

"I hope you don't mind…. But I kind of ordered for everyone."

"My treat, guys…. I think I have what everyone likes coming. There's more to come as well."

Shrimp cocktails, pizza, wings, bruschetta, and cheese balls.

He even ordered a charcuterie board.

"Wow….," Angel's eyes popped, "What a feast! All our favorites!"

"OMG…... You shouldn't have," Ricky remarked.

"Well... This is my way of showing my appreciation for my awesome new friends. Sofia was right.... when she told me I would love you guys!"

"Now.... dig in!" He chuckled.

They all grabbed some food and started eating. The smell was wonderful!

Their server came with another round of drinks. Everyone raved about the food.

They ate until they were stuffed! It was excellent!

"Oh......Man......I'm so full, "Maina sighed, "I have to go to the gym tomorrow and work this off!"

Everyone laughed and agreed, "Yaa.... we all should."

"I feel so fat...," Kaylee added.

"Well... I'm just comfortable," Lenora said, "I guess I just have a bit more control! LOL. It Comes with age, I think maybe."

They all sat back....and sipped their drinks. They kept the chit-chat going for the next hour.

Sofia talked about their cruise and staying in a two-bedroom suite this time.

"OH...That sounds expensive!" Angel said.

"It probably is," Sofia replied, "Frank is taking care of everything.

"I couldn't believe it...He has his own as well."

"He said he'd probably be busy catching up with some crew, especially the Captain; they are good friends. He wants Ashton to get away and just find some peace in what has happened. He thought I might help, " She squeezed his hand.

I think they both could use a nice getaway now.

"Two weeks in paradise sounds amazing," Lenora told them.

"Away from this snow and cold! Think of us! While you cruise the seas, in the warmth, Eh!"

Ashton laughed, "OK...we'll do that! LOL,"

The evening soon came to an end. Ashton offered a ride to anyone who wanted it.

They all thought it was ok to drive now. The streets were looking good, as far as they could see.

As they started to get up...they all thanked Ashton for the fantastic night! The food, the company and everything else.

"My pleasure! I really enjoy this with you guys!" Ashton waved at them.

They headed to the front doors.

"Nice meeting you," Lenora, "They all agreed."

"Yes.... Same here. This was very nice."

Hugs and kisses went all around as they put on their coats.

Paul had sent a text to Ashton that he was there waiting.

"Ok.... You drive safe!... We'll talk to you when we get home!"

Good night, everyone......Ashton, Sofia, and Lenora got into the Limo.

****

"What a great night!" Lenora spoke out, "Thank you for inviting me!"

"Any time," Ashton replied, "The more... the merrier!"

When they reached their apartment, Ashton escorted the two ladies up to the doors.

They said their good nights to Lenora.

Ashton and Sofia stood in the hall and hugged.

"I'll talk to you tomorrow?" Ashton asked.

"Of course," Sofia kissed him.

"Ok, I'll call in the morning. You get a good night's sleep." Ashton patted her head.

"I will," Sofia replied, "Thank You for tonight! That was awesome!"

"Anytime Hun," Ashton replied.

He leaned over, kissed her, said good night, then turned and headed out.

Sofia closed the door and stood there with those so familiar butterflies!

The cruise is going to be even better than how they first started out.

Her feelings for Ashton have hit a new level.

It was late… she decided to just go to bed and fall asleep with the T.V.

Tomorrow, she'll be busy making sure she has everything ready for the trip.

The excitement was building now. Even being nervous about spending that much time with her big boss…couldn't bring her down.

It will work out just fine. She and Ashton will have a great time!

The next morning, when Sofia opened her eyes….

Huge snowflakes were slowly coming down. She closed her eyes again and went back to sleep. Her big down duvet wasn't ready to let her go so soon. It hugged her like a bear.

She remained there for another hour and a half before finally getting up.

The thought of a nice hot coffee cup was probably the big incentive.

She made her way to the kitchen and turned on the coffee machine.

She freshened up and dressed in something comfy.

It looked soo pretty outside. She stood gazing at the snow while waiting for her liquid gold.

Christmas was in the air now. Colorful lights were starting to appear in the area.

The commercials were also in full force.

Hmm... She wondered how it would be this year now that Ashton was so prevalent in her life.

Her cell phone chimed. That was the sound for Ricky and Fred.

"Morning Hun...how are you guys?"

"Morning, dear! We just wanted to thank you again for last night!"

"Ohh....no problem! I think everyone enjoyed themselves,"

"We always do. Christmas is going to be even better! Ashton is just perfect for you, my dear! He adores you,"

"You think so?" Sofia responded.

"OH...Yaa! I watched him last night, and he's completely in love,"

Sofia paused, "I really think the world of him, too! We've just been taking it slow,"

"Well...I think you are so in sync with each other," Ricky said.

"My Dear? Don't take too long! Life is short. You don't want to lose something that's so special. Just saying," Rick advised her.

129

"I know Rick…. Thanks for looking out for me. I respect your thoughts. Your intuition has always been right. I always listen to you. You know that, Eh!" Sofia answered.

"Well, that's just my opinion from what I've observed. You're like our sister; we love you!" They replied.

"Thanks, Hun….I'll keep that in mind. I love both of you as well."

"Hey… I loved your idea for Christmas! Having our own party. And picking names. That will be fun!"

"Yaa…," Sofia agreed, "I think it's what everyone needs. When we return from our trip… we can start making plans."

"Perfect!" Ricky sounded excited, "We'll start giving it some thought."

"Oh…Also, we just wanted to wish you a safe and fun trip!"

"Thanks … I'm hoping so. I'm sure it will be," Sofia replied.

"Ok… call us when you're home, ok?"

"I will...Stay warm, LOL. Enjoy the snow!"

They hung up.

Sofia reached for another coffee. Her thoughts moved to Ashton.

Tomorrow, they would leave. She sat remembering the last cruise.

She thought of Robin…. Walter, whom she met at her dinner table, and the sea waves. She got extra excited about that.

She remembered drifting off to sleep with waves singing to her.

She sent a good morning text to Ashton. He then called her.

"Can't wait till tomorrow! I'm just about ready! LOL," Sofia chuckled.

Ashton laughed, "Great, me too."

"We have an early flight. What we can do is pick up some croissants and eat them in the limo, on our way, or just eat at one of the restaurants there," Ashton suggested.

"After we get through security, we'll have enough time," He added.

"I'm ok either way!... We can decide tomorrow. Is your father excited?" Sofia asked.

"Yaa… I think he is, actually! Since you had that great idea for the ashes… and he'll get to see some good friends. This will be good for him," Ashton replied.

"So… what time will you be here?" Sofia asked.

"Ummm… I think 7.30 should be good," Ashton replied. There won't be much traffic that early. Ok, great… I'll be ready," Sofia said

Ashton told her he had to run out and pick up some new luggage today. He thought his was wearing out. He didn't want to chance it getting ruined, "It may fall apart. I found a tear in the bottom." He explained.

"Ohh… yaa… you'd better! They go through a lot of rough handling," Sofia said.

"Well, I'm just doing a final check… and then relaxing," She added.

"Nice.... We'll have a lot of time to enjoy ourselves. I'll give you a call before we leave," Ashton replied.

"Sounds good," Sofia agreed, "Enjoy your day."

Check in at the airport went smoothly. They had a rather nice breakfast and awaited the flight.

It felt strange to Sofia to be in the passenger position, not the crew.

Once they arrived, they were picked up and taken to the ship.

"Wow! I still can't get over the size!" Sofia gasped, "It's unbelievable! How do they stay afloat?"

Frank looked up…and smiled to himself, "It's been a few years since he was able to sail the seas with his wife. It still felt like yesterday, though."

"She would have loved this," He thought in silence.

"Well…She'll be remaining here forever now. She'll be happy!" Frank smiled.

Once they were aboard…they quickly found their suites.

They were informed that their luggage was soon to come.

Both suites were beautiful, bright, and modern.

Sofia's eyes grew large, "This is even better than the first cabin. I thought that one was awesome!"

"This is like an apartment," she commented. They wandered around, inspecting every corner.

"Look!... we have our own hot tub! Wow!" Sofia jumped in excitement.

Ashton laughed, "Yaa... I'm sure we will enjoy that!"

They each chose a bedroom and then went out on their private deck.

They had views of both the water and the interior of the ship. They could watch the water shows without leaving their Suite.

"This is awesome!" Sofia screeched.

There was a knock on the door.... It was Frank.

"So... how do you guys like your suite? Is that what you need?"

Sofia looked at him, "Are you kidding me? This is a dream!"

Just then...their luggage arrived. Frank thought they could go for lunch after they unpack.

"Sounds great, dad...we'll see you in a bit," Ashton said.

Frank headed back to his suite.

One of the perks of having a suite was that they also had access to a private dining room.

Once they got settled, they freshened up, changed, and headed out to meet Frank.

The private restaurant was just down the corridor and around the corner.

"Ohh… this looks nice," Sofia commented, "Casual with a flair of fine dining.

They were quickly seated. There were only about 20 people there.

The server brought their menu, and they looked it over.

They all seemed to pick the seafood platter.

Shrimp…crab…and scallops, finished in a garlic butter sauce.

That was served with a basmati rice underlay. They also ordered a nice bottle of wine.

"That was easy," Frank laughed!

"Frank!" Sofia spoke in a serious voice.

"Our suite is just wonderful! You really went all out for us. I don't know how to thank you. I never would have dreamed a ship had suites like that." She praised Frank's kind and welcoming gesture.

"It's nothing, my dear! I have a lot of connections. I am a major stockholder; I'm sure Ashton must have mentioned." Frank asked her.

Sofia smiled, "Yes, he did tell me something about that. Well... I really do appreciate what you've done."

"Also...," she said nervously, "Ashton explained about you paying me for all this time off. You don't have to do that."

She looked at Frank. He sat a moment silent.

"Sofia?... I've come to learn a whole lot about you. I've seen the good in you firsthand as well. I also learned about your childhood recently from Ashton. I have to admire your strength and determination. Those are great attributes. I have also observed the way my son adores you. He's all I have left now, and if you make him as happy as he appears? Then you'll make me happy too. I will do anything for him!" There were tears in his eyes. He was feeling the pain of his recent loss.

Sofia also felt tears trickling down and felt his pain.

"Cheers...," Ashton raised his glass. Frank and Sofia did as well.

"Here's to a great cruise! Cheers, they all touched glasses."

It didn't take long for their food to come.

"Wow...," They stared down at their plates, "This looks fabulous!"

They enjoyed every bite as they sat and chatted about the ship.

They kept the conversation light and neutral.

"OK…I'm stuffed," Ashton rubbed his stomach.

"Me too," Sofia added.

Frank laughed, "Yes… I'm done."

"Soo…," Frank stood up, "I think you two should go about your day, and we can meet for dinner in the main dining room. If you're not hungry, then that's ok. I'll be fine. I have people to meet up with and things to do."

"Sure," Ashton answered, "We can catch you later. We'll walk off this lunch, LOL,"

They turned for the door. Ashton turned back around and gave Frank a thumbs up.

Frank stood and watched them leave. He then sat down and poured another wine.

He stared down at his glass in deep thought.

"One day, she'll take him away from me. That's ok. He'll be in the best hands. She's the one!"

He took a sip of wine and exited the restaurant. He wanted to meet Robin as it had been a while.

She was on another ship the last he saw her. He really liked her bright, lively, fresh personality. It made him feel young again.

Ashton and Sofia changed into bathing suits and went into the pool. There were many… so they chose the quietest one.

A lot of people were still getting settled and finding their way around.

"Awe…...this is so much better than the snow we left behind," Sofia exclaimed.

Ashton jumped into the warm water, and Sofia followed.

"Ohh…Yaa… I could take this anytime. I love swimming. When we get out… We'll try the drink of the day! It's blue! LOL. I think I've had it before, and it's so delicious. Just a break from wine," Ashton chuckled.

"Sounds awesome," Sofia replied.

"It does look cool! I really like your dad," she said to Ashton.

"He really seems like a real person. Not some high and mighty business executive. He has the same warm, caring personality …just like you." She added.

"Yaa… he does. It's true, too. He's never acted like a snob or beyond reproach." Ashton replied.

"My mother was the same! So… maybe it rubbed off on me." He added.

Sofia gave him her warm, honest smile.

"Come on… let's order those blue drinks!" She said as she climbed out of the pool, "I'm thirsty,"

They headed to the lounge chairs they had saved.

"We have to catch up with Robin! I hope she's on this week." Sofia informed.

"She should be," Ashton said, "I can thank her in person for looking out for you…after I left last time."

They soaked up the sun for a while, then went back to change.

Sofia wanted to explore the ship with Ashton and was in a completely different frame of mind this time.

They stopped by the main courtesy desk on their tour, and Ashton inquired about Robin.

The gentleman, Zachary, informed them she was in a meeting.

Ashton left his name and suite number.

"Just let her know we'd like to see her when she has some time. Thank You, Zach!" Ashton told Zach.

They carried on out into the main heart of the ship.

The energy was building. The passengers were all thrilled and amazed by the beauty.

"This ship is so grand!" Ashton commented!

"I didn't really get the chance to observe it fully last trip." He added.

Deck by deck…. they explored all the offered activities and choices.

"You know what?" Ashton turned to Sofia, "Tomorrow, after breakfast…How about we try those huge water slides?"

"They look amazing! It might make us feel like kids again, LOL," Ashton chuckled.

Sofia looked at him, "Really? I think you're crazy!"

"Chicken...Ashton laughed, "You're a chicken! LOL. Oh, Yaa...I'm not a chicken…..You're ON! And…. You'll be more scared!" Sofia laughed.

They continued on their tour. They found the deck where they had a Merry Go Round and some games— a Candy Store.

"Ohh…let's go in there," Sofia turned and pulled him.

There was a huge array of goodies.

She grabbed a container and started picking out her favorites.

"This is fun!" She laughed, "Now, this is my way of feeling like a kid again! LOL,"

Ashton just shook his head, "Yes, You look like a kid, LOL,"

"OK…Let's return to our suite and relax before dinner. I'd love to do some reading," Sofia said.

"Yeah… that sounds good. I brought a book with me as well. We have two weeks to explore," Ashton replied.

They took their bag of sweets and made their way back.

"This really does look and feel like an apartment," Sofia commented, "The bathroom is bigger than mine! LOL,"

"Yeah, I know," Ashton replied, "It is nicer than I thought! These ships have really thought of everything!"

"Look! I just noticed...A coffee maker. YAY! We'll get off at the first Island and pick up some good coffee." Ashton suggested.

"Nice...," Sofia lit up, "That's a great idea. I think we're heading to Montego Bay! Remember our trip there?"

"How can I forget?" Ashton laughed, "It was ...quite exciting!"

"Well...Jamaica has some awesome coffee. We can get enough to bring home, too!" Sofia said.

"Cool!" Ashton replied.

Ashton's phone rang; it was Frank. He said, "Hi guys...if you're still coming for dinner... Robin arranged a nice table. We have the 5.30 sitting. She mentioned that we would be pleased with the company at our table."

"Sounds great!... We'll meet you there!" Ashton replied.

Ashton mentioned it to Sofia.

"Oh, nice!... I wonder who our company is?... I guess we'll find out in an hour. I'm going to get ready now. I have to do my hair." Sofia rushed.

"Sure...But you look just fine to me," Ashton smiled.

Sofia shook her head, "I think you need glasses! You always say I look great.... Look at this hair!... It's all tangled and twisted! The wind does crazy things. Anyway... I'll make it quick. It will be nice to see Robin. We really seemed to hit it off." Sofia replied.

Ashton disappeared to his room. He showered and changed into a beautiful shirt and black pants. Then, a splash of cologne.

Twenty-five minutes later, Sofia came out fresh and smelling like a rose.

"Mmm.... Who smells the best here? LOL," Ashton laughed.

Sofia laughed, "I hope it's me.... But you are very intoxicating to me! I think you win."

Ashton smiled with satisfaction, "I think we both win,"

The two went out and stood on their deck. The view was endless.

Blue waters, blue sky, and fresh breeze.

"This really is relaxing...," Sofia commented, "No stress."

"Yaa...,"Ashton agreed, "As my mother felt ... this is my happy place."

It was time to head to the dining room. They were getting hungry.

Hand in hand, they made their way.

The glass elevators were beautiful, offering views of the various decks. Everyone boarding was dressed in attire, exuding a fresh and clean scent. The dining room showcased fine dining.

Frank and Robin were there waiting for them when they arrived.

Everyone looked fabulous.

"Oh, look… there's Robin! Hope she's joining us!" Ashton pointed in her direction.

"Hey… Hi guys… Great to see you again!" Robin greeted them.

Ashton leaned over and hugged her, "Hi there! I hope you're joining us tonight?"

"Yes… your father bribed my boss…. Ha Ha! He has some kind of hold on everyone… I think. Works for me!" She laughed.

"Well, that's great…," Ashton said, "Let's go in. I'm starved now."

"Me too," Sofia added.

The four of them found their table…and who was there? Walter! He stood up and shook everyone's hand.

"Welcome to my table," He laughed, "I hope you don't mind not at all,"

"This is a nice surprise!" Frank smiled.

They all sat down, and their server arrived.

"I haven't seen you in a few years! How have you been keeping?" Frank asked.

"Oh... you know...just traveling and caring for the animals. I have a lot of volunteers now. We've grown quite a bit! That's not a good thing! You know? It's a sad thing." Walter replied.

"Yes... I hear you. It's a shame," Frank nodded at Walter.

"Oh... I'm so sorry to hear about your wife! She was such a wonderful Lady!" Walter sighed, "I just found out yesterday."

"Thanks," Frank responded, "In a way, it was a blessing. She's at peace now. Her cancer returned swiftly, and within weeks, she was gone. The last week was particularly challenging, but at least she didn't suffer for long. That would have been truly awful."

"Oh yes... You're lucky there." Walter said.

"So now, what should we order this evening?" Frank changed the subject.

"I'm so hungry," Sofia laughed, "I'll eat anything!"

Ashton agreed, "Yes... I'm starving! I'll take two appetizers, LOL,"

Walter had taken it upon himself to order a bottle of wine.

The server poured each one a glass.

"Cheers! To a wonderful trip! And to good friends."

"Cheers!" They toasted.

The server took their orders and slipped away.

Sofia was sitting between Ashton and Walter—two handsome men.

Frank was also very handsome and distinguished-looking. Robin was next to him.

They started some little chit-chat amongst themselves.

Walter asked Sofia about her working for Exotic Airlines.

She said it was great, although she has been off the last few weeks.

"Yes, that was sad. And then your cruises. That was nice. Yes, until Ashton had to leave. This one will be different." Sofia replied.

Sofia asked Walter about his Rescue Farm, "Are you full?"

"Oh Yaa," Walter sighed, "I feel so bad for them. I had no idea just how many needed his help." Tears submerged in Sofia's eyes. She stared at the table.

Walter noticed but never said anything. He didn't want to bring attention to her at this moment.

Frank, Robin, and Ashton were lost in their conversation and were busy catching up.

After a few minutes, Walter leaned over and said, "That's ok. My dear... I cry about them, too. It's hard to see some of them when they come in."

The server showed up at that moment with their appetizers.

They all chose some and enjoyed it.

Soon after, their entre's came as well.

"Wow.... everything looks amazing!" Frank commented.

He ordered another bottle of wine.

They began to devour their meals.

"Mmm.... this is fantastic!" Ashton said, referring to his steak, "Soo tender!"

"Mine too," Sofia agreed, "Just the way I like it."

It didn't take long for them to finish. Then, they were full.

"Ok...," Robin said. "I'm done eating for the next week," She sighed.

"I'm completely stuffed," She chuckled.

"Yaa...me too," Frank responded.

"Well...I think Ashton and I should hit the pool. We need to wear this off!" Sofia said.

"I'm game," He said, "Let's go,"

They finished their wine and, again, said how nice it was to see both Robin and Walter.

"You don't mind if we take off? Do you?" They asked.

"Oh no… you kids, go and enjoy! We're ok."

"Thanks," Ashton replied, "We'll catch up with you tomorrow."

They said good night and headed out.

Back in their cabin, they changed, grabbed their robes, and then made their way to a quiet pool.

Most of the guests were having dinner now and getting ready for some of the variety of entertainment. That was just fine with them. They had a pool to themselves.

They dropped their robes and walked up to the underlit water.

It sparkled in the dark skies. It was mesmerizing.

Sofia decided to just push Ashton in. Maybe not such a good idea!

When he surfaced, he smiled, then grabbed her leg.

She went down as well and yelled, "OOOPS!... I didn't mean that!... sorry!"

Ashton laughed, "Yaa…sure...I'll get you for that!"

Sofia assured him.

They swam around and did some laps.

"This is awesome!" Sofia commented, " The water is so warm. We should hit the hot tub, too!

"No one is in there at this hour. We'll sleep like babies!" Sofia suggested.

"Good idea!" Ashton replied, "Let's go!"

"Look!" Sofia pointed to the hot tub area.

"They have a movie screen on the wall!... We can catch a movie!" Sofia said.

"Cool...I'll get us a glass of wine, and we'll call it a date! Ha Ha." Ashton chuckled.

"Sure... Ok... Let's do it then," Sofia jumped in excitement.

Ashton slipped over to the bar and ordered. When he returned, he saw Sofia in the water and watching the screen.

And... of course?... What was playing? JAWS!!!!!

The two of them laughed!

"Perfect," Ashton said.

"This is one of my favorites!" Sofia agreed. She always loved it, too.

They settled in and sipped their wine. A warm breeze and steam was coming off the water. The perfect environment for relaxing and feeling at peace.

When the movie ended, they got out and decided to retire for the evening to their suite. They were heading out early in the morning.

Once they both had changed into their lounge clothes, they made themselves a coffee and sat out on their deck.

They discussed whether they would make any plans in Jamaica aside from shopping for coffee. They left that open.

Ashton texted his dad, telling him they would be gone most of the day.

Frank then returned the text with a thumbs up. He also had plans to spend the day with Walter. He needed someone of one-on-one companionship.

It wasn't long when Sofia stood up and, with a yawn, said, "It is time to get some beauty sleep."

Ashton agreed, and they kissed goodnight. Tomorrow's another day.

And, tomorrow came early. It seemed like they closed their eyes and bam!

First Sofia, then Ashton. They ordered breakfast and ate out on the deck. What an amazing view of Montego Bay! The luscious greens and colorful flowers were so inviting. You could smell the fragrances.

What a way to enjoy breakfast! Their plates consisted of bacon and eggs, home fries, and an array of exotic fruits on the side.

"Simply delicious," Ashton commented.

"I agree," Sofia said, rubbing her tummy.

"We're going to have to work this meal off too!" She laughed.

Ashton nodded and took one last sip of coffee.

"Huh!... I like yours better," he scowled. "But for now, I'll just suffer! Soon, we'll have the good European again. Maybe I'll look online."

"No… Ashton… We'll probably get some when we get back to work! Remember work?... That place we get up and check into each day?" Sofia laughed.

"Oh…Yaa… You're right! Lost my head, ha ha ha." Ashton chuckled.

"Well… Jamaica has some awesome coffee, and we'll pick some up. Come on…let's get this day started! There is some shopping we need to do. Not that you like to shop or anything. He he he," Ashton teased her.

Sofia's head jerked towards him, "Ah…Yaa…No, I don't want to shop at all," She smirked.

Ashton gave a devilish smile. He loved to tease her when he could.

Once they were both ready, they took off to where they got off the ship.

They followed the line of passengers and then hailed a cab when they reached the end of the dock.

Take us to the best shopping on the island! Ashton instructs the driver.

"Ohh… and can you tell us where we can find the best coffee?" They asked.

The driver looked into his rearview mirror and said, "I have just the right place for you guys."

"There's a beautiful shop with a large variety of products you will love. My friend owns it. He has the biggest collection of coffees on the Island. There's beach wear, souvenirs, and all sorts of candy and chocolates, too. You will like his place." The driver explained.

"Sounds great!" Sofia said, "Take us there."

They made their way through the touristy areas and came to their stop.

It was a fairly large shop. The surrounding stores were newly built by the looks of them.

"I hope you enjoy and find what you want... would you like me to wait?"The driver asked.

"No...," Ashton said, "We can call you when we're ready. It might take a while," He laughed.

Thank You....we'll call for you. Ashton took his name and number.

Sofia was already out of the car and looking over the shopping area.

First things first.... COFFEE! They went into the shop.

"Ohhh... nice!... Look! There's so much in here." Ashton spotted a beautiful pair of shorts. The colors were vivid and screamed Island life.

"Sold...," He laughed. These are beautiful! The material is top quality!

Sofia was lost in her own glory. She found some really nice shorts and tops. They were very soft and almost dressy-looking.

"Perfect....," she picked them up and carried on.

While she was focused on the boutique items, Ashton headed for the Coffee area.

"Wow! What an assortment!" He thought. He went to the counter, and asked the lady which was the best kind.

She pointed out the top three, and Ashton took a couple of each.

"This will get us through…..," He laughed, "Maybe! Ha ha."

The woman took his choices up to the counter for him. Ashton went and found Sofia and mentioned the coffee.

"Oh… great," She said, "This place is fabulous!"

On their way to check out… they just had to pass through the Chocolate area.

Of course, they had to sample and then purchase a big bag.

"Mm… this is sooo good!" Sofia rolled her eyes, "I think I need some more!"

"Well… we have what we came for…and then some. How about we head over to that juice place across the lot and have a refreshing drink? It's getting pretty hot out here." Sofia suggested.

Ashton agreed, and they walked over.

It was the cutest, bright, and cheery shop, filled with all the fruits and colorful condiments they'd ever seen.

They each enjoyed a tasty smoothie, then decided to head back.

"Those were to die for….," Sofia commented.

Their arms were loaded with bags, and they called the same cab they had before.

"Awe…. I see you found some nice things!" He laughed.

"I hope you liked my friend's store." The driver asked.

"Oh… very much!" They both said, "Thank You,"

He took them back to the ship, and Ashton gave him a huge tip.

The driver almost cried, "Oh, sir…Thank you!!!!"

"This is more than I could make in a month! Thank You…Thank You!!" He said.

"Just enjoy...," Ashton smiled as he took Sofia's hand and returned to the ship.

They reached their suite…where they had fun going through all their purchases.

Sofia had found a couple of short sets, and Ashton got his swimsuit. They also picked up souvenirs, chocolates, and all kinds of sweet treats. It was a productive morning, I would say. They sorted everything and put them away.

Ashton quickly took one of the coffees and made a pot.

"Great!" Sofia said, "We can try it out and relax on the deck."

These views are just stunning.

They both changed into their comfy clothes.

The aroma filled their suite! Ashton took a deep sniff, and his eyes said it all.

"Heavenly!" Sofia sighed, "That's more like it. Now…we're all set."

"Soo……," Ashton spoke up.

"How about we have a US day….and just enjoy our suite, the views, and the quiet. I thought maybe we could order a fabulous Seafood dinner. Some wine, and then enjoy the hot tub." Ashton suggested.

Sofia raised her eyebrows, considering the idea. "You know, that sounds perfect—total relaxation, no need to get dressed up for dinner. Yes, let's. But what about your father?" she inquired.

"He'll be just fine! He'll be with Walter; he knows a lot of people on this ship. I'll text him and let him know," Ashton assured. He took his phone, sent the message, and received a wink in response from Frank.

"OK…We're good…He has no problem with that," Ashton smiled to himself, "He had an ulterior motive for wanting the time alone with Sofia."

He had a little surprise he had been keeping for just the right time.

Tonight's the night.

He was getting excited and hoped she'd love what he had planned.

They got into their bathing suits and lounged in the sun for most of the afternoon.

Sofia moved into the shade and started reading a book that she had brought.

Ashton just closed his eyes and fell asleep.

The sun grew hotter and hotter, and Sofia thought she'd better wake up Ashton, to get into the shade. He was getting a bit too red.

"Oh…Yaa, thanks," He said, quickly moving to where she was lounging.

"That little nap was just perfect," He said, "I think I'll go have a cool shower and change."

He jumped up and disappeared to his bathroom.

Sofia also decided to do the same. She had her own bathroom, so it was not a problem.

Between the two of them, their suite smelled like a perfume boutique! It was beautiful and aromatic.

"Awe…... That felt fabulous," Ashton commented as he surfaced.

Sofia was still getting ready. He poured them each a juice cocktail and set a few chocolates on the plate.

Sofia emerged and was delighted to see the treats.

"You read my mind," She smiled, "Looks so tempting!"

They took the treats and sat at the table by the doors to the deck.

This time, they stayed just inside for the air conditioning.

"This is wicked…. Ash! You should be a bartender," She licked her lips.

"And… no alcohol," He said, "Just fresh, exotic juices. We should try and stay healthy."

"Oh.. and the chocolates are healthy, too?" Sofia smirked.

"Well… I didn't say everything has to be healthy."

They both laughed.

"I thought about dinner," He said, "How about we start with a delicious Vichy soi! Then, a Seafood feast! I'll order a plate with all our favorites! Lobster, Crab, Shrimp, Scallops, and Italian-style Muscles."

"Wow…," Sofia's eyes lit up.

"So, what are you going to have? Ha ha ha," Ashton laughed aloud.

"Oh…you're funny. That sounds awesome, let's do that," Sofia chuckled.

They sipped their drinks and enjoyed the last of the views until their next stop.

"Tomorrow, we're going to the sea," Ashton mentioned.

"I think we would head to Grand Cayman, not sure yet," Ashton added.

"It doesn't matter to me wherever we go: all the islands are beautiful!" Sofia replied.

"So far, from what I've seen. I would find it hard to get used to so much heat all the time, though," Sofia said.

"It would be hard to live here. Thank God for air conditioning! I'm a fall baby!... I love it when the heat and humidity are gone and before the real cold sets in. I love it when the snow falls in big flakes, covering everything in white. It's especially nice at Christmas time. The lights reflect off the snow and brighten all the streets. The ambiance is wonderful. I do enjoy visiting here, though, anytime!" Sofia mentioned her love for winter.

"Speaking of Christmas…," Ashton said, "Do you have any special plans?"

Sofia just gazed at him in thought, "No… not really. I will be planning a party with the gang, though.

Remember?"

"I hope you'll be there too," She said questionably.

Ashton didn't hesitate, "Of course, I will. That sounds great!"

"So…what about you? Do you and your dad have any plans?" Sofia asked.

Ashton looked sad, "We haven't gotten that far yet. I'm sure we won't this year. It could be a quiet time. We'll see how it goes."

"Ok… now… are you getting hungry at all? It's 5.00 PM." Ashton asked.

"I could eat...," Sofia smiled, "Whenever you're ready."

Ashton picked up the phone and ordered from the best restaurant on the ship, 'Ocean Treasures.'

"How about we check out the gym tomorrow and then book a nice massage. I think we should also see what lavish treatments they offer. This can be a Luxury Spa cruise," Ashton suggested.

"Manicures, pedicures, facials, and whatever else they have! Let's go crazy!" He laughed.

Sofia shook her head, "I think YOU are crazy now! Ha ha."

Ashton gave her a quirky smile, "Nah,… just trying to enjoy life while we're here. Life is short. We will, Hun…We're going to have a great life. And yes,"

"That sounds perfect for tomorrow. First the gym…. then we'll go for a facial and manicure. We can book a massage for early evening, so we're relaxed for the night."Sofia jumped in excitement.

"Great! I'll call now and make the appointments." Ashto said.

While Ashton called the Spa, their dinner arrived.

With that was a complimentary bottle of wine.

"Oh.... How nice!" Sofia thanked the man, and he placed the order on their table.

He smiled at her, and winked; then turned and left.

She began setting out the dishes and silverware.

There were beautiful wine glasses on their bar. They were soo sparkly and unique.

Ashton hung up and joined her at the table.

"Wow...Everything looks amazing! You've outdone yourself, my dear," Ashton praised her efforts.

"Yaa... you wish....I wish!" Sofia said.

"Maybe I will go to culinary school! Then, you could eat like this all the time!" Sofia chuckled.

"That sounds good to me," Ashton laughed, "Do It!"

"Come on....Let's enjoy this fabulous seafood before it swims away!" She laughed.

Ashton poured them each a glass of wine.

"Ahh...French! How appropriate!" Sofia said.

"OH? Why? We're having Seafood." Sofia asked.

"Not a reason…. Cheers," Ashton and Sofia clinked their glasses.

They totally made the most of their meal. It was almost all gone.

"OMG… That was excellent! I'm stuffed," Sofia sighed.

"Maybe we should hit the gym now!"

They both laughed.

"Let's take our wine out on the deck. There's a subtle breeze, and the sea air feels refreshing." Sofia suggested.

They took their glasses and sat at the table in the corner.

Ashton poured a little more wine into both glasses.

"Cheers, Sofia to a wonderful Cruise and maybe some new beginnings." Ashton cheered.

She looked at him with a smile and said, "Cheers!"

"There's something I want to give you," Ashton said as he reached in his Pocket.

"I've been keeping this for just the right moment; this feels right."

He pulled out a beautiful black box. Sofia's eyes lit up in surprise.

"For me?" She questioned, "What have I done?"

"Nothing!... Open it," Ashton urged her.

Slowly, she opened the box and gave out a gasp.

A brilliant diamond tennis bracelet lay glistening on black velvet.

"OMG…This is beautiful! Where did you find something like this?" Sofia asked.

"Paris…I did a bit of shopping myself while you were lost in those stores. Remember the main street where all the shops were? Well... I spotted a fine jewelry shop and snuck in. This was the most exquisite one they had. It is one of a kind. I knew I had to get it for you." Ashton told.

"I've never seen anything so beautiful," Sofia said as tears streamed down her face.

"I don't know what to say!" Sofia became emotional.

"Well, here, try it on." He opened the clasp, "It was a perfect fit."

"Look at the sparkles!" Sofia smiled.

She got up and gave Ashton the biggest hug and kiss. She sat back down and sipped wine.

All she could do was stare at the most gorgeous piece of jewelry she had ever owned, "I can't believe you did this!"

No one has ever given me jewelry before, especially something this sparkly!

"What are you thinking?" Ashton asked.

Sofia looked up and said, "I'm thinking about how lucky I am and how my life has changed since I met you. I'm not sure I deserve all this."

Ashton took her arm and gently moved it into the moonlight glow.

He pulled her up from her chair, "You do deserve this."

"This represents the beauty and shining light I see in you. I know you've never had a sense of closeness in your life. I know you've never really felt the security of a family. Maybe one day…. I can change that for you." Ashton put his arms around her and held her tight.

In that instant, Sofia felt her world blossoming and gleaming like a shining, brightest star ever!

She entered a new, exciting phase, and there was no turning back.

She broke their embrace and stood in silence, gazing into his eyes.

Ashton stood quietly, wondering what was next.

Sofia took his hand, and together they turned toward her bedroom.

He stopped dead and asked her if she was sure. She slowly nodded, and they entered the room.

It was the right time; she wanted him. That night, they made beautiful, passionate love.

Neither one had ever felt what they felt that night.

It was innocent and magical. The morning brought a sense of a whole new beginning.

Sofia opened her eyes. Ashton was still sleeping.

She lay there transfixed on his beautiful face, with those soft yet masculine features.

Her mind played out the events of the night. She smiled with the feeling of contentment.

She had become a woman.

Quietly, she slipped out of bed and made the coffee.

Then, she put in an order for breakfast to be delivered in an hour.

There was a beautiful breeze while they slowly cruised to the next island. The sun was just starting to appear.

"What an experience!" She felt so blessed.

Ashton was still sleeping, so she jumped into the shower and put on her favorite tracksuit, some make-up, and a light, subtle perfume.

The scent of coffee filled their suite. She poured a cup and sat out on the deck to watch the sunrise.

This was a moment to capture for a lifetime.

The aromatic coffee had woken Ashton, and he poured a cup and joined Sofia outside.

"Good Morning!" Ashton said flirtatiously.

"Yes…. It really is," She replied with a smile.

Ashton leaned over and gave Sofia a long, gentle kiss.

She closed her eyes in submission.

"Good Morning. It looks like a beautiful day."Sofia said, feeling exceptionally sensual.

Ashton looked out over the water. The sea was very calm.

"How did you sleep?" He asked.

"Like a baby," Sofia replied.

"I did, too. I don't think I woke up, even once." Ashton replied.

"Oh… I hope you're getting hungry…. Our breakfast will be here soon." She said.

"I am starved," He answered, "You're awesome."

"I'll go take a quick shower and be back in time," Ashton told her.

Sofia sat staring out over the sea. The waves were mesmerizing.

Those butterflies had returned. They were feelings of love.

She glanced down and stared at the beautiful Tennis bracelet.

Ashton had given her the night before. It was sparkling.

How did she get so lucky? How did her life change so much?

Ashton was out and ready just as the food showed up.

"I'm starving too," Sofia bubbled, "Let's eat!"

They set the table and devoured their food. It was so delicious.

Then they both broke out laughing.

"Hey… we have a Spa Day planned… remember? Sofia asked.

"I have to look and see what time. I think around 10.00 AM," Ashton told her.

Ashton went and found his notes, "Yaa…10.00 AM. We have 45 minutes. I want another coffee."

"I'll have one, too," Sofia replied.

"I'm really looking forward to a nice massage and some beauty treatments. It's been a long time since I paid any attention to myself. A facial will make a world of difference for me. My skin feels so dry." Sofia touched her face.

"We're always in the public eye. Looking our best is key when working for Exotic Airlines. All our guests are wealthy and elite. They expect the best of the best. That means us as well." Sofia became over-excited.

"Yaa…I agree; peer pressure things…," Ashton laughed.

"Speaking of Exotic, how about I text my dad and tell him we'll join them for dinner?"

"Oh, yeah, for sure," Sofia replied, "If we don't fall asleep after our treatments! Ha ha. You may want to word it as …. We'll try!"

They both laughed.

"Yaa…Ok,"

****

"Ok…Let's get this show on the road!" They both chuckled.

They headed out down the corridor and around the corner.

This Spa was designated strictly for guests with suites.

"Wow, beautiful," Sofia commented, "Looks so tranquil!"

They were greeted by a very nice-looking man and taken to the desk.

After they signed in, they were both guided to the massage rooms.

And given instructions and their changing rooms.

Ashton had chosen a his and her's massage treatment.

Once in their robes… they met back in a dreamy Zen-type room.

Seductive music, lighting, and relaxing aromas.

There were two beds, almost side by side, and they each took one.

Once they were settled, two women entered the room.

In no time, they were lost in a luxury, almost sleep-inducing massage.

From there, they had a variety of other heavenly treatments.

Ashton also asked for a haircut, and Sofia chose to have hers touched up.

Just a slight trim and some highlights.

They were both very pleased with the day.

By the time they were finished, it was almost time for dinner.

"If we just go back and change quickly, we can make it," Ashton laughed, "I'm so dreary now, but we can do it."

"A cool shower may help," He laughed.

"Yaa… I think we can stay awake long enough to eat," Sofia replied.

They both yawned at the same time.

It took a lot of effort… but they made it to dinner.

Their bodies felt like jelly.

Frank and Walter were there when they arrived.

"Well…there they are," Walter smiled, "We're glad you could join us."

They said hello and took their seats.

"Yaa…," Ashton spoke, "It was very hard," He laughed.

"The Spa Day was more relaxing than we thought." She told them.

"Ohh…my…," Walter's eyes found Sofia's wrist.

"What a gorgeous bracelet! You have exquisite taste, my dear!" Walter praised her bracelet.

"Thank You…but Ashton gave this to me," Sofia glanced over, smiled, and blushed.

"Really?... Well, then, you have great taste," Ashton said.

"I can see the quality from here!" Walter told them.

Frank sat with his hands folded on the table. He was analyzing Sofia and Ashton.

"Am I right in feeling there has been a bit of a change in your relationship, guys?" Ashton and Sofia looked at each other.

"Well, yes… we have been getting closer and closer now that we have been able to spend some quality time together." Ashton turned and smiled at Sofia. He took her hand.

"I thought she was a wonderful person, before… but now… I've come to realize that she is even more than that!"Ashton said.

Sofia looked down towards the table, slightly embarrassed.

"The same goes for me," She added.

We've had the time to really talk and learn about each other.

It's been easy for us to get along and connect.

And this suite we have is like we're sharing a two-bedroom apartment.

It's been really great!

"I'm so glad to hear that!" Frank raised his eyebrows, "I wasn't sure how that would work out. I just crossed my fingers."

"Ok… let's order before you two fall asleep at the table!" Everyone laughed.

The Steak seemed to be the popular choice. It came with baked potato, asparagus, and a tasty sauce.

"Mmm…," They indulged in the food.

It was cooked to perfection and seasoned just right.

It was quite a bit for everyone, but they managed to finish it off.

No one had any dessert.

"So… Can I assume you two will be heading back to your suite early this evening?" Frank laughed.

"Oh, yaa… You assumed right," Ashton said sleepily.

"In fact… I think we should have our coffee up on our deck. Not that we don't want to spend time with you.

Tomorrow night, we'll be more awake. I hope you don't mind." Ashton said.

"Not at all," Walter added, "You two go!" He laughed.

"We'll be fine here. I think the next massages we get will be after dinner," Ashton said to him while Sofia nodded.

The two excused themselves and made their way back to their suite.

Once the coffee was ready, they sat out on the deck.

Sofia yawned and laughed, "I feel so relaxed and dopy. Those treatments really were awesome!"

"Yaa…," Ashton agreed, "I'm the same. Maybe they spiked our health drinks," He commented suspiciously.

Sofia glanced at him. "Yaa… sure they did."

"Well… whatever it was… I feel great! I'll sleep like a baby tonight." Ashton chuckled.

"Soo…anything you'd like to do tomorrow?" Sofia asked.

"Oh…yes.! I'd like to get ahold of Robin. Maybe at one of our stops, we can get off and find some authentic Caribbean cuisine. And…do a little shopping, of course," He laughed.

"That sounds awesome! Give her a call!" Sofia said excitedly.

"I will, in the morning. She's probably busy right now with all the entertainment and activities tonight." Ashton replied.

"I know there's some competition going on in the theatre, so we can catch her before she starts her day tomorrow," Sofia said.

Sofia poured them another coffee. Then fell into her lounge chair.

"Ahhhhh… This is heavenly!" She gazed out over the seas, with the breeze blowing through her hair.

Ashton's heart melted. Just seeing her in the moonlight made his heart race. He sat transfixed and felt truly blessed.

"What a beautiful day," He said.

Sofia agreed. They closed their eyes and let the gentle wind wash away any lingering stress.

Ashton turned to Sofia, "Last night was Beautiful…... I loved sleeping next to you."

Sofia smiled, "Yes…. I loved waking up this morning in your arms."

Ashton paused, "Can I sleep with you tonight?"

Sofia didn't hesitate, "I was hoping you would. Every night, I felt so safe and secure.

They both smiled and closed their eyes again.

They actually fell asleep for a while. How could they not?

Between the warm winds and the sound of the waves, who need sleeping pills? The perfect natural drug of the seas.

They were out for quite some time. When Ashton woke up, it was 9.00 PM.

"Oh… it's still early," He thought. Sofia was still asleep.

He was a bit hungry, so he slipped inside and ordered a wonderful Charcuterie Board.

He also had some fresh juices to go along with that.

Sofia woke up and was surprised!

"Ohh…Wow…where did this come from?" She asked.

"I'm actually getting hungry!" She said, "How did you know?"

Ashton laughed, "Well… I'm hungry too," He replied as he poured them each a glass of fresh, exotic juices. He made his own blend.

"Oh… Yum….," Sofia perked up, "Looks and smells amazing!"

As they enjoyed their delicious snacks, they got their second wind.

"I'll see if there are any good movies playing," Ashton said as he got up.

"I'm feeling awake now." He said.

"Ok," Sofia said and followed him back in.

"Just no horror films! I don't need to have nightmares," She laughed.

They found and settled on a light comedy.

Together, they curled up on the couch and got comfy.

"What a great ending to a perfect day! The best day ever!" They both hugged each other.

When they couldn't keep their eyes open anymore, they slipped into bed and were off in dreamland.

They both slept through the night with no problems at all. They were totally done in.

The next morning, Ashton woke up first. He made the coffee and put in a breakfast order.

He slipped into the shower and came out ready for a new day. He sat quietly on the deck with a coffee.

Sofia then surfaced and did the same. She showered, got dressed then grabbed a coffee.

"Yesterday was an awesome day! Now, today, I'm relaxed but far more energetic." Sofia chuckled.

"I think we needed that," Ashton added.

"What shall we do today," He asked.

"I'd love to check out some of the sports," Sofia stated.

"You know…. The one like you're skydiving, and the one like you're surfing. Then…. if you're up to it, we could go ice skating!" Sofia suggested.

"Ice skating!" Ashton screamed, "We're out at sea…the Caribbean! Not New York?"

Sofia laughed, "Don't be a wimp! It could be fun."

"Yaa…sure…. fun." He teased her.

"Oh…. Our breakfast is here! I'm famished!" Ashton jumped up to answer their door, "Smells great!"

They loaded their plates and went back out to the table.

****

Another gorgeous day at sea.

"My eggs are perfect," Sofia commented, "And…this Canadian bacon is to die for! I think this is my favorite. Well… my sausages are soo tender and tasty, as well. It's hard to choose."

When they finished…. they sipped their juice, then another coffee.

"I don't care what we do today," Sofia said lazily, "I'm happy here, no matter what. We can lounge by the pool and have a hot tub. I brought a couple of books, so I'm set."

"Oh… I want to call Robin; tomorrow, we will be at Grand Cayman," He picked up his phone…and hit her number.

She answered right away.

He asked about going for lunch and shopping, but she had to recline.

She has soo many activities on the go but said she'll stop in the dining room and say hello…. if they're there.

"I'm sorry. I've been very busy with some new ventures, they have added." She replied.

"Ohh… too bad. I thought I'd give it a shot anyway. We will see you at dinner then." Ashton replied.

"Great…I'm just on my way out. I have to make sure everyone is doing their thing," She laughed.

"Ok…," Ashton said, "Talk to you soon."

They hung up.

"So… I guess it's just us tomorrow," Ashton told Sofia, "We'll catch up with her sometime. She said she'll stop by at dinner."

"OK…That's fine; we are capable of hunting out shops and food," She laughed.

"I have a built-in GPS, you know." She chuckled.

"Yaa… I know that," He smiled.

"I was thinking maybe we could take my dad on a tour of the ship today. I don't think he's really done that." Ashton suggested.

"Ohh… Yaa… We should!... He can see what his stocks have helped to create!" She replied.

Ashton laughed, "That's for sure....He has enough of them."

"And… Let's choose a time and place to take care of my mother's ashes." He further added.

"Yaa…Good idea, Hun that will help to ease his heart a little." Sofia replied.

Ashton called his dad and proposed his idea.

Surprisingly, he thought that was a great plan. He hadn't really seen the entire ship after it was completed. He was excited at the thought.

"OK… how about an hour from now," Frank agreed.

They all got ready in their comfy clothes and shoes.

The ship is like a city in itself, huge, and a lot of walking; there are so many decks. Most of which have different activities.

It's not bad unless, like them, you're trying to see everything in one shot.

It's really better to break it up, but this will be just a quick overview.

They made their way, starting at the first deck with points of interest.

Deck by deck, they showed him all the highlights.

Frank seemed very excited at what he observed.

At noon… they even stopped at the hot dog place. They found them delicious.

Franks thought the entire ship was very impressive!

That made him feel content and satisfied with his heavy investments.

"Hmmm… Maybe I'll invest more!" He laughed.

The true tour allowed him to really get a better feel of the ship rather than just seeing drafts and pictures.

He could feel the life of the passengers and their excitement.

Simple renderings could never duplicate that.

When they reached the end, Frank thanked them for the nice gesture.

"That was a great idea," He said.

"I have a much better perspective now. Perhaps I'll go call my financial advisor and pick up some more stocks." Frank added.

Ashton and Sofia broke out laughing, "OK… whatever you think, Dad! Have fun."

"Well… that was fun, guys; thanks again. I think I'll go relax for a while, And hopefully, see you two at dinner." Frank said.

"Yes…We'll be there. We'll meet you there."

"Great! Walter will be happy, too. He's always asking about you." He said.

"We've been having a great time catching up and reminiscing. I need this right now. I need a close friend my age too. It's been so long. I spent soo many years just concentrating on your mother, and I lost touch with so many friends along the way. It's funny how you don't even realize it until it's too late that they're gone." Frank became emotional.

"Anyway…to change the subject… I'll see you soon," Frank said.

Ashton nodded and said, "OK."

He turned, and they went to their suite. The mood was heavy. There was just soo much, he didn't realize. He was young and carefree.

He was finding his place and where he wanted to be, between work and friendships. Ashton's face went straight, and years of guilt suddenly washed over him.

How could he not see what was going on with his family?

All he knew was his mother would be unwell for bouts at a time.

Then she would be ok.

Sofia sat beside him and wrapped her arms around him, "It'll be ok, Hun. It's not your fault. How were you to know?"

Tears were streaming down his face, "I should have known…. I should have paid more attention. Maybe I would have done more to help out!"

Sofia spent the next half hour comforting Ashton.

Then he got up and went to lie down. He needed time alone.

He came out an hour later… and appeared a bit better.

He smiled and thanked Sofia for understanding, then made a coffee. They talked it out until, finally, Ashton agreed to stop feeling so guilty.

They will not discuss it again. He jumped in the shower and got ready for dinner. Sofia did the same.

It was time to head out for dinner. Sofia managed to get a smile out of Ashton.

Soon, his demeanor started to change back to his happy self, and Sofia was delighted. She held his hand tight as they approached their table.

Frank and Walter were there and greeted them with big smiles.

Walter motioned for Sofia to come sit beside him, and so she did.

"Nice to see you, my dear! You two seem to be enjoying your cruise."He laughed, "It's a treat to have you for dinner."

"I know…sorry," She replied, "We will be joining you more now."

They ordered and enjoyed a casual chit-chat.

Robin popped in and sat for a few minutes. She and Sofia hugged.

They were happy to see each other again.

"I'm sorry, guys…my plate has just been so full lately. They've incorporated so many new activities, and it's been totally demanding. I barely have time to think anymore. I'd love to have some time with you. Maybe next week! I'll have to check." Robin informed.

Sofia and Ashton looked sad.

Frank sat quietly, listening. He wasn't that pleased. No one should be so busy that they can't enjoy a meal with friends. The poor girl looked exhausted.

He asked her a few questions, then remained silent.

Robin tried to catch up really quickly, then had to excuse herself.

She said she'll try to find some time for them.

"We're hoping so…" Ashton raised his voice as she briskly left the dining room.

Frank then turned and started by saying that Walter had been telling him all about his Animal Rescue. He had no idea that he was so involved.

He added, "Walter has asked me to come and stay with him for a while and see for himself what he really does. I think I'll take up on the offer."

"He has a large guest house and never has any guests!" They laughed.

"There's nothing to keep me at home now.... And he's just as close to Exotic as our house is, so why not? It might do me some good." Frank said.

Ashton thought that was an awesome idea! Sofia agreed, "That would be wonderful for you. Cheers!"

They raised their glasses.

Their food then arrived, and they were all hungry.

Tonight is Pasta night; they all chose their favorite. There were three types of salads to choose from.

 The aromas were as delectable as always.

"Another fine meal, too much food as usual," Walter laughed, "We'd better take some evening walks to wear it off."

"I think you're right," Frank added, "I could sure use the exercise,"

The whole table agreed; they all needed it.

Ashton decided to bring up the topic of his mother's ashes. They should pick a day.

Frank sat in deep thought, "How about...Friday? We can go to the very tip of the ship."

A tear trickled down his face as he spoke the words.

"It's ok, dad. Remember, this is her happy place," Ashton nodded.

"Yes... you're right. It will be a good day." Frank replied.

They sat for a moment in silence.

Then, Sofia spoke up, "Hey guys, How about a show? There's also a comedy night. All their spirits seemed to lighten."

"Sounds good!" Walter replied.

"I haven't been in a while. I've never been," Frank added.

"Ok...well, let's get out of here and go see which we want and if there are any tickets still. It's getting late." They stood and headed out.

The music show was all sold out, but the comedy show tickets were available.

Sofia was secretly hoping for that one, as everyone needed a mood lift.

They checked and were told they had an hour before the show started. So, they went to the nearest little night spot and had a glass of wine.

"This was a great idea," Sofia said, "I would have just gone back to my suite and fallen asleep reading."

They had some pleasant conversations about the ship.

Frank was completely blown away by the décor.

He had never really stopped and absorbed what he was looking at; he was impressed.

The intricate details in every piece of furniture, wall hangings, color scheme, and lighting was just supreme!

Sofia saw him just nodding in approval and with a smile.

"Looks like my investments were put to good use!" He said with satisfaction.

"Ok….it's time to go. I'm sure there will be a lineup."

They finished their wine, and off they went. It didn't take long for the people to get in. The line went quickly. They got settled and awaited the show.

The comedian came out…. And in no time, they were all laughing!

"This guy is a real card!" Frank commented, "My mouth is starting to hurt."

Walter was killing himself as well.

Ashton and Sofia were laughing at the comedian and the two supporting men.

They hurried back to the same night spot when the show was over.

They sat, massaging their faces.

"I haven't laughed so hard in a million years. I'm exhausted!" Frank said.

"Well, that says a lot about the entertainment," Sofia said, "We're glad you came out and had a good time."

"Yes, thank You, guys. Now, I'm ready to retire for the night; that did me in," He laughed.

"Maybe we'll see you at breakfast," Ashton told them, "We're getting off for some shopping."

"Ok, great," Frank said, "I'll see you in the morning."

Walter said good night as well.

"Thank You," He nodded.

The two gentlemen headed back up to their cabins.

Sofia and Ashton stayed to finish the last bit of wine.

"That was awesome; I'm so glad you thought of that. I've never seen my dad laugh like that. Cheers to you!"Ashton appreciated her efforts, and Sofia tapped his glass.

"I think we should hit the bed early, too. We have a busy day tomorrow." Ashton suggested.

"Sounds like a plan, "Sofia responded, "Let's go."

They didn't sit out this time; they just decided to catch up on some sleep.

It didn't take long for Sofia to fall asleep in Ashton's arms.

This is probably the most wonderful part of their relationship. She felt so safe, and wanted, something she had never felt before.

Morning came in an instant, it seemed, but they were ready to start their day.

The earlier-than-usual bedtime helped. They quickly showered and dressed for their venture.

Breakfast with Frank and Walter was soon.

They had time to enjoy a good coffee before leaving.

What a perfect day to shop around Grand Cayman; a gentle breeze kept some of the heat at bay.

From what they could see from their deck, the scenery was breathtaking. The crystal-blue waters and vibrant flowers brought happiness.

The snow in New York, however, was not so inviting. Despite this, they were set to have a great day, starting with breakfast, as both of them were hungry.

"Come on…. Let's go!" Ashton said eagerly.

"Coming…. Coming…. Coming…...," Sofia laughed.

"Someone's hungry, I think?" Sofia asked.

"Yes, I'm starving!" Ashton replied.

"Well, I am, too! It must be the sea air!" They both agreed.

"I've got Blueberry waffles in my head!" He laughed, smothered in whipped cream.

"I want my favorite: Canadian bacon and eggs, home fries, and toast. Mmmm….," Sofia chuckled.

They joined the men at their table and, right way ordered.

Coffee was served, and they started with a fresh pastry from their server.

"You two look lively this morning," Walter commented.

"That's because we went to sleep early for a change," Ashton replied.

"I guess it's good to get more beauty sleep now and then," He added.

"We could all use that," Frank said with a laugh, "I know, I do!"

"Well… I'm just beautiful, with or without sleep," Ashton replied.

Everyone paused, then broke out laughing.

"Yes, you are," Frank said and rolled his eyes.

"We are going to head out today and do some shopping and probably lunch, " Ashton told the guys.

"There's nothing like authentic food on the islands. All the ingredients are fresh and locally grown, and they make your dish in front of you." He further told.

"Ohhh… that sounds good," Frank said.

"Would you like to join us?" Sofia asked him.

"No, dear, but thanks for asking. Walter and I have booked some time in the spa." Frank replied.

"Oh great," Ashton said, "You'll feel good as new. You'll love it!"

"I think we're only going for a massage…then for a swim. There are a group of regulars, that Robin introduced us to. They love to play cards. We thought we'd go and check it out." Frank told them about his plans for the day out.

185

"Nice," Sofia said, "You might just enjoy that."

Their food arrived, and they gobbled it down.

It was still early, so they had another coffee.

They decided to head out after some small talk and letting their food settle.

"Ok, you gentlemen, enjoy your day." He said.

"Stay out of trouble, too." Everyone laughed.

"We'll try," Walter added, "Or maybe we won't. Haha,"

"We should be here for dinner," Ashton said as they waved goodbye.

Hand in hand, they made their way off the ship.

They climbed into a taxi and asked to be taken to any nice marketplace.

Their driver was very friendly and eager to point out any sights and notable attractions. They enjoyed that.

Grand Cayman is a very flat Island, but even without the mountains, it has its own beauty. They make up for that with their fragrant and colorful gardens.

One of the highlights is swimming with the stingrays. And their beaches are breathtaking.

Sofia saw an iguana as they drove slowly up to their stop.

"Oh, look! It's so cute! It looks like a mini-Dragon!" She was fascinated by its subtle colors.

It also surprised her that it didn't run away.

She stood watching it for a few moments.

"Come on, let's get into some shade," Ashton called out to her, "It's getting hot."

"Ok...," She laughed, "You're right....it is hot now."

They slipped into the first little store. They really didn't come for anything specific. It's just fun, looking around at what they have to offer.

They made their way through the different stores one by one, picking up a few trinkets here and there, but nothing major.

They spotted an ice cream parlor and had to have some.

Sofia had a hard time bypassing those as they were like magnets to her.

"Ice cream...Gelato....it's all good," She said as she finished.

It was a welcomed cooling treat.

"Where to now?" Ashton asked.

"Oh, how about we go back and relax? The ship will be half empty. We can have a hot tub and read while getting some rays." Sofia recommended.

"Sounds good to me," He replied.

They stepped outside and began to walk toward the main entrance of the shopping mall. There were vendor tents all around as well, including indoor and outdoor marketplace/mall.

It was quite unique.

Hand in hand, they strolled, checking out all the sellers.

An older woman is in front of them, carrying a couple of bags.

She was walking slowly.

Just as she reached the corner of a small store, a young boy jumped.

Out, knocking her down, he grabbed her bags and took off!

Sofia gasped, "OMG,"

Ashton didn't hesitate! He shot off, running after the guy.

Sofia quickly ran to help the old woman laying on the ground.

She kneeled down and rested her head on her legs.

"Are you ok? Are you hurt?" Sofia asked.

The woman was in tears.

"I'm ok," She said in quivering words.

"He took my food! It's all I have. I don't know how I will be able to eat now." She cried, and seeing her made Sofia emotional.

"I have no more money!" She cried.

Sofia rocked her, telling her things will be ok.

Someone who saw what happened had called the police.

Two officers approached them and made sure the woman was okay.

They asked for the details and made notes.

Ashton came back.... he couldn't catch the man who did this.

He was out of breath and sweating.

One of the officers ran off to try and find the guy.

They were able to sit the woman up and then into the cruiser, where it was cooler. Sofia took her hand and helped.

The woman was sobbing so sadly. She has no more money for food.

Sofia was crying now as much as the woman.

"It will be ok," Ashton reassured her, "Don't worry."

The officers had what they needed and offered her a ride home.

Ashton asked if they could go along and get her settled in.

"Sure," The one said, "That is very nice of you!"

They all got in, and it wasn't far from where she lived.

When they reached her home, Sofia saw nothing but a small hut-type structure. There were no windows, just open spaces.

She couldn't imagine having to live there.

The officer got out and escorted them into her house.

It was sparsely furnished.

There was a small kitchen with a small fridge.

Before the officer left, Ashton asked him to call for a cab.

The officer offered him a ride.

"Please take me to a grocery store. I want to replace her food. That's so nice of you," The cop said, "Come on, let's go."

They spotted the other officer as they turned the corner.

"No luck," He said, "He's long gone."

Ashton told them to drop him off; he might take a while.

"That's ok…. We'll wait for you." They replied.

He went in and bought all kinds of fresh fruit and veggies.

The fridge she has is small, so he wanted to pick up a lot of Canned food. He also bought a can opener in case she didn't have one.

He bought up a ton of good healthy foods and drinks. Rice and peanut butter were on the top of his list. Canned vegetables, beans, soups, juices, etc. He came out, and the officers helped load the bags.

They were very impressed with this young tourist and his girlfriend.

"You are very kind!" The one officer commented.

They returned to find Sofia and the woman sitting in tears.

But when they saw the guys walk in with all the food, the old woman smiled from ear to ear.

"You are too kind," She said, "I don't know what I would've done! Thank You, Thank You!"

"How can I ever repay you?" She said with tears in her eyes.

"There's no need," Ashton said, "You just take care of yourself."

"I will try," She responded.

Sofia helped her put everything away. There was enough food for a month at least.

When the woman wasn't looking, Ashton slipped 200.00 dollars in the fridge under a bottle of juice.

Sofia was calming down now. They stayed for a few more minutes and then had to return.

The officers offered them a ride to the ship. On the way, they thanked them again for all their kindness.

Sofia just sat looking blankly out the window.

As they reached the dock, one officer mentioned that they were welcome to come back anytime and even encouraged them to look them up if they did. They exchanged handshakes and bid their goodbyes.

Sofia was quiet and out of sorts as they headed to their suite.

Ashton knew she was very upset after seeing the living conditions of the elderly woman.

So, he let her be in peace.

Ashton made them a coffee, and they went out to the deck.

Sofia just kind of dropped into her chair.

"Are you OK?" Ashton asked.

"Yaa," She said. I just feel so sad about that woman. It must be so scary for her, being alone and poor. She's just so vulnerable.

Ashton ordered a light lunch for them.

His phone rang, it was Robin. She said she'd be joining them at dinner as long as nothing came up with work.

"Ok," Ashton replied, "Great, Sofia will be happy to see you. Me too, of course," He laughed, "We'll see you there."

They hung up, and he mentioned it to Sofia about Robin.

She managed a smile and nodded.

"That's great," She gave her head a shake.

"Ok… I'm ok." She replied.

They sipped their coffee and enjoyed the sun and gentle breeze.

Frank and Ashton had decided that it would be nice to go for a quiet dinner in one of the famous restaurants.

Afterward, they will take his mother's ashes and sprinkle them out over the sea.

"That sounds nice," Sofia responded.

Their lunch arrived, and they kind of picked at it. Neither one was very hungry.

They shifted over to their lounge chairs, and both fell asleep in the shade, a well-deserved rest.

The fresh air does wonders for that.

They slept for about an hour, then showered and changed for dinner.

It was early, so Ashton suggested they go down to the boardwalk deck and wander around.

Sofia looked at him and said, "There's candy there! Let's go!"

"That's my Sofia," Ashton smiled.

"I'm feeling better Now," She said, "I know we can't fix everything or everyone. It just upsets me, that's all. All we can do is help out where we can and carry on. I'll have to work on that."

Ashton listened intently, "You just be you, I'll help you get through the rough stuff."

They embraced each other.

"You're special," He told her, "The world needs more like you."

"Come on…. Let's go for some treats!" She practically ran out the door.

"Hey! Wait for me!" Ashton ran after her.

The two of them were laughing as they got on the elevator.

"We have to get there before they sell out!" Sofia squealed.

"Oh… I doubt that's going to happen," He laughed.

They reached the deck and got out.

"OK, now go gather all the treats you want, but then give them to me," Ashton told her.

Sofia looked at him in surprise and asked, "Why?"

"Because," He said, "You'll eat too many, and we'll have dinner soon."

Sofia pouted, then said, "You're right. Ok, I will."

They laughed.

"I know you so well, my love," Ashton chuckled.

She turned and went straight for the candy store. She entered and picked up a bag.

"Where to begin?" She said to herself, "How about the start?"

Slowly, she moved around, adding one thing after another.

Soon, she needed another bag.

"Ok….I think I'm good, for now anyway!" She said.

Ashton waited outside but could see her.

He watched with a smile on his face. It was great to see her happy.

He glanced at his watch just as she came out. It was time to go.

"Perfect timing," He said, "We should head up to the dining room."

"Ready!" She replied, "I'm hungry, too!"

"Ohhh… here…," She handed Ashton her bags as promised.

Two large bags stuffed with chocolates and other sweets.

Ashton laughed and took them from her, "Good Girl! You can have them later when we get back from dinner."

"You bet I will," She said with an assuring look.

As usual, Frank and Walter were there first.

They took their seats and settled in. There was a bottle of wine already on the table. Frank poured them each a glass.

Their server appeared, welcoming them. He informed them it was Italian night on the menu, so they each chose their favorite.

"Pasta dish." One of them said.

They gave their order.

"So," Frank took a sip of wine, "How was your day, guys?"

Sofia and Ashton looked at each other and exhaled.

"Well," Ashton spoke first, "It was not the way we had planned, but it all worked out." He squeezed Sofia's hand.

"You tell the story," She said.

Ashton proceeded to tell them all about what happened at the Market place.

He gave them all the details about what had happened, the woman they helped, and what they did for her.

Sofia had tears in her eyes as he relived the events.

Walter noticed; he, too, felt the sadness.

Frank raised his eyebrows in surprise.

"Really?" He commented.

Sofia shook her head, "It breaks my heart to see someone living in poverty. It just kills me and that look of fear when the guy took her only food, however meager, she had to stop. This shouldn't be. I'll never forget her helpless face; she was devastated."

Ashton jumped in, "We took care of that."

He told them what they did to manage her food at the grocery store.

"I just hope she's okay. She lives alone." He described her run-down home if you can call it that.

****

Sofia looked up, "It was very sad."

"We were glad the two officers came to help, too. They took me to get the food for her," Ashton told them.

Frank listened in silence; he knew how people lived on these Islands.

He has seen the downside behind the pretty beaches and jewelry shops.

Tourists only see the beautiful scenery and highlighted activities.

After their morning rundown, there was a sense of quiet calm.

Frank broke the solemn mood by bringing up their next night's dinner and taking care of the ashes afterward.

They were looking forward to that, setting his wife free!

Frank Thought, "It would be a sense of closure."

Their food was served, and they all perked up.

They changed the subject and enjoyed some light chit-chat while they ate.

The entire dining room smelled like an Italian restaurant.

Frank had chosen a restaurant for them the next night, but now he thought he would change plans.

After this big meal, like most others, he thought they would make it something lighter.

He also invited Walter to join them, and Walter felt honored.

"Thank You," He said.

Ashton was very glad that he was there so that Frank would have someone to be with afterward. They could hang out for a while.

Once dinner was finished, they said their good nights, and Ashton and Sofia headed out.

They wanted to walk off their meal.

Ashton placed his arm around Sofia and gave her a hug.

"Come on…. let's go for a swim. It might pick you up a bit. After that, we'll go up and relax with a nice strong coffee. You can snack on some chocolates!" Ashton tried to lift her mood.

"Oh…Yaa…I forgot!" She laughed.

"Ok…let's go!" She nodded.

They had the pool to themselves. Everyone was either eating or getting ready for one of the shows.

They enjoyed the warm waters for at least an hour. It was still refreshing.

When they were finished, they went to their suite and changed into comfy lounge clothes.

They sat under the stars and sipped their drink. Sofia also put out some goodies.

"Awe... This is heaven," She said, holding her cup close.

"This really is peaceful. I'll never get tired of listening to the waves." She kept admiring the starry sky and kinky waves.

"Well," Ashton reminded her, "I think we only have 4 days left."

"I'll have to check. I'm not even sure what day this is." He laughed.

"Oh... Tomorrow, I'd like to go see the captain. It's been a while, and I'd love to check out the Bridge on this ship."

"I sent a text to Robin, and she said she would arrange a time when he could spend some time with us," Ashton informed her.

"Oh...That sounds great!" Sofia responded, "He's very nice. I thought it was fascinating up there."

"Good, I'm looking forward to it."

They both laid back in their lounge chairs and closed their eyes.

The night breezes lulled them into a relaxed mode.

They had to force themselves to get up and go to bed.

The salty sea air seemed to have a drug-like effect on them, especially after a long swim. But soon, they were sleeping like babies, and neither of them woke up in the night.

Ashton had set his alarm for 8.00 AM. He quickly shut it off and let Sofia sleep a little longer.

He awaited his text from Robin.

Sure enough, it came through, letting him know about an 11.30 AM time for the bridge.

After a tour, the captain said he'll take you for lunch.

"That's great," He said, "We'll meet you there."

He jumped up and made the coffee. Then ordered some pastries.

He thought it was time and woke up Sofia. She was a bit groggy, but after a shower was as good as new.

He filled her in on the plans, and she was very pleased.

"You'll love it," She said to Ashton, "It's so cool."

The pastries arrived, and the coffee was ready. They took it all outside.

"I think we're at Sea now for a couple of days," Ashton said.

"Then… I think we are in the Bahamas. That will be our last stop." He added.

Sofia frowned, "This almost feels like home! I hate to leave now."

She stated, "But…. I know all good things must come to an end."

Ashton looked out over the sparkling waters.

"I know how you feel. I really do not want to leave either." He replied.

They sat in silence for a short time.

"We'll see what happens," He kind of said to himself.

"Pardon…," Sofia looked at him.

"Oh… nothing, just thinking out loud. I love the Bahamas," He said, changing the subject, "It's my favorite. And close and easy to get there."

"We'll do a short tour, then try out their fabulous new Water Park! It looks amazing!" He added.

"Sure," Sofia looked at him with suspicious eyes.

She was sure that he said something she might want to hear.

"Hmm anyway…," She spoke up, "I'm glad to see Captain John again."

"He's very handsome, you know! Dreamy eyes and a sharp nose." She added.

Ashton shot a jealous look at her.

"Do I have some competition? He asked.

Sofia laughed

"Maybe." She said coyly.

Ashton pouted, "Nah…. Just kidding."

"I hope not," He said, touching his nose. Sofia got up and kissed him.

"You're all I want," She assured him.

"Thanks," He said, playing sad, "I only want you too."

There was a knock at their door, and Ashton jumped up to answer.

Frank and Walter were standing there.

"Are we disturbing you two?" Frank asked.

"No, come on in." Ashton offered them a coffee, and they went outside.

"Morning!" They said to Sofia.

"Oh…Good morning! What are you two gentlemen doing today?" Sofia asked.

"Oh…. We just thought we'd stop by and run something past you." They answered.

"Sounds intriguing!" Sofia said, "I'm listening."

Frank and Walter pulled up a chair.

"Mm.... your coffee smells wonderful!" They exclaimed.

"So," Frank began.

"We just came from a short meeting with Robin, the captain, and a few others. Just a brief informational meeting on our stocks, etc. But... afterward, I was talking to Robin about how the staffing was working out. I had heard they were short a few key positions. The magnitude of this ship, some positions, require double staff. For one, ... Robin is very overworked. There really should be two Cruise Directors on a ship this size." Frank explained.

"Anyway, in talking, she suggested letting Sofia stay on as an assistant for her. She was laughing. I think she was joking, but it made me think. That might be an excellent Idea! I mean, if you would agree. We would also find a position for you, Ashton, maybe in Customer Service with Zachary. You two are a lot alike." Frank added.

"It could just be temporary. We could test the waters, so to speak, and see if it might be something you might enjoy. It's clear to everyone how you love the ship. You both have a lot of experience with the public, and both of you are very personable. " He said.

Sofia and Ashton looked at each other and stared in shock.

"I'm speechless," Sofia broke the silence.

"What about Exotic? Don't you need us back there soon? I already feel so funny, about being away, so long!" She laughed guiltily.

"My dear, I own the company and make any decisions I want! Don't you feel bad about anything? You mean more to me here with my son. You have been a Godsend to both of us." Frank adored her.

Sofia just blinked in silence, "I don't know what to say!"

Ashton agreed.

"This is a complete surprise," He said.

"You don't have to decide right this minute," Frank Laughed, "Take your time. If you are interested…. You'll have a month at home to prepare. Your training will be on the job, but nothing you haven't really done before."

"Also, you can keep the suite you're in now…... because I have a lot of pull. Ha ha Ha. It pays to invest heavily sometimes." Frank chuckled.

"Hmm… OK, maybe we'll think about this." Ashton replied.

"Hmm," Sofia smiled, "Yes…. we will. It sounds like a great opportunity, actually."

"Ok… That's all we came for. I know you're leaving soon to meet Robin. She may start bugging you to take the offer, so… be prepared!" He laughed.

"She's all excited." He added.

"Ok, Dad…. Give us some time, and we'll think it over." Ashton said.

"Great," Frank said, "We'll catch up at dinner tonight at 5 .00 O clock. We'll be there."

The two men left, and Sofia and Ashton went back outside.

They sat staring at each other, not knowing what to say. Sofia shook her head, "Wow... I wasn't expecting that,"

"Yaa, neither was I," Ashton said.

"Any thoughts?" He asked, with a puzzled look.

Again, Sofia just shook her head.

"We can discuss it more later tonight. Now, we should go meet Robin." He said.

They cleared their table, put everything ready to be picked up, and headed out.

When they reached the Bridge, Robin was just coming off another elevator.

"Hey, great to see you guys!" She led the way.

They found the captain standing at his post. He was instructing the co-captain with all the details.

He spotted them and started their way.

"Hey…. Ashton! Great to see you again. How have you been? It's been a while!" He inquired.

"Great," He said as they shook hands, "You're looking good!"

"Sorry to hear about your mother. She was a fine lady. I really thought about the world of her." He felt sorry.

"Thanks," Ashton replied.

He then told him of their plans for that night.

"Oh, she would really love that. This was her Dream place, I know." He said.

"So! What do you think of my new home?" He laughed.

Ashton looks around, "This is fabulous! Lucky you!"

"Yaa... I did luck out here, didn't I? It's just wonderful." He chuckled.

They did the little tour, and the captain said, "I'm taking you for lunch."

He led them out to the private dining room, where only the Top suites were available.

They were greeted and taken to a lovely table with a view of the water.

It was a delightful lunch, with a lot of reminiscing.

Ashton was just young when he started cruising with his parents.

They always took him to meet the captains.

Captain John was his favorite for the past few years.

Ashton mentioned his father's proposal.

The captain was aware already. Robin had mentioned it. He asked if they were considering it at all.

"I don't do the hiring, but I would put in a good word for you." He laughed.

Sofia said they would be talking it over later that night.

"Good.... I hope you decide to join us, even for a while," He said, "It would be a pleasure having you here."

Sofia and Ashton glanced at each other and nodded.

"This is a beautiful ship"! Ashton said again, "We love it!"

They had a very nice lunch and visit with the captain. Ashton was so glad to spend time with him again.

Soon, he had to get back to the bridge. He asked them to consider the opportunity again.

"No Pressure!" He laughed.

"We will, John....," They chuckled.

Sofia and Ashton shook his hand and gave him a hug. Then, they headed back to their suite.

They thought they would just lay low for the rest of the afternoon.

They would have a wonderful dinner and would spread Ashton's mother's ashes into the Sea.

A bittersweet celebration.

Ashton ordered them each a smoothie. A strawberry for him and a blueberry for Sofia.

They sat quietly on the deck, both pondering over the thoughts of working on the ship.

It would be a big decision.

They would be gone for weeks or months at a time.

A lot to think about!

When their drink arrived, they moved to stretch out to the lounge chairs.

"I'm just so torn….," Ashton said, thinking out loud.

"I know," Sofia agreed, "Me too. We've been working so well together at Exotic! But we are still young and have a lot of time and choices to discover! We can do anything we want. And we can work well, no matter what we decide or wherever we are."

"Ok… Let's just relax. We'll figure something out later. My brain is tired," Ashton exhaled, "This isn't easy! We have two days left. Let's try and enjoy the Sun and the scenery. We'll be going back to snow and cold weather."

They closed their eyes and dozed off for a while.

Sofia woke up first, and after a refreshing shower, she put on one of her new outfits. She wanted to look special for this important evening.

Ashton soon followed. He, too, chose something dressy.

Although it was a beautiful gesture for his mother, he still found it difficult to accept. Sofia could feel his sorrow and gave him a big hug.

She managed to get a smile and was glad to be there for him.

They made their way to the special dining room Frank had chosen.

He was there with Walter, Robin, and Captain John.

"Oh... this is nice," Ashton commented when he saw the others there.

"I asked them to join us since they all knew your mother, and she would be happy to have them here," Frank said.

"Now it's a real celebration as it should be," Ashton replied.

"Sofia, you look amazing!" Walter commented, "Ashton you too."

"Thank You, Sofia blushed, "I think we all look great this evening. This restaurant looks beautiful."

Their server arrived with Red and white wine that Frank had pre-ordered. Along with that were some appetizers.

The server poured each one, with their choice, then slipped away.

"Oh...they look delicious," Ashton remarked.

Frank stood up, "Ok... Here's to Maria...may she enjoy her new home, where she's always wanted to be."

"CHEERS…CHEERS!"

Frank sat down, and they all engaged in chit-chat.

Soon, their server and another came out with an assortment of different dishes.

They were all luxurious seafood steaks and vegetables; everyone could take what they liked.

"Wow," Walter spoke, "This looks wonderful! I'm hungry he licked his lips. This is a real feast!"

"Well… I want everyone to just enjoy," Frank replied.

"Also, I want to thank each of you for being so nice to us over the years. It's meant a lot to us."

"CHEERS!" He raised his glass.

"CHEERS," They all toasted.

After that fabulous meal, they headed up to a quiet place where Frank brought out the urn.

He opened it, and after a short prayer by the captain, he began to Sprinkle the ashes into the sea.

There wasn't a dry eye among them.

Tears Flew freely; some were even happy tears.

The captain said one last prayer. And after some warm hugs, they slowly brought it to a close.

"She is at peace now." Everyone muttered.

Ashton decided he'd just like to go back to their suite and have a coffee. Sofia thought that was a good idea.

The Captain and Robin returned to work, and Frank and Walter went their own ways.

"See you in the morning," Frank said.

Walter nodded and gave him a wave. Frank headed up to his suite with tears streaming down his face.

Deep inside, though, he was happy for his wife. Maria really was at peace now.

Sofia and Ashton took their coffees out to the deck, and they just dropped into their chairs.

It was over. There was a sense of relief in the evening moonlight.

The gentle breezes felt warm and had a calming effect on them both.

Ashton stood up and lightly shook his head, "OK! Now we have some decisions to make!"

Sofia looked up and nodded, "Yes, we do!"

They sipped at their coffee and sat in silence, thinking.

One thing we should keep in mind is that Christmas is coming soon.

"What... around a month or so. We do have plans. Also," Ashton added, "I can't leave my dad alone at this time either. We have to have a plan if we do consider working here. Then, we'd have to see if it could be done. There's no way we can leave before Christmas. We have to be home!"

"Yes," Sofia agreed. "That's another thing we should think about! We have a party to plan! OMG..." They laughed.

"OK……Let's go to bed early and then get up early with a fresh start. We'll concentrate a lot better after a good rest. It's been an emotional day for everyone." Ashton said.

"Sounds good," Sofia agreed, "This could be complicated."

They got ready and climbed into bed.

There, Sofia fell sound asleep in Ashton's arms. Ashton laid awake for a while in deep thought. But soon, he, too, was in dreamland.

He was just too exhausted to think anymore.

The next morning, Ashton got up and made the coffee. He ordered them a big breakfast with their favorite pastries as well.

Sofia soon joined him out on the deck.

"Good morning, Hun… How did you sleep?" He asked.

"Like a baby," She replied and gave him a kiss.

"You were right!... I needed that extra rest. Now, I'm ready to face the day. Our last real day, and tomorrow, we'll head home." Sofia said.

Their breakfast arrived, and they enjoyed every bite.

More coffee, and they were then ready to go over all their decisions.

Ashton had also ordered a notebook and pens from customer service.

They came a short time before their food.

Ashton made some titles and divided up some pages.

There were three titles that were important.

Christmas Party….. Christmas…..Cruise Ship.

"We should pick two dates to offer our group. Then, decide about our own Christmas together. Then…. If we should choose to accept their offer? We should decide when we could start. Also… How long might we stay on?" Ashton asked.

Sofia nodded, "We'll start with the party. Next week is December! We have to make sure we can get into Alexanders on the date we choose. We let the gang know as soon as we get home."

"Yes," Ashton said, "We are cutting it short. We should pick a date and a backup date. That way, no one will miss out. We'll have to call Alexanders as soon as we're home."

"Right," Sofia agreed.

They checked that off and moved on to their own Christmas.

"I'm hoping you will spend Christmas with my dad and me. Perhaps we can have our own turkey dinner. I know he would love that!" Ashton said.

Sofia laughed nervously, "I've never cooked a turkey before; maybe you should rethink that!"

Ashton laughed, "We can have that done for us," he shook his head, "We can have it all ordered."

"Whew…," Sofia exhaled, "You scared me there. And you'll have to help me with a gift for your dad. I wouldn't know where to begin."

"No gifts needed," Ashton replied, "Just good company. For that matter, we can even go out as long as you're with us."

"Ok, now, the big one! The Hardest One!" He said.

"Do we join the Cruise ship or return to Exotic?" He paused, went and stood at the railing. The water looked so intoxicating.

Sofia joined him. She, too, became entranced.

"I'll be ok with whatever you decide," She spoke, "As long as we are together."

Ashton put his arm around her. They gazed out over the sea.

"Come on… let's sit and figure it out." He said.

"I wouldn't mind trying it out for a while anyway. What do you think? Maybe we can sign on to try it for just a month or so. Would that be ok with you?" He asked.

Sofia took a sip of coffee, "You know…. I think that might be great! We're young!... no responsibilities! Why not give it a try?"

"Your dad is behind us, whichever we choose. So why not?" She said.

Ashton smiled, "Yaa... that's true."

"So, does this mean we are in?" Ashton asked nervously.

After a brief pause, Sofia blurted out, "Yes! Let's do it!"

"OMG.... Who would have thought? This is crazy," She squealed.

Ashton just nodded, "Yaa... It's weird!"

"So... now what do we do?" Sofia poured them more coffee.

"I'll text Robin and ask her to come here when she has a moment," He picked up his phone.

"So you're really sure?" He asked one last time.

Sofia jumped up and kissed him, "YES, YES, YES!"

Robin texted back she could be there around 4.30.

"Great," He replied, "We'll be here."

Ashton spoke out, "It will be quite a change in duties, you know? But.. we both have a lot of experience with the public. I know you and Robin will also work well together! I've watched you so many times, plus working with you too."

Sofia nodded, "I'm not concerned about that. It was just a shock out of the blue,"

She laughed, "S o many things have been going on. I'm only one person you know. But like I said... If we're together, then I'm game for almost anything. We can always go back."

They went inside and changed to meet Robin. They had lots of time, so they decided to go for a stroll through the ship.

This time, they took mental notes of all the details. It would be like studying for their jobs.

There really was a lot to learn.

It was approaching the time to get back and prepare for Robin.

They tidied up a bit and ordered a bottle of wine.

Soon, she was at their door.

"Come in!... Let's go out to the deck." Ashton brought their glasses and the wine.

He poured them each a glass. Robin, just a half, since she's working.

"Hi guys… what's up? It's your last day! How sad!" She asked.

"Yaa… I know," Sofia stated, "I hate to leave. But… we do have to get back."

Ashton jumped in, "We discussed your opportunity for us to work here. We decided that we would love to try it out! Maybe even for a month or two. The only thing is we can't start until after Christmas. We have too much going on right now."

Robin smiled, "That would be awesome! I'm so happy! What I'll do is arrange for you to talk to the head office, and you can work that out. It would probably be a Zoom call since you leave tomorrow."

"Great," said Ashton, "That sounds perfect."

"It sounds exciting!" Sofia added, "So unexpected."

"We're hoping we can work out some kind of schedule that works for everyone." She said.

"I'm hoping so, too. I could use the help. Sometimes, it's just a bit overwhelming, and I'd love to work with you." Sofia relied.

"Let's cross our fingers! .... Now I must get back! I'm just so busy!" Robin jumped up and gave them each a hug.

They walked to the door and told her they'd talk soon.

"Have a safe trip home, guys!" She waved.

"Hopefully, see you soon," They waved back.

Ashton closed the door, and they went back to their wine outside.

"Cheers!... to new adventures ... maybe?"

"Cheers!"

"I guess we should think about packing!" Sofia suggested, "I think we have an early flight!"

"Oh yeah ...I should check that out. We'd hate to miss it," Ashton replied as he went to his suitcase for their tickets.

He glanced over them and said, "Not too bad. Our flight is at 10.30 AM. We'll have time for breakfast without rushing."

"Oh…nice," Sofia spoke up, "I love a leisurely breakfast."

"OK… Now, We'd better get ready for our last dinner. We have to say goodbye to Walter." Ashton said.

"He's such a wonderful man," Sofia commented.

"I'd love to visit his Animal rescue," she said as she stared at the table.

Ashton studied her intensely, "The emotion in her words and the look in her eyes."

He said, "I knew you loved animals, but I didn't know how much."

Sofia looked up, and he saw a tear in her eyes.

"When I was young, one of my foster homes had a little puppy, Mika. She was a small black poodle. I think she was the only one that showed me any love. She slept with me every night. I loved her so much, and she never left my side. But then I was moved and never saw her again."

"I cried for weeks! My heart felt torn into pieces. After that… I've been afraid to have another. Once I was on my own, it was not fair to have one because I was not home enough. So…what could I do? Secretly, I still think of Mika. I wish I had her back," Sofia fought back more tears.

Ashton, too, had tears in his eyes, feeling her pain.

"Anyway... maybe one day, I'll find a way." She cried.

Ashton stood and pulled Sofia up. He held her tightly.

"You will Hun…... One day, you will." He said.

Sofia shook her head and said, "Come on... let's get ready. I'm getting hungry now. She changed the subject.

They showered and put on something special for their last night.

It was time to meet Frank and Walter.

They headed out, hand in hand. Sofia wore the beautiful tennis bracelet Ashton had bought her.

It picked up every light from every angle.

Their mood soon lightened, and they smiled as they entered the dining room. They took their seats and were greeted by Frank and Walter. Everyone seemed in a great mood.

There was wine and rolls on the table. The server came, and poured them each a glass.

"So guys... this is it. Are you looking forward to leaving tomorrow?" Walter asked.

"No, not really," Sofia answered, "We love that suite we have; it feels like an apartment."

"I feel like we're leaving home!" She laughed.

"Thank you again, Frank! I feel so spoiled." She said.

"Don't mention it, my dear."

"Oh," He continued, "I didn't tell you, but I bought the suite outright."

He took a sip of wine.

The table went silent.

Sofia and Ashton sat with their mouths open.

"I got a good deal!" He laughed.

Ashton looked at him; his expression was questioning.

"What!... Did you buy our suite? What made you do that?"

Frank laughed, "Well… Since I've been spending this time with my good friend here, I've decided that I want to spend even more time here. I have nothing to keep me home anymore. It's a huge, lonely place for me. And…by the way, I've decided to stay another week, maybe two. You'll be going back without me."

"Good for you, Dad! I think that's a great idea. You can run your business from anywhere for the most part."

"Yes, I can," Frank stated.

"Cheers!" Ashton raised his glass.

They all cheered.

"To new beginnings! New journeys! New life!" Sofia spoke up, "I feel so blessed to have you all in my life! It really feels like a dream."

"We feel the same about you, my dear. I've never seen Ashton so happy!"

They toasted, then said, "Let's order."

Sofia told Frank that he had to come back for Christmas with them. "And Walter, we'd love it if you would join us too!"

"Oh, that's very nice of you. That sounds wonderful!"

"Great! Then we'll have a special Christmas."

Just then, Robin showed up with some papers. "I hate to interrupt your dinner; I just have the applications for you two."

"Great," Ashton reached for them. "We'll fill them out tonight and leave them with Zachary for you."

"Perfect," She said, "I'm really hoping to see you guys soon. Take care, and have a safe trip back."

"Thanks," They replied. Robin gave them a hug and said good night; she then left.

Their food arrived and looked delicious. They all enjoyed it thoroughly.

Sofia brought up their plans for a Christmas party. She told Frank and Walter that they both had to come.

They said they would try. They didn't want to impose on their friends, didn't even think of that. You're coming she stated with authority.

Frank and Walter looked at each other and laughed, "Ok! We'll be there."

"I guess you've been told," Ashton laughed, "CHEERS! We'll let you know the date as soon as we get back and check the availability. It will be at Alexanders. It should be in two weeks, just before Christmas. You'll both love our friends. They are very special."

They finished their dinner, and Sofia and Ashton decided to go for a swim before heading to their suite.

They stood, hugged the men and said their goodbyes.

"We'll call and let you know the details as soon as we have them." They informed.

"Great!... Have a safe flight!" Frank and Walter bid farewell.

"Thank You…and you enjoy your stay!" Ashton was very happy.

They turned and headed out arm in arm. Frank and Walter watched with smiles.

Frank said, "I'm so happy Ashton has found such a wonderful girl as Sofia."

"She really is amazing," Walter added.

"Mark my words, she is his soulmate! Forever!" He slipped his wine.

"Cheers to that!" Frank said.

The next morning, breakfast came early, and they savored the last views of their suite and the beautiful weather before heading to the airport.

So much had happened on their trip. They would share it all with their friends when they get back.

They decided to grab a shuttle, along with 10 other people.

The airport was not far away, so the ride was short.

They passed through security in no time and soon were on their way.

"They have forecasted snow for New York," The pilot announced.

"But the temperature is fairly mild. Enjoy your flight!" The pilot added.

Sofia and Ashton looked at each other and frowned.

"Well... maybe it will look pretty," Sofia said hopefully.

"The Christmas lights should be on now. I love them," She said.

Then, they closed their eyes and slept away the time.

Both were awakened by the captain's voice, saying they were on their final descent, "New York, 61 degrees....and light snow. Thank you for flying with us."

Sofia and Ashton sat up and buckled their seatbelts.

He held her hand and watched out the window as they landed.

He sent a text to Paul, who was there waiting, "We're on our way out now."

Just as Sofia had thought, It was very pretty outside.

It was beginning to look a lot like Christmas.

They climbed into the Limo and asked Paul to take them both to Sofia's.

As they were getting out of the car, Paul asked Ashton if he would need a pick-up later.

Sofia looked at Paul, shaking her head.

"Oh…," Paul blushed.

"Ok, just text me when you need me," He smiled.

Paul turned, tipped his hat, and got into the Limo. Ashton and Sofia giggled. They headed up to her apartment.

They put their luggage down and headed for the kitchen.

Coffee was made, of course.

"I was hoping you would stay here," Sofia said, "She kisses him."

"You don't have to worry about leaving your father alone now, Walter is with him staying on the ship for a while." Sofia comforted him.

Ashton's eyes lit up, and he nodded, "Yes… that was great! He and Walter will have more fun, too. It will help with the changes here at home. He's in great company."

"We can slip over to your house tomorrow and pick up some clothes."

"You'll need warmer stuff. Aweeee," Sofia laughed.

"But for now…. Let's get comfy and get started on our plans."

They got changed and set up at the kitchen table.

"We need two dates," Sofia said, "Just in case anyone can't make it."

She picked up her phone and called Alexander's.

She asked them to hold the Friday and Saturday for two weeks.

They agreed and began calling their group.

When all was said and done, they all agreed on Saturday.

Ashton called the restaurant and gave them a definite date and time.

Sofia checked that off the list.

"Ok… so now the menu. How about Italian?" Sofia suggested, "Everyone will be having Turkey at

home, anyway."

"Sounds good to me," Ashton smiled.

"For starters, we'll be serving salad and rolls. As for the main course, guests have the choice of Chicken Parmesan, Mushroom Ravioli, or Fettuccini Alfredo, ensuring there's an option for everyone, including vegetarians. For dessert, the options are Tiramisu or Chocolate Cream Pie."

Sofia meticulously penned down the menu, and after Ashton reviewed it, he deemed it quite satisfactory.

"Great," Sofia remarked.

"They can be prepared for us then. We'll have to call with a count soon, too. I think we have our list made up. Also, I would like to have a nice little gift for each by their place setting. I'll give that some thought. Ok, the following week is Christmas." Sofia said.

"What should we do for our own dinner? I have never cooked a turkey before! There's no way I try that for your father," She laughed.

Ashton laughed as well, "No… we can have that catered in."

"Ok…. Whew!" Sofia exclaimed, expressing her relief, "I was getting worried."

She poured them another coffee.

"Oh… look! It's snowing hard out there," She pointed at the window.

They stood and went over to check it out.

"Glad it came now rather than when we were just coming in," Ashton said.

"Yaa… that could lead to delays," Sofia said.

"A great night to get cozy, make some popcorn, and watch a movie," Sofia recommended.

"You read my mind," Ashton agreed.

They sat back down.

Sofia picked up her pen. "We have ***You, Me, Fred, Ricky, Maina, Angel, Kaylee, Lenora & Yvonne. There are nine of us. That's great for Alexander's. So, who will be at our own Christmas?" She asked Ashton. "Do you get together with anyone else in your family?"

"Not really," Ashton shook his head. "It's just been my mom and dad for the past bunch of years. Now, just my dad and I and You!"

"Well," Sofia said, "we could ask Walter If you think he might come. He's alone."

"Oh yeah…. we should! Great idea! There you go again…. Always thinking of others. That's what I love about you." Ashton appreciated.

Sofia blushed, "It's just the way I am."

Ashton grabbed his phone and sent a text to his dad, asking him to invite Walter.

Moments later, he got a response, "Sounds good, I will do that."

"It's nice that Walter is from New York as well. He and Frank can get together when they are home, too. That will help Frank get over his loss., at least a little. He's a great distraction." Ashton said.

"OK…I'm getting hungry now!" Sofia stated, "I think some Chinese would be nice for dinner. How about you?"

"I'm always in for Chinese…. Let's do it! Order anything…. I love it all!" Ashton said.

"Great!" Sofia said as she picked up her phone. Of course, she had the number on

Speed dial!

"Hi, it's Sofia De Carlo. I'd like to order for delivery, please: 1 number 3, 1 number 7, 2 extra egg rolls, and 2 Won Ton Soup. 45 minutes? That's great! Thank you. Yes, you have my address and number."

"Ok, now… where are we! What's next on our list?" Ashton sat thinking.

"How about some gift bags for the gang? We can pick out some nice ornaments, with the year on them, and add some beautiful chocolates and goodies." Ashton suggested.

"Awe…that sounds good." Sofia agreed, "We'll find some shiny bags and sparkly ribbons and bows. They'll look nice beside each plate."

"Perfect!" Ashton remarked.

"Hey… we're doing great! So far. What's next?" Sofia said excitedly.

Ashton stared out the window in thought, "We should think about the Cruise Ship's position. They'll be getting back to us very soon."

"Yaa…," Sofia nodded, "I'll go with whatever you think is good. I'm easy!" She laughed.

There was a silence in the room as both began pondering which way to go.

Sofia started clearing their notes to make room for their food.

She set the table and pored them each a cold drink.

"I'm Hungry!" She squealed, "Hope it comes soon!"

Ashton just laughed at her.

Soon, their order arrived, and Sofia was happy.

They took a little of each item and started devouring their food.

"Mmmm…. This is awesome! I could eat this every day!" Sofia chuckled.

"Me too…," Ashton agreed.

Just then… his phone showed a text from his dad, "Walter will be joining us for Christmas. He was grateful for the invitation! I told him it was Sofia's idea, and he said to thank her."

"That's great, Dad," Ashton replied, "I'll let her know! Have fun, and we'll see you soon."

He ended the text with some hearts and smiley emojis. Sofia was so happy to hear the news.

"Now, your father won't feel like a third wheel. He'll have his friend to keep him up in spirits." Sofia said.

"Yaa… I hope so," Ashton added, "That's good!"

Sofia sat staring out at the snow.

"It's so pretty," She commented. I love it when we have nowhere to be and in comfy clothes, and it's storming out. Rain… Snow…. It's all good!"

"This is my paradise," She said.

"I feel so bad for the homeless people. I can't imagine what it is like to be laying on the cold ground and wet. There shouldn't be anyone in that position! It breaks my heart!" Tears were forming in her eyes. Ashton felt the same.

"I know," He replied, "It always bothered me too. Then, I feel guilty for everything I have. No one should be without a home, dry, clean clothes, and food!"

After a long pause in silence, Sofia spoke up, saying she was going to spend a lot of time helping at the soup kitchens.

"They always need help serving the less fortunate. I want to help out and give back for what I've been blessed with." Sofia said.

Ashton stood up and hugged Sofia. He felt her trembling in his arms.

"I'll be right there with you, Hun! We'll do it together!"Ashton took his phone out and began Googling soup kitchens.

He copied a list of those that were close by. Tomorrow, he'll make some calls and arrange for where they need help and time.

Sofia's face lit up, "Thanks, Hun… You're the best!!!!!"

"I did this last year. It felt so good to help others. I would, however, go home and cry my eyes out. I just wanted to help them all. I would wonder how they got to that place in their life and why. How could I help get them out? Could I? or anyone? Anyway… It was very emotional for me. But…. I did what I could. It should be a lot easier this time as you will be with me." She leaned over and kissed him.

"I'm so thankful for having met you!"Ashton said.

Sofia smiled her sweet, innocent smile. Ashton smiled back.

He took her by the hand and led her into the bedroom. They made passionate love. They lay in each other's arms for hours.

Ashton's phone chimed. It was Robin. He quickly jumped up and answered, "Hey! Robin. How are you?"

"I'm great Ash…... I have some news for you." Robin replied.

"Ok, shoot!" He replied while putting on Sofia's robe.

He slipped into the kitchen quietly, not to disturb Sofia.

The coffee was still hot, and he poured a cup.

Robin continued, "So, you two are hired if you choose to work here. They can offer you a three-week schedule and one week off. With all the new ships coming out so close together… there's a real shortage of help. They will accommodate your needs. I had suggested maybe a month-by-month contract. Then, you can decide from there. I'm just thrilled to have some help even if for a short while."

231

"That is awesome, Robin," Ashton said, "When do they want us?"

"When can you start?" She laughed.

"We can start right after Christmas. I can book us a flight on Dec 26th; there's a lot going on up until then."

"Oh… that would be just great," Robin answered, "I'm so looking forward to having you guys here."

"I know Sofia and I will work well together," Robin added.

"Yes, you will," Ashton responded.

"Ok… I will inform the head office, and they can take it from here. Let's keep in touch!" She said, "oh, and Merry Christmas, guys!"

"Yes… You too, Robin."

They said their goodbyes.

Ashton put down his phone. He turned, and Sofia was standing there.

"Ohh… Good morning, Hun! Did I wake you up?" Ashton asked.

"Morning… No… I heard the phone. Soo… Are we all set to go then?" Sofia yawned.

"Yes, it looks that way," Ashton replied.

"Oh, Great! I need a coffee!" Sofia said.

"I'll have some too, please." Ashton requested.

He was writing in his notes.

He wanted to give a report to his dad and figure out how they might work it out with Exotic.

There may not be a way to keep both.

Sofia sat down with both coffees. She yawned again and shook her head, "Soo... what's the scoop! When do we start?"

Ashton looks up from his notes.

He proceeded to fill her in on his conversation with Robin.

Sofia sat listening and nodding. She was still waking up.

"So, three weeks on and one week off? I guess that's ok.... What do you think?" She asked.

"I'm ok with that if you are. Plus, if we decide it's not for us, we can end any contract monthly. So... it's not like we're stuck for a year or anything." Ashton replied.

"Hmm, sounds good to me," Sofia sipped her coffee.

"The great thing is we can stay in our suite," Ashton said.

"Oh, Yaa... perfect!" Sofia lightened up, "I love that suit. Now... it's like our home away from home!"

"I know, plus it has special memories for us," Ashton smiled shyly.

Sofia blushed, "Yes ...very."

"Ok, we are now Cruise ship workers! CHEERS!"

They clinked their cups.

"It will be a big change from working on the planes, but we both have years in customer service and dealing with the public. It will be a great experience, I think. And we can always go back at any time! So... why not take the opportunity? Then, there is another bonus.... The weather! No Snow!" Ashton explained.

Sofia smiled and said, "Yes! Love It!"

"We'll have a lot to tell our friends." They chuckled.

The two of them spent the rest of the day doing laundry and some cleaning. They emptied their suitcases to re-pack again.

They wouldn't need their warm weather clothes until they leave.

They'll be working this time, so half of their outfits will not be needed.

That lightened things up a lot! They would be in uniform most of the time.

It was late afternoon when they had finished everything they wanted to do.

They decided to order some steak subs for dinner.

"I'm starving," Sofia said, "Then I think I'll make some calls after we eat."

Ashton said he would review their list of things to do and ensure they covered their checklist.

It was a very productive day for them both!

****** Coleen*******

When their food arrived, they both devoured it.

"I guess I was as hungry as you!" Ashton laughed, "That was delicious!"

"Yaa…," Sofia said as she stood and cleared the table, "Mine was awesome!"

She noticed it was really snowing hard outside, "Look! We must have 3 or 4 inches of snow! It's almost a whiteout!"

"Oh, cool," Ashton replied, "It makes it so cozy when you don't have to go out in it."

"OK, I'm going to call a few friends. You do your thing with our list." Sofia headed to the living room with her phone.

Of course, Maina was first. But she must have been working. There was no answer.

Next, Kaylee. She was excited to hear from Sofia. They chatted for a while, but Sofia never said anything about their new plans. They were saving that.

Angel was next. She only had a few minutes because she had company coming over. They spoke about Christmas and the party mostly.

"It was great hearing from her," She said, "It seemed like a long time."

"I know," Sofia said.

Then, she let her get going and said they'll see each other soon.

Last but not least, Rick and Fred. They were like a warm hug before she would go to bed.

They were her big brothers, her fathers, and her whole family, all in one.

The family she never had. They made her feel wanted and secure.

Fred answered the phone with his gentle, "Hello, darling! Where have you been, so long! We miss you!"

"Same here," Sofia replied with a moan, "We're back now… for a bit…," She hinted.

"Ohh…," Fred said, expecting her to tell him why.

"What do you mean? A bit?" He questioned, "Are you leaving us again?"

There was silence. Sofia just said, "Well… I'll get into that later."

Ricky kept asking when you were coming home… but she wasn't sure.

"We are so looking forward to our Christmas party. It's going to be fun. How is that new love of yours, my dear?"

"He's just beyond wonderful, Hun! We've really had the chance to get closer."

"OH… my… sounds delicious!" He laughed, "Well… we're very happy for you."

In the background, Sofia heard Ricky yelling. "Hi Sweety…. I miss you!"

She replied, "I love you too! Can't wait to see you guys again!" Sofia felt such sadness coming on. She thought about being away for long periods of time. She didn't let on.

Ricky took over the phone, "Hey, sweety! Glad you're home! We are overdue for a shopping frenzy! What do you think?"

"The cutest little shop just opened, down on 5th Ave. We have to Go!" She said.

"OMG…. I'd love to! How about Tuesday?" She asked.

"Sure," Rick answered.

"It looks like a really cool shop, with all kinds of vintage and modern styles. Bring your other half too!" He said.

"I'll ask him… I'm sure he'll love that! I'm all excited!" She replied.

"Great," He said, "We'll call you on Tuesday around 9.00 AM. How about we go for breakfast first? Then go from there!"

"Perfect!" Sofia responded, "Sounds great! OK… we'll talk then."

They said their goodbyes and hung up.

Again, Sofia felt a sense of sadness after talking with the guys. She was going.

To Miss their sporadic plans and get-togethers. She just loved their company.

She sat quietly, staring down at her phone. A tear trickled down her cheek.

It was going to be a big change for her again.

She shook off the feeling and wiped her face. She went into the kitchen and checked on Ashton. He was face timing his Dad on his phone.

"Hi, Frank," Sofia cut in, "You're missing all the snow!" She laughed.

"Awe… too bad!" He lied, "Maybe I should rush home! Ha ha."

She took the phone and aimed it out the window.

"Yaa…. I miss that all right," He laughed, "Think I'll stay, though."

They ended the conversation, and Ashton said goodbye.

"My Dad seemed to be enjoying himself," He said, "I'm so glad he stayed on with Walter. He will be back for the party, though. He's even excited about that."

"Oh…I'm so glad. I was hoping he didn't feel too lonely after we left. I'm glad he's also coming to our party.

Everyone will love him too! After all…. He's your father! They all love you." Ashton smiled.

"I'm sure he'll fit in ok. Plus… it's Christmas. Everyone will be in a cheerful mood." He said.

"Oh… That reminds me," Sofia blurted out, "We should get all our gifts together. I'd like to have each gift on their chairs. We'll have to pick something up for our newest guests, Frank, Lenora, and Yvonne."

"Also, something for Walter and your Dad, for our own party," Sofia said.

"Yes, you're right! We can slip out tomorrow if you like. We only have a week left now. I haven't got a clue what to get either of them." Ashton frowned.

"I'll put my thinking cap on." Sofia offered, "We can find some beautiful gifts."

"I really want to get something nice for Paul, too. He's been such a great help to me, to both of us. He's always at our beck and call. He never complains about going out in the bad weather either." She said.

"Yes… good thinking! We'll do that," Ashton agreed, "We can go early in the morning."

They were getting tired now and decided to head to bed early.

They snuggled up and fell off to sleep.

Sofia has never felt so safe as when she's in Ashton's arms.

Her heart still pounds when he's close.

The morning brought blue skies and sunshine. It was still cold, but not that bad.

They decided to drive themselves in Sofia's car. It is mid-sized and has a large trunk. Perfect for shopping.

They headed to the mall not far from the apartment. They wandered.

Through all kinds of stores, with special and unique items.

They refrained from going into the clothing and fashion boutiques. That day, they had a mission to accomplish and wanted to be done.

Store after store, they searched for some beautiful gifts. Then, they found.

Some shiny, colorful bags and bows. Sofia couldn't remember if she had

Enough or not, she always has a need for them anyway.

With their arms full of bags, they headed back home.

Most of the afternoon, they sorted all the gifts and then wrapped them.

They made sure they didn't miss anyone.

They stacked them up in a corner, ready for Christmas.

"Whew!" Sofia threw herself on the couch, "That was a great day!"

"Tomorrow, Ricky wants us to check out a new boutique! I meant to tell you. I said we'll probably go. Are you up for it?" Sofia asked.

"Sure," Ashton nodded.

"You know me!" He laughed, "Great! We can have lunch after that. I'm really going to miss those guys when we're away all the time. But…. I'll just have to adjust and ensure we see them when we're here."

"We'll figure things out as we go along, Hun. We can handle anything when we're together." She comforted him.

"Yes…. That's for sure! I'm learning that more and more every day." Ashton replied.

Sofia took out her phone and called Ricky. She told him they were excited to go and should go for lunch.

"That was great," He said.

"They would pick them up at the apartment around 10.00 AM." He said.

"We'll be ready," Sofia replied.

"See you then!" He replied.

"OK… what's on the menu tonight?" Ashton asked.

"Something light, I hope," Ashton laughed, "All we do is eat, it seems."

"I hear ya," Sofia replied, "Hmm… I know! Wonton soup…. And some Chow Mein. We can add a couple of egg rolls, too."

"Great! Sounds good to me."

After enjoying their meal, they watched a bit of T.V. Soon, they were off to sleep. They'll need their rest for a shopping morning.

Morning came upon them with a beautiful sunny day. The weather was Mild, and the snow was melting.

They chose to have just coffee and bagels so they wouldn't be too full for lunch.

They put on their comfy clothes for shopping. They picked clothes, that were easy on and off for trying on anything they liked.

Rick and Fred were there right on time. Both had big smiles on their faces.

Everyone was happy to see each other again.

Multiple conversations were going on while they made their way to the new mall and new fashion boutique.

Sofia had mentioned Frank staying on the cruise ship until just before the party.

She brought up Walter, and as it turned out…. Ricky and Fred were very familiar with him. In fact, their home is just down the street from him.

"Sofia was amazed! What a small world!" She gasped.

Fred was telling her all about his animal shelter. He said it was beautiful.

"Wow," She said, "I had no idea! I just thought he brought in a stray and found their home!"

"Well… yes, that's what he does… but so much more." He replied.

Walter is very well known for his big heart and big donations to other facilities. All of them pertain to animals in need.

Sofia sat listening in awe. She could feel her heart melting.

Rick spoke up, saying that she should go for a tour and see for herself.

She envisioned what he was saying and was staring out the window, lost in her thoughts.

"Sofia…So…fia? Hello?" Ricky laughed. Fred said, "WE LOST HER!" He laughed as well.

Sofia turned and said, "Sorry, I'm just so intrigued! I was picturing everything. You were saying."

"Welcome back," Ashton said loudly, "Just in time! It looks like we're here!"

Ricky turned into the most beautiful, exotic-looking mall they had ever seen.

It was ultra-modern, and like it should be somewhere like in Miami.

"OH… nice," Sofia's eyes widened, "This is outrageous! It's huge!"

"I heard this place was nice," Ashton said, "But this is Awesome!"

"OK guys…. Game On! Grab your credit cards! Let's go shopping," He yelled in excitement.

Inside, the mall was even more modern and exciting! There was cool music playing, and waterfalls. The whole atmosphere was invigorating.

They shopped from store to store, exploring all there was. This mall was like no other.

The center of a large group of vintage boutiques showcased a huge circular glass aquarium filled with exotic fish.

That in itself was totally amazing!

"Wow….," Sofia gasped, "This is the most beautiful mall I have ever been in!"

Ashton agreed.

Ricky and Fred caught up with them and soon were inspecting the aquarium. They were both awe-struck.

They'd never seen such rare and beautiful Fish.

Everyone grabbed their phones and took selfies a group pictures.

After that, there were still a lot of shops and quaint boutiques to be checked out.

This new mall was more like an adventure park. In fact, there was a water park for kids at the far end.

There were another two hours of exploring until the four of them were done.

As they made their way back to the car, Sofia announced she had found her new favorite shopping mall!

Everyone laughed but agreed.

When they were in the car and ready to go, Ricky turned and said, "OK… Who wants coffee?"

Sofia replied we can have coffee at our place; we have some good Jamaican.

"Well… I thought We could go for a little ride!" Ricky stated.

"Oh… Ok, sure!" Ashton answered, "I'm game."

"Me too," Sofia added, "Where are we going?"

"Oh… You'll see soon enough," Ricky said mysteriously.

Hmmm, Sofia and Ashton looked at each other, "OK! Let's go!"

"Another adventure! What a great day!" Everyone laughed.

"You're so refreshing, Sofia!" Fred commented.

"I love it!" Ashton hugged Sofia, "Yaa, she's quite a gem."

Sofia just blushed.

They drove for a short time down winding roads and beautiful country settings. Nothing like in the city.

They passed Rick and Fred's house. Sofia wondered why. But said nothing.

It wasn't far when Ricky turned into a long driveway. Along both sides were gorgeous flowers and trees. Beyond that, they saw a huge ranch-style home. Everything was immaculate!

Sofia's eyes lit up, "Where are we? This is beautiful!"

They came to a stop, and all got out.

"This, my dear, is Walter's home. You can't see from here, but his Animal rescue is in the back. I think you'll be impressed."

Sofia and Ashton followed Rick and Fred around to where the animals were kept.

Everything was clean and looked well-maintained.

"You're right! I am impressed." Sofia exclaimed.

"Walter is very strict about cleanliness and appearance. He wants everyone to know how well they take care of their animals." Fred replied.

There were different areas where they kept animals other than dogs and cats.

They had a few goats and pigs as well. Sofia smiled with delight as she saw a baby goat come towards her at the fence.

"OMG…she reached out to pet the baby. She's so beautiful! Who would want to abandon this sweet little doll?" She had tears forming in an instant. The thought made her upset.

Fred walked over and put his arms around her, "Look! She's so happy!"

Before going to their forever homes, they all have a great life here.

"Don't be sad." He squeezed her tightly.

"Yaa… I guess you're right," She sniffled.

"Come on… let's catch up with Ashton and Rick. There's more to see. You'll love it inside." Fred said.

They turned and picked up a brisk pace. Then, the four of them entered the building, where a nice young girl greeted them.

"Hi," She said with a big smile, "Can I help you? Are you here to adopt? Or just a tour?"

"Just a tour, sorry." Ricky felt kind of bad.

"We know Walter wants to show our friend here his facility." He replied.

"Oh… sure, no problem." The girl nodded, "The name on her badge was Emily."

"We can take Sofia around ourselves; we know it inside and out." He replied.

"You must be new," Fred said.

"Yes, this is my first week. Elsa has some health issues, so she had to retire." She told.

"Well, welcome, sweety. You look very sweet, and I'm sure you'll fit in very well." Ricky smiled that movie star smile of his.

"Thank You," She blushed, "I love it here."

"Go right ahead. The animals love company." She said to them.

They turned and followed the corridor down to where they housed the animals awaiting their new families. As they slowly strolled along, each pet jumped up and stood at their doors. These were mainly dogs and puppies, their tails wagging and the looks of hope in their eyes.

Sofia's heart melted. And tears were streaming down her face.

Ashton quickly moved toward her and held her tight. He, too, had tears.

As they passed each one… Sofia could feel the pain of feeling unwanted and alone.

Some of them had their little paws, arms, or heads wrapped with bandages.

They had been hurt and or abused.

"Who the hell could ever hurt any of these precious souls," She thought.

Her sadness turned to anger.

As they reached the end, there was a small little puppy staring up at her. As she got closer, she saw there were four more along with it. They were the cutest, sweetest puppies she had ever seen.

Her spirits changed to excitement. She went down on her knees and touched the glass.

"OMG," She said to Ashton, "Look at them. They're just babies! Where's their mother? They need her."

Fred walked over and read the note on the top of the door. It said the mother was hit by a car and didn't make it. The puppies were found in the grass by the road. She had just given birth.

Sofia stood up, her lips quivering. She stared down at the little one and whispered that she was sorry. The puppy seemed to be begging her to take them home. Ashton knew it was time to explore other areas of the complex, perhaps somewhere not so sad.

He turned to Ricky and Fred and gave them the look of it's time to go.

"Hey!" Ricky said, "Let's go check out those goats outside. They are the funniest things to watch."

Sofia nodded, "Ok...I need some fresh air."

They thanked the girl at the reception desk and headed for the exit.

Fred paused and said, "Go ahead. I'll be right there."

He went to the desk and gave a large donation to the Rescue.

"Oh…Thank you so much," The girl said.

"We really appreciate this a lot! You're very generous! You must really love animals." They said.

"Yes, we do," He replied, "Thank you for letting us tour the building."

Fred headed over to where the rest were. They were laughing at the goats. There were bags of food on a table, and for a small donation, you could purchase one and feed them. That was just to help the Rescue, towards their care.

Sofia grabbed a whole bunch and left a very large donation.

She was having a riot with them. It was great to see— her mood had lifted, and she was happy again.

They stayed for quite a while before leaving. As they drove down the winding driveway, Sofia looked back with sad eyes. No one had any idea how much the rescue would affect her.

She felt such a connection to all those animals, more than she had expected.

They pulled up to the apartment complex and sat chatting for a few minutes. They talked about their Christmas party coming up soon.

Sofia hinted that they would be making an announcement but left them hanging with that thought.

"Fred hates when he's got to wait. He blurted out! Are you pregnant?"

"No...," Sofia laughed.

"Are you getting married?"

"No," Sofia laughed again.

"You'll find out at the party! Bye loves....," She waved.

"Ok...," Fred said.

"I hate you!" He laughed.

Ricky waved, and they pulled away.

Ashton put some coffee on while Sofia jumped in the shower. She needed to escape the emotional afternoon at the Rescue. "Emotional" barely touched the surface of her feelings. It hit her heavily.

"You smell fabulous," Ashton remarked, "Let's sit for a bit, then check out our packages."

"Oh...Ya.... I forgot about that! We did find some amazing fashions." She jumped.

"I need a distraction," She added.

"Those tiny puppies... they just stole my heart. They really made me feel like I should be taking them home. I wanted to take them all home! Make them feel wanted! I seemed to really relate to them." Sofia said.

"I have to say...," Ashton spoke up, "Walter really has a beautiful setup there. You can see they really take good care of all the animals. They really put their heart and soul into helping those poor things. I feel the same as you do. So... keep that in mind. They're in good hands."

"Yes... you're right! They are in great hands. That's a bit of a reprieve."

"Ok, now.... Let's open our bags and have some fun!" Ashton brought out their goodies.

They had found a few unique items to add to gifts for Christmas. They chose a very cool outfit for Robin to bring back on the ship.

By looking at her, Sofia felt she had a good judgment of size. They took a chance.

They were happy with everything they found. The prices were very reasonable too.

They took care of all the add-ons for their gifts and then modeled their own items. A fashion show, so to speak.

Sofia started to come back to life; fashion had that effect on her.

With every article of new clothing she put on, it was like reinventing herself. This was something she did as a young child. She always dreamed of being someone else, someone worthy of love.

Fashion seemed to fill that empty void in her life. Every piece gave her a sense of a fresh new beginning. She felt beautiful when she saw herself in something new.

That long-ago world was still deeply embedded in her heart. The need to change things was her only way to stay positive. It was her way to deal with her emptiness.

Soon, they both were getting hungry and decided to have some leftovers in the fridge.

They were also tired from the busy, emotional day.

The rest of the evening, they made popcorn and dozed off watching a movie. Later, they dragged themselves to bed.

The next morning, Sofia was the first up. She had a restless sleep.

Walters Rescue played out in her dreams.

She thought her strong European coffee might help but to no avail. She was still tired.

"Hmmm...I should have made our Jamaican," She thought out loud, "Or... a blend."

She looked out to see a blustery, snowy day. It was coming down hard!

The wonderful aroma had awakened Ashton. He came out with his nose in the air.

"Ahh... Smells like heaven in here. Wow...it's snowing heavy! How did you sleep, Hun," He asked her.

"Not well, thank you. Too many dreams of those poor animals. I can't get that little puppy out of my mind. I feel like she was with me, sleeping all night. I could almost feel her by my side." Sofia said with teary eyes.

Ashton just nodded, "I know it was difficult to see, but remember what we said. They are in the best hands, and it's only going to get better for them all."

Sofia said, " I know that."

"Soon, they'll be adopted by people and families who really love and want them. I know, you're right." She smiled.

"I was thinking we should have Lenora over for coffee. We haven't talked lately. We can remind her of the party in a few days. Maybe I'll call Yvonne as well. We have enough cheese, crackers, and deli meats.... I'll put together a little snack plate. Or Charcuterie board." She said.

"Sounds fine with me," Ashton replied, "No one is going anywhere in this bad weather. Look at it out.... It's crazy now! The wind has picked up even more!"

"Yaa... I love it. It's mesmerizing! And we're safe and warm inside." Sofia took her phone out and called the two ladies. They were happy about the invitation and quickly accepted.

"Great! How about 1.00? I'll have some appetizers." They both agreed.

Ashton had jumped in the shower, dressed, and ready to start the day.

The two had a light breakfast. They made sure everything was clean and tidy for their guests.

Sofia started preparing a nice array of snacks.

Ashton knew that having company over would be a great distraction for Sofia.

She already has perked up.

Sofia was pleased with her creation. The goodies looked so tempting; she had a hard time not eating them herself.

"Ok, ready," She announced, "Time for a coffee."

She looked outside and saw the snow was still coming down hard.

"Wow," She commented. Maybe we should order a bunch of supplies.

We may be snowed in, or worse! Lose power! Ashton went to the window. You could be right!

We'll give it an hour, then decide what to do. Soon, it was 1.00. Right on time, the doorbell rang.

Lenora and Yvonne were at the door. Lenora had MIA in her arms.

"OMG…. Look at this beautiful baby in a new dress."

Sofia took the puppy from her and said, "She's mine." She hugged and kissed Mia. And Mia was all excited.

They all laughed; Ashton couldn't believe the change in Sofia while holding the little dog.

Later, after telling the ladies about the Rescue they went to, Sofia found out Mia was also a rescue puppy. She was so surprised.

"That is just wonderful," She said, "There are so many in need of homes."

"Oh, I know, Hun! We donate regularly to rescue and other animal services."

Sofia just kept playing with Mia, "Oh… I love this little baby doll! Her dress is so pretty. Where did you find that?"

"I went online…. There's nowhere around here that has any nice pieces. No variety."

"Oh… good idea!" She exclaimed.

Ashton looked on as Sofia held little Mia. He could see the love in her eyes. Even more, he could sense the love for a pet she'd never been able to have.

They sat chatting and snacked on goodies with their tea and coffee.

Ashton just kept quiet in the background.

He found them very entertaining!

Soon, the party was brought up. Both ladies were thrilled to be invited.

Then, after a while longer of chit-chat…the ladies headed back to their apartments. It was good they didn't have to drive.

Ashton went over and looked out again. The snow was slowing down.

The snowplows were out, and the roads were not too bad.

"Oh good," He said, "Maybe we dodged a bullet."

Sofia peeked out and said, "Oh yeah, now it's just looking pretty Good!"

Sofia spent the rest of the day calling her friends.

Whoever she was able to reach spent an hour or so on the phone with her.

Ashton called his dad, which was only 5 minutes.

Frank said he'd be flying home once they docked.

The next few days went by quickly. Christmas was in the air.

Sofia and Ashton went for many drives, where they were showing.

A lot of festive displays and colorful lights.

It was so beautiful seeing the decorations. Some people spend a ton of time preparing.

With the snow so soft and fluffy... the lights were sparkling bright.

Christmas music played loudly in all the shopping malls.

The perfect touch for shoppers.

Ashton and Sofia spent a few cozy, romantic evenings. They talked about their upcoming plans.

They went over the differences between working at Exotic and the cruise ship.

They were by no means similar.

Ashton got a call from Robin and informed, "Their uniforms would be given to Frank to put in their suite. Any alterations can be done after they arrive."

She was excited. It was beginning to feel real for them now. It wouldn't be long.

Frank flew home for a couple of days, eagerly anticipating their Christmas party.

He planned to stay at home until after Christmas, and Walter would be flying in to join them for their own little family dinner.

Sofia was excited about the opportunity to talk to Walter and share their experience of visiting his animal rescue.

She had many questions and was eager to learn more about how it worked.

Finally, the night of the party arrived! Sofia and Ashton were brimming with excitement as they prepared to gather with their friends.

Frank was ready and waiting at home, and Paul was designated to pick them all up.

They planned to arrive early to place the gifts and ensure that everything was perfect. They also brought along a few decorations to add to the festive atmosphere.

Ashton received a text from Paul indicating that he was at the curb and had already picked up Frank.

He relayed the message to Sofia, and they eagerly headed down to join the celebration.

They arrived at Alexander's and were greeted by their favorite host, Robert, who had been there for about three years or so.

There was always a smile and a twinkle in his eyes, indicating his genuine enjoyment of working with people. He was a born natural.

He quickly led them to their favorite corner, where a fireplace was going, and the tables were set beautifully.

"This is so nice," Sofia said.

They began sorting out the gifts and placing them by each chair.

After a little bit of decorating, they were done.

Frank ordered them each a wine as they had time before the others came.

"This is a gorgeous place," He commented, "No wonder you always come here."

"Yes," Ashton nodded, "They have great food, great service, and they are the most accommodating restaurant you could ever find. We just love it here."

Their wine arrived, and since it was close to the others showing up, they brought out some cold appetizers.

"Oh, that looks wonderful!" Frank exclaimed.

Beautiful plates of cheeses, croissants, specialty meats, and sauces were placed all down the table. Sofia had them arrange the table in a square. With this setup, the servers could enter inside and serve the food much more easily.

"And this way, everyone could face each other and talk. It's the best idea, and it feels cozier too."

The guests began to arrive. Ricky and Fred were the first, and Sofia had them sit next to her and Ashton.

Maina was next, sitting beside them.

Then came Angel, who took a seat next to Maina.

Kaylee soon followed.

Lenora and Yvonne were the last to arrive, having been caught in some traffic.

Sofia had them sit on the other side of Frank, with Lenora beside him.

The servers were prompt, placing white and red wine all around.

Fred ordered an espresso, and Sofia opted for a Caesar for a change.

Ashton stood up and welcomed everyone.

After they all had their drinks, they raised their glasses for a toast. He introduced the three new guests - Frank, Lenora, and Yvonne.

They all exchanged greetings, and everyone was in great spirits.

Laughter and conversation filled the air as they delved into the food.

Sofia looked around with bright, excited eyes; these people were her family, and she loved them all.

"What are all these gifts here, my dear," Ricky said, shaking his head, "You really shouldn't have."

"Oh…Those are from Santa! Not me," She laughed, "Just some little goodies."

Fred elbowed her, "Ya sure. She gave him a hug."

Sofia now stood and gave a very short speech and thanked everyone for coming.

"Let's enjoy this awesome food, and even more, let's enjoy being together again. Now, the food is on its way. Mangia!" She laughed, "There Is more to come!"

She sat down.

Everyone applauded, and the feast began.

The aroma of fresh pasta, homemade sauces, and soft, warm rolls filled the room. Two salads were served in large bowls.

Sofia sat back and watched everyone dive into the fabulous food.

Their excitement and smiling faces brought her comfort, and she wondered when they would get the chance again to gather.

Fred nudged her, "Eat!"

He said, "Eat while it's still hot!"

"Oh… Ya… I am," She assured him. She reached for the Seafood platter.

The dish was piled high with lobster, shrimp, and Crab legs. Scattered throughout were Garlic Butter Scallops—her dream food.

It felt like they ate for hours.

Finally, everyone was more than full. Moans and groans came from every seat at the table.

"I think we should all go out and run around the block a few times," Ricky shouted.

Everyone agreed.

"They may have to roll us out of here," Maina added.

"Well, dessert is next, guys! I hope you have a bit of room left!" Sofia laughed.

"OMG, My clothes are going to hate me tomorrow," Kaylee sighed, "But…. This dinner was worth it!"

Ashton and Sofia both stood up again.

"So!" Ashton started, "We have an announcement to make."

Everyone slowly became quiet.

Ashton said, "There have been some new opportunities offered to us recently. We have been asked to work on the largest Cruise ship."

The room went silent.

"This will mean we will be gone for weeks at a time. It was a very difficult decision to be away so long at a time, but we're trying to work things out. This may or may not be a permanent move; for the time being, we are mostly filling in where they need us. With all the new ships, and because of their huge sizes, they require more help in a lot of their main positions." He informed.

"Wow," Maina shouted, "You never mentioned this to me. I'm going to miss you so much!"

"Yaa...," Everyone agreed.

"When do you leave?" Kaylee asked.

Ashton said they would be flying out a couple of days after Christmas.

"Awe...that's so soon!" Ricky pouted.

"We'll see how it goes, guys! Who knows, maybe it won't be so bad. We can arrange some get-togethers when we have our time off. That would be every month. Not too bad. Three weeks on, one week off. Of course, we'll fly in.

"Well, I'll have some adjusting to do!" Maina grunted, "I'll miss my Bestie."

"Yaa, me too. But like I said, who knows how it will go? We may only stay a few months or a year. We're really just supposed to be filling in until they've had time to hire and train more staff.

Their standards are high… so… they are looking for those who really want this to be their lifestyle. They don't want people who just come and go.

Frank has been so supportive. I feel for him. He's alone now… and here he's giving us the O.K. to try something that will take Ashton away from him for long periods as well." Sofia explained.

"Well, I'll miss you," Maina repeated, "Maybe I'll take a cruise on that ship sometime. Then, we can visit."

"Yaa, that would be awesome," Sofia replied, "Shop on the Islands! Get the girls together and come aboard!"

Fred then joined the two and gave Sofia a hug.

"You never let on," He pouted.

"Ricky and I will miss our little sister! But who knows! Maybe we might have to take a cruise also!"

"That would be great," Sofia responded, "You guys would love it so much."

As everyone caught up with each other and shared their stories, the atmosphere lightened up, and the Christmas spirit came back.

Ricky started tapping his wine glass to get everyone's attention.

"I'd like to thank Sofia and Ashton for arranging this wonderful party! And thank you for the wonderful gifts! Everything was beyond perfection—the food, the décor, but more than anything, the company. Here's to a lifetime of staying best friends! Cheers!"

Everyone raised their glasses and cheered, "Friends forever!" Ashton jumped in and said, "Yes, friends for life! Cheers!"

Frank then stood up and said, "Thank you for welcoming me into the group. And... THIS PARTY'S ON ME!"

Everyone started to insist that they should all contribute towards the bill, but Frank wouldn't listen. He had already called ahead and settled it.

"You are a great group of friends," He said to them, "Again, thank you for including me in your party!"

Angel spoke up, "Cheers to Frank!" Everyone joined in, raising their glasses and cheering.

They continued with their conversations, and it was a delight for Sofia to see.

It's usually hard to get everyone at the same time. Perhaps it's the Christmas magic in the air, too. Fred got up and moved beside Sofia.

"This was a beautiful evening," He told her, "I just want to say I hope the two of you enjoy your new adventure, even though we won't see as much of each other."

"It's good for you to explore different opportunities until you find your happy place. You'll know when it happens." Fred said.

"Thanks, Fred… We'll see how it goes. I'll miss you a lot, too," Sofia gave him a big hug.

The group started to make their way out, exchanging "Merry Christmas" and best wishes with Sofia and Ashton. It was almost sad for her. She hated nothing more than goodbyes. Sofia smiled and nodded a thank you to everyone.

Only five of them were left: Frank, Sofia, Ashton, Ricky, and Fred. They sat and sipped their wine, and a quiet atmosphere settled in. Ricky was deep in conversation with Frank, while Ashton and Fred discussed the cruise ship.

"We've been on a number of cruises," He mentioned, "I have to say, they are our favorite kind of vacation. It's nice to have all the options, from laying on a beach or just hanging out. And the entertainment is fabulous. We always get a balcony suite, so at night, we can sit out and just relax with the fresh sea air."

"Truthfully, I could sleep out there," He laughed, "but Rick thinks I'm crazy. I think it would be kind of cool!"

Ashton said he could sleep out there, too.

"Why Not!" He added.

Sofia sat quietly, listening to the different conversations. Her mind was elsewhere.

She still had such a feeling of sadness at seeing those poor animals without homes.

She was looking forward to talking to Walter.

There were so many thoughts going through her mind. Even she had no idea what effect that Rescue shelter would have on her? It really surprised her.

"Sofia? Where are you, dear?" Ricky tilted his head questionably.

"Are you still with us," He laughed.

Ashton had a good idea of where she was. He knew that one particular puppy grabbed at her heart. She hadn't had time to get over that little face yet.

He knew she was envisioning all those misfortunate animals.

Sofia slowly glanced up and smiled, "I hear Hun! I'm just enjoying the last of the evening."

"Yaa... OK," He said, not believing her.

"Well, guys, I think it's time for me to head out! I have a bunch of business calls to make tomorrow. It's almost Christmas, and a lot of companies will be closing down for the holidays. I'm sure my mailbox is filled," He laughed.

"Yaa, I suppose it's that time for us too," Fred said. "I think Ricky has an audition for some soap commercial. He still loves to have fun, even though he's retired. Me, I'm just fine with no commitments."

They got up and headed for the door, thanking Frank again for picking up the tab. "Next time is on me," Ricky said with a serious look. They wished each other a Merry Christmas and made Sofia and Ashton promise to call them as soon as they got back.

"Oh, you know we will, sweetie! We'll miss you."

"Okay, safe trip home! Good night! Hugs and kisses."

Paul was waiting for them out front. They dropped off Frank before heading to Sofia's. Ashton told his dad he'd call him in the morning and said goodnight.

Once they got settled in, Ashton put the coffee on. It was now beginning to snow. As much as he loved the warm weather, there was just something about relaxing in comfy clothes inside while it was cold and snowy outside. They sat at the table and talked about what a great night it was.

Now, Christmas with Frank and Walter. They should decide where and how. Order in or go out to someplace special.

Ashton sat in deep thought. It was still so soon after losing his mom. He was hoping to keep his dad's spirits up. Perhaps it might be best to go out. There were a lot of wonderful places open and having Christmas dinners.

That was another thing. Do they want a traditional Turkey dinner? Or something like Italian or Chinese. After all, it's all about being together, not what you're eating.

Sofia decided to go online and bring up some of their favorite fine dining establishments.

Surprisingly, most were open, and offering special menus.

She showed Ashton, "Oh, wow! So many! I guess it's quite popular to dine out!"

"When you think about it, most people here in New York do not have room or parking for too many guests. It only makes sense that they meet somewhere." She said.

"Yeah… you're right there. Hmm, OK, I think that may be the best. Christmas is an emotional time, as it is. It may be very hard for my dad to celebrate in his big home without my mom." Ashton replied.

"Ok… so… where should we go? Let's think!"

The two of them sat staring at the table, deep in thought.

There were a lot of choices.

"We just had a huge Italian-themed dinner. So, I say maybe something different. How about that quaint little place we went to before? It is Seafood, but also has other styles as well. I can't remember the name, but maybe you can find it." Sofia suggested.

Ashton looked up and said, "That sounds great! I know which one you mean. That was an awesome restaurant. The food was so fresh, and they gave you so much. They also have a wide variety of other foods. I'll try and find it."

He scrolled through numerous places, slowly reading each one.

"Here... maybe this is it. Silver Seas! It sounds familiar." He said.

He clicked on the menu. The pictures were beautiful. They were even offering a Turkey Dinner special, just for Christmas. This would give everyone a choice.

"Sounds great... you'd better call right now." Sofia stated, "We only have a few days."

"Oh ya... I'm on it." Ashton called and inquired about availability.

Since there were only four of them, there was no problem.

Their larger tables were totally filled, though.

"Great!" Ashton booked them for 6.00 PM.

"OK, we're all set. I'll let Frank and Walter know." Ashton informed.

Paul was picking up Walter in the morning. Frank was going for the ride.

Ashton was pleased that his dad was keeping busy. Walter was a big help.

"Now.... I'm tired! Let's call it a day." Sofia agreed, "I'm done."

The next couple of days they spent going through their luggage and getting ready for Christmas. They wrapped their gifts beautifully.

They verified their reservations and ordered some wonderful appetizers.

These would be set out just before they arrive. They would be arranged strategically around the table in a decorative design.

"That's genius!" Ashton praised Sofia, "What a cool idea! You have a flair for entertaining."

"I try," She replied, "I just love to make people smile and feel good."

Ashton kissed her and said, "Well, you're doing it right!"

"I'm so glad Walter is coming! He's such a nice man with such a big Heart. What he's doing for those poor animals is just awesome. I can't get that out of my head." Sofia became emotional.

"I know," Ashton said sympathetically, "I know your heart is with them. When we come home, on our time off, I promise we'll go and visit them again."

"Oh…... That's awesome," Sofia shrieked, "I'd love that. I want to see those adorable puppies, too. That smallest one seemed to want me to take her home! I've named her ASHLIA! You know…Ashton…," Sofia chuckled.

"There was just something about her; I felt so attached. I felt her desperation." Ashton shook his head.

"You're too much," She smiled away in her usual coyed demeanor.

"I should have known," He smiled.

The two of them laughed.

"Yeah, well, I can't help it. It's just the way I am. Beneath the smile are hidden tears."

Sofia went to lie down for a while. Their plans were all done.

One more day, till Christmas. Then, one day after that, they would leave for the ship.

Ashton sat in the kitchen thinking. He got this very strong feeling they would be ending up with a puppy soon.

"That was great," He thought, "But how do they work it with being away so much?"

"Hmm……..,"

He got an idea, but he'll have to talk to Lenora first.

Maybe if she could take care of a puppy while they're away, then it could work out.

He thought about what he'd love to do – surprise Sofia with a Valentine's puppy. What an awesome gift, on the best occasion! Valentine's is all about love.

"Perfect!" He thought, keeping his excitement a secret. Sofia had fallen asleep, so he quietly snuck out the door and went to see Lenora.

She was happy to see him.

"Come in," She said.

"Oh, where's Sofia?" Ashton explained.

He sat and went over what he had in mind. Lenora was all for it.

She thought that was a great idea and had no problem with taking in their puppy.

Together, they both thought that she should take Mia to visit those little puppies at Walters.

He described the ones she loved, particularly the smallest one.

They should make sure they would get along okay.

Lenora said she could go any time; her first trip would be the next day. She would probably go a few times before letting Ashton know.

Ashton gave her his number and email. He asked if she could take some pictures of them together.

"Sure," She nodded.

"This is exciting," She said, "I love giving surprises!"

"I really appreciate this, Lenora! Sofia will go crazy!" Ashton thanked her.

"I'd better sneak back before she wakes up. We'll keep in touch, good night."

Ashton slipped away. He was feeling very excited about his idea.

He could almost see Sofia's face lit up.

He managed to creep in and back to the kitchen, passing Sofia on the couch.

He exhaled, "Whew!"

"That was fun," He thought.

Sofia soon woke up, and they both went to bed.

One last day till Christmas.

Ashton couldn't hide his great mood.

When Sofia asked what he was so extra cheerful about, he brushed it off as being excited about going back on the ship, framing it as a new adventure.

"Yaa… I'm getting excited, too," Sofia said.

Falling asleep came easy.

All their plans were complete, and they were ready to enjoy a nice holiday and then… off for a new experience.

The wind was howling, and the snow was coming down hard.

The two fell deep into la la land.

The morning brought a whole different picture. They awoke to a winter wonderland. It was so beautiful. Blankets of white snow covered the ground.

Sofia gazed out the window, and the sun's reflection almost blinded her, "Wow… We slept through a bit of a storm, it looks like."

Ashton stepped closer to see, "Ohh wow… and we missed it he said with a pout. I love a good snowfall."

"At least they've been clearing the roads. Paul is picking up Walter soon. Hopefully, his flight is ok. It would be a shame for him to miss Christmas Dinner. I'll check online." She showed her concern.

"He's good," Ashton reported, "No delays."

Sofia was thrilled as she really wanted to talk to him.

Plus, she wanted him to enjoy Christmas with them, too. He's alone, just as Frank is now.

They prepared a nice breakfast and savored the rest of the day without any obligations or having to do anything at all.

They cuddled on the couch, enjoying some alone time. Then, began getting dressed for dinner.

As Ashton took his shower, his thoughts were consumed by the little puppy he was surprising Sofia with. He couldn't wait to see her face.

That alone was worth a million dollars.

As he was getting dressed, he received a text from Lenora.

No words, just a beautiful picture of Mia and the puppy side by side at the Rescue.

Lenora was in the background, smiling.

Ashton's heart beat faster! That was a great sign.

When Sofia asked who the message was from, he replied, "Oh… just advertising as usual," He lied.

He had to hide his grin.

"Yaa… I get so many, too," Sofia stated.

"I'm just about ready!" She told Ashton.

"How about you?" She asked.

"Yup… I'm good to go," He replied, "I'll text Paul."

He quickly deleted the photo and sent a text.

Paul said he was just leaving to get Frank and Walter.

Ashton told him they'd be at the door ready.

They gathered their gifts, plus the gift for Paul.

Frank and Walter greeted them as they entered the Limo.

Both looked all dressed up….and in cheerful moods.

Ashton was happy to see that. The traffic was light, so it didn't take long to get to the restaurant.

They pulled up out front of the main entrance, and Paul got out and opened the Limo doors.

As Sofia and Ashton stepped out, they handed Paul his gift.

He wasn't expecting that. His face beamed with surprise.

"Thank You so much," He said, "Merry Christmas. Enjoy your dinner."

The group was greeted by a very beautiful woman who escorted them to their table.

Menus were handed out, and right away, their server appeared with two bottles of wine, one red and one white. He set them both on the table.

"May I pour," He inquired.

Frank said, "Please."

Each received a full glass he quickly slipped away.

"Cheers!" Ashton raised his glass.

The rest followed, "CHEERS."

They sipped their wine and enjoyed light conversation, mostly about the cruise ship.

Then, Sofia changed the subject. She had been waiting to talk to Walter more about his Animal Rescue.

He was more than delighted that she had enjoyed seeing it and taken such an interest.

Ashton mentioned how emotional it was for her. He didn't bring up anything about the puppy; he himself was going to rescue it.

Sofia asked a lot of questions. Walter walked her through the steps for adoption.

And how they're very careful who they allow to take their animals.

Sofia listened, absorbing all she could. Walter was pleased; he could fill her in.

The Rescue was his life project, and he took a lot of pride in what he was doing.

Meanwhile, Ashton and Frank discussed what was going on at Exotic Airlines.

The business had been picking up, with new clients pouring in. Maybe that was a good sign that the economy was improving.

Frank reassured him they were more than okay with him and Sofia being gone.

Many top Hosts need the extra time to recover from their losses from the two years or so of Covid.

He told them to take their time, deciding where they wanted to be.

Ashton thanked him and said how grateful they were for the opportunity.

Soon, the night came to an end.

They let Paul know, and he was there in no time to pick them up.

After hugs, kisses, and Merry Christmas, they all were home safe and sound.

Ashton told them they would catch them soon on the Cruise ship.

Frank and Walter were staying home for a week. Ashton and Sofia were leaving right after New Year's. They just had a quiet celebration themselves.

"There were enough parties going on TV," Sofia commented as they got ready for bed. Walter was very eager to discuss all about the rescue. "I feel a little better, knowing how well they're being taken care of," Sofia said.

"That's good," Ashton agreed. "That's what you have to concentrate on."

It was after midnight, and both were yawning.

"I think I'll call it a night," Sofia said sleepily.

Ashton agreed, "Tomorrow is our last day. Then we're off!"

The next morning, Ashton received an email from Lenora.

He and Sofia were having coffee, so he slipped into the bedroom and opened it up.

There was a picture of her and two of the puppies at the Rescue.

He smiled and stared at it.

Underneath was a message. Lenora informed him that the rest of the puppies were adopted last night.

There was only the one he had held and one other, a boy. She let him know that if they take the one, that would leave the other all alone.

Ashton sent Lenora a text:

Are you trying to butter me up and take TWO PUPPIES?

She replied:

Well.......? Wouldn't that be awesome? You could each have one.

Ashton laughed to himself. He pictured them both with little carriers.

"Are you able to take on two puppies with Mia?" He responded.

"You're going to have them for a while until we figure out what our plans are. If we decide to stay on the ship…. I'll have to check and see if they'll let us keep the two with us in our suite!"

There was a pause. Ashton was thinking and staring at the two puppies.

They were adorable. Having one each could be a lot of fun.

He bit his lip, "OK…. go ahead and have them hold the other as well."

"OMG…..You're the best," Lenora replied.

"Don't worry…. I'll take great care of them. If things don't work out, I'll keep them myself. OK… I have to go…. Sofia has breakfast. Text me later, and let me know how it goes; he deleted their texts." He replied.

The smell of bacon lured Ashton back to the kitchen.

"Mmm…..You're making me hungry!" Ashton replied.

"Good…," Sofia replied. I have eggs almost ready and the toast as well.

Ashton set the table. He also poured them each a coffee.

So, our last day here for a while he said excitedly. I'm starting to think about the sun and water.

"I know," Sofia replied, "Me too. I think I've had enough of the snow and cold for now. This cruise should be interesting, too."

"We have an early flight tomorrow. I think it's 8.00 AM. Can you double-check that for us? I'd hate to miss it." She said.

Ashton got out their papers, "Yup... you're right."

I'll text Paul and give him our itinerary. He took a picture and sent it on.

They enjoyed the homemade breakfast and then sat back with their coffee.

There was nothing left to do but relax. Sofia had the ship on her mind.... Ashton had other things.

He was picturing them walking hand in hand through the park. Their other hands held a puppy on a leash. Their puppies were wearing matching outfits.

Lenora never said whether the second puppy was a girl or a boy!

Not that it mattered. He would love them both the same.

He checked his emails and texts frequently for anything from Lenora.

It was hard keeping his excitement from Sofia.

But, he also loved surprising her when he could.

"Oh… Look…. More snow! Just what we wanted." Sofia shouted from the kitchen, "I'm glad we will leave tomorrow!"

"Yeah, so enjoy it all today!" Ashton laughed.

Another text from Lenora, "We got them! Then a big thumbs up."

Ashton said, "Thank You. We'll be in touch."

He deleted those as well.

They spent the afternoon hanging out and watching a couple of movies.

Eventually, they decided on Chinese cuisine for dinner and placed an order.

The delicious food left no leftovers, and both of them were completely stuffed.

Realizing that three weeks was a substantial time to be away, they decided to make some last-minute calls to their friends.

Sofia sat at the table. She was talking loudly with Maina. Ashton went to the living room.

He quietly spoke to Lenora.

She told him, "Everything was good. But they were lucky! Another couple was very interested in the second puppy.

"Thank god you were there, Lenora! The more I thought about having two, the more I love the Idea.

I owe you a big one!"

Lenora responded, "No, just let me babysit."

"I've fallen in love," She wrote, "They'll be in good hands."

Ashton thanked her again, "OK, let me know when you have them at home. I want to see a beautiful close-up."

They said goodbye and deleted it.

Sofia was talking to her friends. Ashton called his dad, "Hey, Dad, just touching base. We'll be off early tomorrow, so I guess we'll be seeing you in a week or so."

"Yes... not sure when, but we'll get there soon. I promised Walter I'd help out with the Rescue. Mostly making calls to big corporations." Frank was used to that.

"Anyway, have a great trip. Call me when you're settled in. Oh... Say hi to Robin." Frank said.

"Sure, I will. You have fun with Walter. We'll catch up soon. They hung up."

When they were both finished making numerous calls, they decided to call it a night.

Ashton wanted to go for breakfast before going to the airport.

They set their bags at the door and went to bed.

The morning came in a flash, it seemed.

They jumped up and showered, and Paul was there to meet them.

After a brief stop to eat, they were on their way.

Paul stated he would miss them for so long.

They said the same.

"But… we'll be back," Ashton assured him.

Paul pulled up at their gate and unloaded their luggage. Sofia gave him a big hug and thanked him.

She told him we'll see you soon as she turned and began walking to the doors.

Ashton shook his hand and said, "Take care! See you in three weeks."

Ashton ran to catch up to Sofia. They had no trouble at security and then found a seat by the window to await their flight.

They had about a half to kill before leaving. Both were pumped up and eager to go.

They checked, and there were no cancellations.

"Great," Ashton said, "A few hours from now, we'll be back in the sunshine."

"Our suite awaits us." Sofia smiled.

"I love that suite," She said, "It's almost like an apartment."

They watched other planes come and go; Sofia sat, reminiscing about their flights with Exotic. It seemed like a lifetime ago. She wondered how it would work for the cruise line.

"It will be different." She thought.

Soon, they heard their flight being called. They got up and started to board.

Once seated, it was only minutes before they took off.

Benefiting from tailwinds, the flight turned out to be shorter than expected.

Ashton held Sofia's hand as they peered out the window at the perfect white fluffy clouds with the sun shining through.

In that moment, they felt completely at home.

Upon landing, they quickly headed for their luggage pick up.

It took a little while, but they soon found theirs. There was a car waiting for them from the cruise line. They were picked up and soon boarded.

They went straight to their suite and started unpacking.

Robin would be there in about an hour to bring their uniforms and brief them on what was to come.

They went out on the deck to take in the warmth of the sun.

What a change from where they came from. They had to change into lighter clothes.

Sofia quickly unpacked all the coffee and specialty treats they had paid extra for in order to bring.

They had a suitcase filled with their favorite supplies.

COFFEE being the most important, of course. To them, it was like fine wine!

There was a knock at their door. It was Robin.

They were happy to see her. They exchanged hugs, and she was all excited

They were there. She had their position information in her hand.

Ashton made some Iced Tea, and they headed outside.

Your uniforms will be here shortly, she told them.

After talking about Christmas and the holidays, they got down to business. Sofia would be assisting Robin in her day-to-day duties, a much-needed position.

With the great number of passengers, it was taking a toll on her to provide the service they offered.

Ashton will be working with Zachary.

With all the newly added activities and bonuses, he's been running in circles trying to keep up with the demand.

Robin was so grateful that they were helping out.

They've never had this problem before! They've never had such a staff shortage.

Hopefully, they will get that sorted out.

Robin went on to say that because of their experience with the public… their training will be very short. Mostly just learning the computer

System. The rest is dealing with the general public and foreign passengers.

Both Sofia and Ashton had quite a bit of experience in that field.

Robin welcomed them to the Cruise line again.

She informed them that they would be joining the captain for dinner.

"Ohh…Great!" Ashton replied. Sofia was happy as well.

"So I must go now," Robin said, "Dinner is at 5.00 PM. I'll see you there."

They all stood and hugged goodbye. We'll be there with bells on Sofia said.

Robin turned and headed out.

Before getting ready, they had a couple of hours to enjoy the warm breeze.

They also wanted to watch the ship pull out at 4.30 before heading for dinner.

"This feels so good," Ashton commented, "Almost like we're home again."

"Yaa, it feels so comfortable in this suite," Sofia added.

They sipped their iced tea and absorbed the hot sun before getting ready.

Once the ship pulled away from the dock and into the open waters.

They headed to the private dining room to meet the group.

Sofia was getting hungry. Ashton was as well.

Robin and the captain soon joined them.

They sat at the table, where there were a couple of bottles of wine awaiting them.

"I thought I'd take the liberty," John said.

"So, it's nice to see you guys again!" Captain John smiled, showing his pearly white teeth.

Welcome aboard he raised his glass and toasted. I heard you were coming on for a while to help out. We really appreciate

Ever since coming back from Covid, the number of employees quitting has been off the charts. No one wants to work anymore.

With all the new and larger ships being launched, Robin has told you that there's been a major shortage.

Any bit of help is great. We must keep our guests happy. They expect top-quality service. We're doing our best.

Ashton spoke up, "Well, thanks to my dad, we can do this. You know how he and my mother have been cruising forever. Myself as well. Plus, with all the stock he owns. He should help protect it, Ha Ha," They all laughed.

"Just kidding," He added.

This is one of the best cruise lines anywhere. We're glad to help out.

The server showed up with a fine array of rolls and specialty breads.

He took their orders.

"Anyway," Ashton went on, "They have made up a schedule to allow us to return home every three weeks. That was nice of them, and we got to stay in our own suite while we were working. Once things get back on track, we'll see what and where we will be the best place for us."

Their food soon arrived, and they sat chatting about everything under the sun.

"The meal was excellent!" Sofia praised the chefs.

"So, I guess we will start bright and early tomorrow. That's ok."

"I'm always up before the world," She laughed.

"Yes, she is," Ashton added, "I like it, too, so I'm good to go at any time. We'll be starting a new adventure.

"Well... I'd better get back to the bridge. Who knows where we'll end up if I'm not there," He said jokingly.

Everyone laughed.

"Thank You for the wonderful dinner," Sofia said, "Hope to see you soon."

"Yes, if they don't fire us first!" Ashton laughed.

Sofia just shook her head. Well, you never know, Ashton tried to look serious.

"Come on," She said, "We have to try on our uniforms and get a good night's rest."

They said goodnight, and everyone went their own ways.

Back in their suite, they made some coffee.

The gentle sea breezes were calling them outside.

Sofia stated, "It feels like we never left."

"I know…," Ashton said, standing at the railing. Yet, so much has happened since. It's funny how time does that."

They both took out their phones and were checking for messages.

Sofia was laughing at one from Maina.

She sent a sad, crying face that said, "MISS YOU! Wahhhh!"

She responded, "I know, dear… mommy and daddy will be home in three weeks."

She giggled.

Ashton had only one text he was hoping for. That was from Lenora.

There were no new messages. Perhaps that's a good thing, he thought.

He decided to send HER one, "Let me know when you have the puppy's home with you. Check your email... I've sent an E-transfer for the adoption fees along with money for Food and any other supplies you need. Can't wait to see them! Sofia is going to freak out! Now I don't know if I can wait till Valentine's Day! LOL."

He received a new picture of the three puppies together a moment later.

MIA was kissing the two babies.

There was a message, "Have you chosen the names yet?"

"Give it some thought. Then let me know. There is something I want to do."

Ashton thanked her for the picture and said he'd think about that.

"There's a girl and a boy. Ok.... I'll be in touch."

He erased their conversation. He saved the pictures she had sent.

He poured a fresh coffee and went outside. Sofia soon joined him.

"Awe...... this is nice," Ashton said, "Fresh sea air. I think I'll go to bed soon. I want to be awake and alert tomorrow. It should be interesting."

"Good Idea," Sofia agreed, "I'll do the same. These hours are longer than what we're used to. And I have no idea what all Robin does in a day. I guess I'll find out tomorrow."

They finished their coffee and then went to bed.

They were both up early and ready to go. They had a pre-ordered breakfast, which was delicious. They both headed out to where they were meeting Robin.

First, she brought Ashton to where Zachary was making up his schedule. They knew each other, so it was an easy meet.

Then, Robin took Sofia and started going over her routine.

Sofia was starting to understand why she was desperate for some help.

There were just so many details, game plans, tours, and specialty events, and time was sometimes crucial.

In between all that, she had to mingle, entertain, and manage events.

Robin had sheets of paperwork to go through each day.

With Sofia's help, it would be much easier and more efficient.

Sofia suggested breaking down the list, and they each took charge of different tasks.

Sofia wouldn't finalize anything before having Robin's approval.

"Perfect. Here, point out the things you think you can do. I'll conquer the more involved projects." Ashton Suggested.

"Works for me," Sofia said energetically.

The two got down to work.

"This is fun," she said, "But I see everything does take time. With the huge ship, it takes longer to go back and forth preparing for each event."

There was a wine tasting, a meet-the-captain party, and a bingo session, just to name a few.

Pool parties, kitchen tours, and information about shopping on the islands also had scheduled meetings. All these and more had to play out smoothly over the course of a day.

Those were just the beginning.

"Wow," Sofia gasped in shock.

"I think you need help!" She laughed.

"I see it now. Well…. Let's get started."

They divided the list up and began their work. Sofia had to learn where to go and who to deal with for each activity and event.

This slowed things down, but it will work for the best in time.

Robin is a very patient instructor.

By the end of their day, Sofia was exhausted. So much to learn, so much to absorb.

They made it through and then had a light dinner. Robin told Sofia not to get too stressed out, and she was still a big help.

Sofia wasn't sure she believed her.

They finished their meal and headed out for the night.

Ashton was already in their suite when Sofia got in. He had a cold, refreshing juice waiting for her. She threw herself in a chair and moaned.

"That was a very hectic day," She said, "There's just a huge amount of details and running around to do. A great deal of responsibilities. This is going to take a little time to get used to."

"My feet are killing me," She laughed.

"How was your day?" Sofia asked, "How is Zachary doing?"

"It was good! We connected very well. He's really good for the public. I really enjoyed being with everyone and actually talking to the guests. With the airlines, there are limited short conversations compared to here. It's very different. I had a great time offering discounts and add-ons and giving out information. Quite a lot I already knew from all my years of cruising."

Sofia sighed, "That's great."

She said, her eyes half closed, "Well, Tomorrow's another day. It should be easier. Now, I'm going to bed. I know it's early, but I'm done."

Ashton stood, taking her hand, "Come on, I'll give you a foot massage. You can just go to sleep."

The next morning, Ashton had coffee, juice, and bagels with cream cheese, waiting for Sofia when she got up.

She looked refreshed and ready for another day.

"I feel much better after that massage and long sleep. I'm not going to get it. I am so stressed out today. I learned a lot and will just take one step at a time. I think I was trying too hard," Sofia expressed.

"Good for you! I know you can do anything you set your mind to. Just be you and go out there with your usual positive attitude," reassured Ashton.

Sofia smiled and nodded, "Yeah, I was just nervous."

They ate their breakfast outside. It was already getting warm.

"That was delicious!" Sofia said, "Good cook!" She laughed.

"Thanks! I've been practicing!"

"Ok, I'm off!" Sofia turned and gave Ashton a hug and kiss.

"I'll see you later, Hun. Have a great day!"

"You too; I'll be here when you're done."

Ashton quickly reached for his phone. He had thought of names for the puppies, 'TIA and TAO.'

It was early, so he texted Lenora rather than called.

He thought they were short and cute.

It was soon time for him to go to work. Just as he was about to get on the elevator, his phone rang. It was Lenora.

"Good morning," He answered and stopped in the corridor, "What do you think of those names?"

"I think they are adorable! Just like these little Yorkie poos," She giggled.

"They are going to be very small, teacup puppies. I found out that the reason they were turned in was that they are not purebred. The breeder was annoyed and dropped them off. Such a shame." He vehemently expressed his anger.

"Anyway, I will pick them up tomorrow! I'm so excited!" He said.

"They are being checked over now. I will send pictures when they are here at home." Lenora informed.

"Thank You so much Lenora! This means a lot to me. I can't wait to see Sofia's face. I'd better stock up on tissues," He laughed, "For both of us!"

Lenora laughed, "You're going to fall in love! Trust me."

"OK, I'd better get to work! I'll be in touch tomorrow. Thanks again."

They hung up.

Ashton quickly headed to his service desk. He was doing alright. Zachary greeted him with a Latte.

"Good morning, guys."

"Wow, thanks, Zach! This is great! I'm ready and set for the day. Anything special I should know about?"

"No…," Zachary said as he sipped his coffee, " only that it would be a beautiful day. Since we're at the dock, it will be very light. Most get off the ship."

"That's good for us. I can go over more things with you with fewer interruptions." Ashton replied.

"Ya…you're right! I'm good with that. You wanted to show me some computer tricks for looking things up. I'm ready when you are. There's a lot to learn yet." He added.

Half a dozen guests came to the desk, and Zach let Ashton take charge. He stood behind him for support.

The way he handled their requests was impressive, and he efficiently kept the line moving. He felt good about his performance.

Ashton effortlessly connects with the guests, exuding confidence with his bright smile and light, wavy hair, capable of calming anyone facing a problem.

As they delved into the computer, Zachary shared numerous shortcuts for checking events and tours. They covered everything from finding seats and times to backup dates.

After an intense session, they decided to take a break and enjoy some lunch.

The following day, Zachary continued to guide him through the remaining tasks. The rest of that day unfolded seamlessly, with small groups of guests returning aboard.

Many of them had questions about their bills or were purchasing tickets for the evening shows.

Amidst the routine, Ashton found moments to ponder about Tia and Tao. In his mind, he envisioned them in matching outfits, sporting cool hairstyles that added a touch of charm to his thoughts.

After his shift, he rushed up to their suite and called Lenora.

She laughed at him, "You sound more like a father expecting a baby!"

Ashton laughed as well, "Yaa... I feel like one, too!"

"Well," she said, "I brought them home two hours ago. All is good! They're in perfect health and happy as could be."

"My little Mia is very inquisitive around them. She's also very gentle. So far, no problems. Here, I'm sending you some pictures. You'll love them!" Ashton looked at the two puppies in their bed. His heart melted.

Just then, Sofia walked in.

Ashton hung up and sent a text to Lenora, "Sorry, Sofia came in! Thanks, I'll be in touch later."

"Hey, you're back early!" He turned to Sofia.

"Yaa... we had a great day! Less running around and fewer activities while at the dock. That gave us a chance to show me more without interruptions. It was fun!" She replied.

"Oh, great," Ashton kissed her, "We can have a relaxing dinner and evening."

Sofia jumped in the shower and changed into comfy clothes.

Sounds good hun.

Ashton followed after... then took out a bottle of wine.

"This is what I love the most," He said.

"Enjoying a nice evening with my sweetheart! The breezes off the sea made it even more special. Fresh air and a glass of wine." He added.

Sofia ordered their dinner. She was in a great mood.

"Robin and I seem to work in sync," She said, "We get along so well. She needs to meet a nice guy!"

Ashton nodded, "Yaa... she really has a great personality. We'll have to keep our eyes open."

He sat staring at Sofia with a smile he couldn't contain.

"What!" She said with a questioning look, "What's in that head of yours?"

"Nothing," He lied, "Just enjoying the moment."

The truth was he was picturing the two of them in the park, each with a puppy on a leash.

"Sure…sure…," Sofia smirked, "Anyway, dinner will be here shortly."

"I'm getting hungry," She said.

I heard on the news that New York was in for a major snowstorm on the weekend.

"I hope everyone stays safe!" Sofia told Ashton.

"I'll have to keep in touch with the gang." She said.

"Oh really! Good thing my dad and Walter are coming on Friday! I hope they're ahead of the weather!" He replied.

"I think they'll be ok, Hun. They always take an early flight. The storm will be hitting in the afternoon to early evening." She calmed him down.

"Ok, good!" He sighed.

"It will be nice to have them back here. I'm already missing our friends. I guess maybe knowing we are here for weeks at a time, we'll have to adjust to this." He said.

Sofia smiled, "We can do this, even if just for a while. Remember, we're only helping them out right now! Nothing is in stone."

"Yaa, I try and keep that in mind. I DO enjoy my job so far. I think I've been thinking too much of us living together back home. I was just settling in. It felt soo right!" Ashton expressed his feelings.

"I know," Sofia smiled, "We seem to really connect. At least we're together here also. Let's see how it goes…. Then, as things start to get back to normal, we can see about cutting our hours. Maybe 2 weeks on, 2 weeks off."

Ashton's thoughts turned back to their puppies. He pictured coming through the doors and being greeted by two fluffy babies and Sofia.

Grinning broadly, Ashton agreed to whatever was discussed.

Little did she know the thoughts running through his mind!

"Come on," Sofia said, "Let's go for a nice hot tub. It's a beautiful night."

"Sounds good; I'll pour us a wine," Ashton replied.

The remainder of the evening unfolded in relaxation, with Sofia and Ashton exchanging texts with their friends.

Sofia took the opportunity to FaceTime Ricky and Fred, inquiring about their weather.

With a mischievous grin, she turned her phone around to reveal their beautiful deck with a hot tub, showcasing the absence of snow.

In response, the two friends playfully expressed their surprise with a few not-so-proper words.

Sofia and Ashton burst into laughter, offering mock apologies.

"Ohhhhh, we're sooooo sorry!" They chimed in with amusement.

They did the same to the rest of their friends. It was fun.

The next couple of days were routine. They both adjusted well into their positions and felt more relaxed.

Ashton kept secretly in touch with Lenora and the puppies.

Due to the storm, Frank and Walter put their arrival off for a few days.

They were afraid of being stranded at the airport.

Ashton agreed it was a wise choice.

The storm arrived with a vengeance, just as predicted.

New York found itself buried under almost three feet of snow, causing the cancellation of most flights in and out of the city.

Meanwhile, Sofia and Ashton enjoyed the spectacle from the comfort of their deck, basking in warm Caribbean breezes and the view of the blue sea.

With the weekend off, they indulged in a couple of massages and some leisurely swimming.

Docked in Grand Cayman, Ashton took the opportunity to slip out and restock their coffee supply cupboard.

Not stopping there, he also made a quick visit to the wine store, ensuring they were well-prepared for a relaxing time onboard.

It was a beautiful, romantic weekend. They concentrated on relaxing and enjoying the weather and even more on themselves.

Their next stop would be St. Lucia. Frank and Walter would have to meet them there.

The two days off flew by, and it was back to work for Sofia and Ashton.

Both were growing more comfortable in their positions and, surprisingly, found themselves genuinely enjoying the experience.

Their easygoing personalities made the work more manageable, and the staff quickly warmed up to them.

As planned, Frank and Walter boarded the ship.

They organized a delightful dinner with Sofia and Ashton on a day when the ship was at the dock, making it easier to step away a bit early.

Eager to catch up, they discussed various topics. During the conversation, Ashton discreetly mentioned the puppies to Walter and requested him to keep them under wraps.

Walter was pleased with the trust and assured him, "Mum's the word."

In the following weeks, Sofia and Ashton dedicated themselves to their jobs.

They enjoyed occasional dinners with Frank and Walter, deepening their connections.

During these gatherings, Walter observed that Sofia's passion revolved around the Animal Rescue.

She shared her plans with him, expressing her intention to return for another visit once they were home.

Walter was genuinely pleased to hear about Sofia's commitment to such a meaningful cause

"Well," Walter said, kind of joking, "We are always looking for help!"

Sofia's eyebrows raised. "That might be a great idea!" She said.

"Maybe even a day or two on my days off!" Walter nodded, "We're always grateful for any help."

Ashton spoke up, saying that they were very impressed with his setup.

It was very clean and organized.

They had no idea there were soo many pets in need.

Sofia said with tears in her eyes, "It broke my heart to see some of them were greatly abused. They are just soo helpless!"

Frank ordered another bottle of wine.

"Perhaps, my dear, you are in the wrong business!" Frank commented.

"Maybe you should be in the animal world," He smiled.

Sofia wiped her eyes. "I love my career with Exotic," She said, "And we've both been enjoying it here on the ship, but since visiting the Rescue, I've had this heavy feeling. I've had to work so hard to support myself after being too old for foster homes. I think there is so much going on in this world that we just don't see. We become oblivious to what's in front of us. It really opened my eyes."

She added, "Lately, another thing that has affected me is the amount of homeless people on the streets. Since Ashton and I have been together, I seem to be in a limo a lot. I've been able to actually look around and see what's out there. It's so wrong!"

"Anyway, let's change the subject. We only have a couple of days before going home for a week. Ashton and I are looking forward to seeing our friends. Maina's been whining about missing her BFF. She's planned a get-together when we're back." She chuckled.

"So...Dad!... How long are you staying on the ship?" Ashton laughed.

"Should you be changing your address?" He asked.

Frank laughed, "Ohh...who knows! I've been able to take care of most of my business, from here. Most meetings now are over Zoom. I've finally got the hang of that."

Sofia laughed, "Yaa, everything is on the computer now. You can do everything while lying on the beach! It's great! Except, I don't think our jobs at Exotic would be possible."

Everyone laughed.

"You're funny," Walter grinned, "You're also right."

"I've really been enjoying my time on board," Frank said, "Walter and I have connected so well. We have made other friends here who are doing the same. It's like our own community. I need this now."

"Well, that's great," Ashton nodded, "It's time to enjoy a little now. You deserve it!"

Just then…his phone chimed. It was Lenora, with new pictures.

He quickly ended it and put it in his pocket.

"Who was that?" Sofia asked.

"Ohh… just advertising…you know," He lied again.

"Now, I think it's time we head up. I'd love to soak in the hot tub." He suggested.

"Oh, yeah…that sounds good. We'll have three days more work then our week off. Strange shifts, but it works. We told them we were flexible, so that helps them a lot. I'm ok with whatever they need." She replied.

As the evening came to a close, Ashton and Sofia rose from their seats, warmly hugging Frank and Walter, bidding them goodnight.

"We'll join you for dinner tomorrow night if we can."

They left the dining room.

Walter leaned over to Frank and said, "One day, Sofia is going to be your favorite daughter-in-law."

"My only daughter-in-law," Frank laughed, "Now we don't know that for sure?"

"Mark my words; I watch how Ashton looks at her! He's deeply in love. And she feels the same."

Frank agreed, "I know,"

He said, "She's a wonderful young woman. I would love to welcome her into our family."

In their suite, Sofia and Ashton relaxed in the hot tub as the ship sailed through clear skies.

Ashton set the mood with romantic music, and as he moved closer to Sofia, they shared a passionate kiss. When the kiss ended, Ashton, with a racing heart, contemplated expressing his feelings.

Just as he was about to speak, Sofia closed her eyes and declared, "I LOVE YOU!" Opening her eyes, she kissed him again, tears of happiness streaming down her face.

Overwhelmed with joy, Ashton held her close, reciprocating the sentiment.

They shared smiles and fell into each other's arms, later heading to bed, where they shared a beautiful moment of love.

The next morning, Ashton ensured he was up before Sofia, ordering a fabulous breakfast and a single red rose.

With coffee ready, he eagerly awaited her presence, filled with excitement.

The day held multiple sources of joy: living with Sofia, the surprise with the puppies he had for her, and the realization that they loved each other.

Sofia, waking up and jumping into the shower, emerged ready for work.

To her surprise, Ashton had everything prepared on the deck. He greeted her with a kiss, and she blushed, noticing the beautiful rose.

"Wow... Someone's in a great mood! Oh, what a beautiful rose! For me? Thank you!" She exclaimed with a smile.

Ashton served the coffee and juice and then sat down to eat.

He looked at her and asked, "Did you really mean what you said? You know that you loved me?"

Sofia looked into his eyes, "Yes! I really love you!"

Ashton stood up and moved towards her. Sofia stood up. They embraced, and he kissed her most lovingly. They sat and finished their breakfast.

Sofia was staring down at her plate. Ashton asked what she was thinking about.

"I never thought I would ever meet someone like you," She said.

"You've been loving, caring, and always watching out for me. It took me a while to adjust to that. I wasn't sure how to react! But...deep down... I think I knew you were special.

I felt a bond. Even before I knew who you were!" She let her heart out.

"Then, you told me who you really were. I panicked inside. I didn't feel worthy of you. But it was too late! I fell in love. I've played it cool, expecting you to be gone at any time. You're so handsome. And charming, you can have anyone you want! Why would you want to stay with me?" I thought.

"You never left," Sofia went on, with tears in her eyes, "You're still here!"

Ashton grabbed her.

"I'm never leaving," He said, "I'll be here as long as you want me. They embraced for what seemed like forever."

"OMG," Sofia wiped her eyes, "I have to go to work."

She gave him a kiss, and then turned towards the door.

"We'll have a special dinner tonight," Ashton said, "I'll let my dad know we won't be there."

"Sounds great," Sofia replied, "See you soon. With a smile on her face, she was out the door. She practically bounced down to meet Robin."

She made it on time. Robin showed up a moment later.

"Good morning," She sang out.

"Good morning," Robin replied.

"I think it's going to be very busy today." She said.

"No problem," Sofia replied, "Bring it on!"

Robin looked at her, surprised, "Wow… someone's a little more than cheerful this morning?"

"Yaa… I had a good rest, and now I'm good to go," She laughed.

Robin informed her that they only had four days left before they would be off for the week.

This was due to the scheduled port stop providing the opportunity for them to disembark.

"Ohh… That's cool," She replied.

Excitement bubbled within her at the thought of surprising Ashton with the news.

They both focused on their duties, with Sofia approaching each task with great joy.

Together, they efficiently managed to accomplish everything needed for the day. Robin was so grateful for the help.

"I'm very glad to have you here," She told Sofia.

"So, how are you enjoying it so far?" She asked.

"It's been great! Do you think you could work here on a more permanent basis?" She replied.

Sofia sat down and thought for a moment.

"I'm not sure," She replied.

"It's not been easy being away for so long at a time. We miss our friends, and it's been kind of funny working somewhere we had been coming on for a vacation." She said.

"I'm not sure about Ashton. He hasn't commented about it yet. I'll try and get his thoughts on it. He has said that he's enjoying what he's doing. Staying on full-time may be another thing. We are glad to help out, though, any time. It's been fun so far." She said.

"Great," Robin said.

"We are doing some training classes now. It's been difficult finding good, serious workers. Everyone wants to work from home anymore! You can't do that on a ship," She laughed.

"Yaa, I guess that would be hard," Sofia laughed.

"Anyway, we're here to fill in for now. So, we'll see. Ok, let's get to work!"

They grabbed their sheet of tasks and started knocking them off.

There was a lot to do, just as Robin figured.

Ashton threw on a little light cologne and made his way to his desk.

Zachary was on the computer, hunting for some info for a guest.

"Morning!...Morning!"

"Ready for a busy day? I've already received some calls," He stated.

Ashton gave a salute, "Aye, Aye, sir, ready and able!"

They both laughed.

Zach gave Ashton some sheets of paper. There were requests for shows and other activities that guests wanted to book.

"Wow, do people not sleep in on their vacation? It's only 8.00 AM!"

They both started taking care of the bookings.

Ashton was in a mood like never before! It was hard keeping a smile off his face.

First, it was the puppies, and now what happened between him and Sofia.

He felt overloaded with excitement. Zach noticed and mentioned it.

Ashton told him about the surprise puppies. But left out about Sofia.

He just said they were getting closer every day.

Zach thought the surprise was awesome, "I rescued my puppy, also! It felt great!"

Ashton took out his phone and showed him some pictures of the two babies.

He was feeling like a proud father.

"OMG, they're beautiful! How did you manage to find two designer-style Puppies at a rescue?" Zach asked.

Ashton explained about the breeder, "They are not pure bread."

Zach then understood.

"Some breeder," He said, "It's all about money! The poor pets suffer because of it."

"Yaa... I know! It really sucks. A friend of ours owns a rescue. We took a tour. Sofia was in tears most of the time. She always wanted a pet, so to see all those poor pets just thrown away by people really hit her hard. That's when I got the Idea." Ashton told him.

"It turns out we'll be on board for Valentine's Day, so I've made arrangements to have the puppies ready for next week when we're off.

Our neighbor has graciously agreed to take care of everything, and I've sent her more than enough money to ensure she can pick up everything needed - from food and toys to a carrier, harnesses, treats, beds, and more.

To add an extra touch, she mentioned finding a couple of matching outfits online for the puppies. I can already imagine how beautiful they are going to look!" He further added.

"Awe...that's fabulous!" Zach said, "I wish I could be there to see her face!"

"Yaa, I'm just beside her." He replied.

"Tia and Tao are short and sweet, just like them." He said.

"Awe.......Well, take lots of pictures!" Zach demanded.

"Oh, I will, for sure."

"OK, let's get this day taken care of. I'm too wound up to relax." Ashton said, "I'm full of energy!"

They both laughed and got to work.

The day flew by. Ashton couldn't wait to get back to Sofia! He was in Love!

As soon as he returned to their suite, he ordered a special seafood dinner for the two of them.

Uncertain about when Sofia would finish work, he informed the kitchen that he would let them know the exact time.

The meal would commence with a light salad, followed by a platter of her favorite seafood delicacies.

This included lobster tails, garlic butter scallops seared to perfection, open crab legs, and mussels in an Italian tomato sauce.

The mere thought of it made his mouth water – he loved those dishes, too!

He set up the table with candles and a bottle of wine on ice.

Once that was ready, he jumped in the shower and into a dressy tracksuit.

A spritz of Channel Blue cologne, and he was almost ready.

The weather was beautiful for an outdoor dinner. The hot tub was bubbling.

And he set up the umbrella over the table.

Soft music filled the air.

He sat with a refreshing juice and picked up his phone.

It's time for a check-in on the puppies.

He called Lenora, and she answered right away. She knew he'd be wanting to see them; she had them dressed in one of their matching outfits.

They are truly gorgeous puppies. They are light beige and fluffy.

Their big black eyes look up at you with love.

"OMG...They look beautiful! I can't wait to hold them. Those are the cutest outfits for them. I see they couldn't have been in any better hands! Thank You! A few more days!" Ashton filled her in on the plans to surprise Sofia during their week off.

He informed her that they were scheduled to work over Valentine's Day, but he decided to celebrate it early. As it turned out, it worked just as well. Keeping this surprise hadn't been easy, and he was relieved to finally share the exciting news.

They had to figure out the best way to present them. And when Lenora had another set of outfits. Those ones have their names on them.

Then, she surprised Ashton with a picture of them sleeping in matching pajamas!

"OMG," He sighed, "So gorgeous!"

The door opened, and Sofia entered the suite.

"I got to go… she's back! Talk later……," He replied.

"Wow…. This looks great!" She said as she bent over and kissed Ashton.

"What's on the menu …I'm starved!" She asked.

"You'll see," Ashton replied.

"Well, I'm going for a shower. I'll be out soon." She said.

"Ok, Go ahead. No rush." He replied.

He called down to the kitchen and told them to start preparing.

They were ready.

When Sofia came out, he poured the wine.

CHEERS!

They toasted another day, but more than that, it was a new stage in their relationship.

They sat discussing their days. Both were happy with their progress.

Ashton took a sip of wine and asked Sofia if this was something she might want to do permanently.

She tilted her head in thought, "I'm not sure," she replied.

"I am enjoying what we do, and Robin and I work so well together. It's just that I do miss Exotic a lot.

Being here feels more like we should be on a vacation." She shared her feelings.

Ashton nodded, "I know what you mean. Well... we can decide whenever we want. Now we will enjoy a nice dinner. It should be here soon."

"Ahhh…...This is wonderful!" Sofia stated as she gazed over the open sea.

Her blonde hair flowed around her face.

"This is what I love! After a busy, hectic day…This is heaven." She loved every bit of it.

They both stood, taking in the peace and tranquility, until the food came.

"Oh…Wow… What a delicious-looking tray of seafood! You went all out with all my favorites!" Sofia leaned over and kissed him passionately, "You are the romantic."

They savored every bite and left nothing behind. It was delectable!

Afterward, they soaked in the hot tub.

Oh, Sofia broke their quiet moment, "Robin told me they have training going on now. She said it's been very hard finding serious employees. I know things will get back to normal soon, but I couldn't help but feel bad for her. She really does need an assistant. One she can count on. It's crazy how much she has to contend with every day. I don't want to leave her stuck."

Ashton listened and agreed, "Yaa… It's not fair, really. Most businesses are in the same boat, so to speak. Well… we can arrange to stay on as long as they need us. We can also make ourselves available after that in case they need temporary help."

"Ok…," Ashton stood to get out of the water, "Let's call it an early night. We have another busy day tomorrow. I'll talk to Robin tomorrow and see if we can get together with my dad and her and come up with some different scenarios.

My dad has no problem with what we decide. So…maybe we can find a way to keep everything running smoothly. If we decide to go back to Exotic… I don't want to leave them here short."

"Ok…sounds good to me," Sofia said.

"I am enjoying this at the end of our day. Maybe a little too much," she laughed, "After running around all day…this is total bliss."

"We have two more days before our week off. Let's do what we can, then we can enjoy seeing our friends." She suggested.

"Yes…," Ashton whispered under his breath, "and other surprises?"

"What?" Sofia asked.

"Oh...nothing," He said, "Just thinking about the weather

Sofia looked at him, puzzled, "Ok...."

The next day, they arranged to have dinner with Frank and Walter.

Robin would join them once she cleared her time.

They discussed the different ways Ashton and Sofia could be of help.

"If Robin can create a schedule with any new staff, she could work in time for extra training, using Sofia as a fill-in. Ashton's department was comparatively easier, and he could also serve as a fill-in. It may seem a bit complicated initially, but I believe it will work out just fine." Everyone thanked Frank for allowing this to happen.

"You know....," he said, "You just have to take one day at a time. You make things work."

Frank, for someone of his stature, wealth, and position, is such an intelligent, problem-solving man. He has such a calming demeanor despite all his responsibilities and pressure. Sofia looks up to him as if he were her own father. Walter is very similar. Perhaps it comes with experience and age.

"Well...," Ashton said, "It's time to turn in. We have some packing to do. Tomorrow after work, we head out for the airport. We've got a 9.00 PM flight home. Paul will meet us when we arrive. Hopefully, we'll be home around midnight."

"Our friends are looking forward to seeing us. Maina was working on a plan to get together, last I heard. We only have a week, so. It will be busy for us." He added.

Walter smiled, "It sounds like you two have some wonderful friends!"

Ashton nodded, "Yes, we are very fortunate."

Sofia stood, "I guess we'll see you two in a week or so."

"Enjoy the warm weather, and think of us in the snow," she laughed.

"Good night, guys…see you soon. Good night."

Ashton and Sofia returned to their suite, diving into their luggage and placing it by the door. After work, they planned to simply grab their belongings and go.

Ashton suggested a brief soak in the hot tub to help them relax, ensuring a restful sleep for the night.

Sofia agreed, recognizing that the next day would be long and busy, and a good night's rest was essential.

Ashton stole a quick glance at the puppies before closing his eyes. The excitement was building, knowing he would surprise Sofia early the next day after they got home.

After breakfast, he thought; that way, she would have a full week to spend with the adorable pups.

He kissed Sofia goodnight, falling asleep with a huge smile on his face, anticipating the joy their new furry companions would bring.

The next morning, they both awoke early and headed off to work after a quick bite. Both were in a great mood.

The day flew by. After saying their goodbyes, they headed for the airport.

Ashton suggested getting some sleep, even if just an hour.

Sofia wondered, "Why?"

"Well, we might be busy tomorrow! You know? We'll need some rest." He said.

"Ok….," she said, looking at him questionably.

They both closed their eyes on takeoff.

Upon arrival, Paul greeted them, and soon they were home.

"Not bad," Paul said, checking the time, "12:15 AM. I was pretty close."

"Yeah, but I'm wide awake now," Sofia replied, "Let's have a quick coffee."

"Okay… Then into bed," Ashton told her with a playful laugh, "I need my beauty sleep."

"Sure… I guess I could use some, too," Sofia agreed, and they headed for a quick coffee before settling in for the night.

The next morning, Ashton had coffee and bagels waiting for Sofia.

He had picked up some fancy jams in Grand Cayman to have with some soft cream cheese.

Sofia was famished when she woke up.

"Oh…. Yum!" she squealed, "Starving here!"

While they had their breakfast, Ashton informed her that they would be having company soon.

Sofia looked baffled.

"We are?" She asked, "Who?"

"How do you know someone's coming over? I didn't invite anyone?" She inquired.

"Oh, a little birdy told me," He laughed.

"So, when you're finished here, get dressed. Put on something comfortable." He instructed.

Sofia shook her head, "Ooo…k, You're up to something."

"I won't ask….," She said and went to change.

Ashton quickly sent a text to Lenora. She was all set.

He made some fresh coffee and set out some pastries.

Sofia came out in one of her sweatsuits.

"Is this ok?" She asked.

"Perfect," He responded.

"What's up with you?" Sofia squinted her eyes at him.

"Nothing," He lied.

"Just want you to enjoy your day," He smiled.

The doorbell rang. Ashton turned toward the bathroom and asked her to answer it.

Sofia opened the door. There stood Lenora, with the two babies, in matching pajamas.

Two beige fluffy balls of love.

Sofia's mouth dropped open, and the look on her face was priceless, "OMG.... you got two more puppies! OMG!"

She quickly picked one up, "Ohh.... they're beautiful!" Her eyes teared up.

Ashton put his arms around her, "Come in, Lenora."

He poured her a coffee and offered the pastries. Sofia excitedly threw herself on the floor, hugging and kissing the puppies.

Ashton winked at Lenora, and they both watched with joy as the puppies played.

"So... Sofia! What do you think of them?" He asked.

Sofia said she was in love.

Ashton glanced at Lenora.

"So, when did you decide to get more puppies?" She asked.

Lenora looked at Ashton. Ashton put his head down.

"Ohh, I've thought about it for a while now,"

She lied.

Ashton stood up.

"Sofia......... These puppies are for you! Happy Valentine's Day! Hun. I know it's a little early...,"

Sofia froze, "What? These are mine? Ours?"

"Yes," Ashton nodded.

Sofia could speak no more. She was in tears. She couldn't stop hugging the puppies.

"Really? OMG? I love them! Thank You.... Thank You! OMG!"

Now, the three of them were in tears.

"Their names are TIA and TAO unless you want to change them. I've been babysitting and training them for two weeks now. Ashton must really care about you," She stated.

Sofia ran to Ashton and fell into his arms.

Tears flowed down her face.

"I Love You," She whispered in his ear.

Then, Sofia's tears turned to laughter as she teased and played on the floor.

"I think they like me," She smiled.

Ashton and Lenora went down the hall to bring the rest of the things for the puppies. Together, they showed off some cute outfits, adding to the joyous atmosphere in the room.

"OMG!" Sofia stopped playing, "we're gone for weeks at a time!"

"Don't worry, Hun. Lenora wants to babysit while we're away. Mia is used to them."

"Ohhh…. Great! Thanks, Lenora! You're the best. This is too much!"

Ashton filled Sofia in on how they secretly texted each other, then deleted them. He also told her where they came from.

She was so happy about that!

"And…. Walter? He knew about this too," She asked.

"Yaa… I told him as well." He told her.

"Wow! I had no idea." She replied.

He explained how he intended to get her the small puppy she fell for, but all the other puppies had been adopted except for two.

The thought of leaving one all alone was heartbreaking for him, so he decided to bring both home.

"Awe… I'm so glad you didn't. I love them both! Thank you so much! Guys… Best present ever!" Sofia exclaimed with joy and gratitude.

Ashton and Lenora went into the kitchen to leave Sofia alone with her new puppies.

He poured them a coffee and sat at the table.

"The look on her face was worth the surprise," Ashton said.

"I'm glad it's over, though. Now I can really enjoy those little fur balls. They're only going to be about 5 pounds," Lenora told him.

"They are tea cups," She added.

"Ohh... wow!" Ashton seemed surprised, "I didn't know that."

"She'll love being able to take them more places. I'll pick up a couple of those carry bags. They'll fit in them, and no one will know!" He laughed.

Lenora had a huge smile on her face, "I loved taking care of them."

She said, "When you go back to the ship next week... can I babysit?"

Ashton lit up.

"I was hoping you would!" He exclaimed, "I trust you."

"It's nice that they also have an outside friend, Mia. Thank You so much." He said.

"No.... It's my pleasure. They are just gorgeous and also comical! They're great company for me." She replied.

Sofia walked in and showed off her new babies. She had one in each hand.

"Do you like their names, Sofia? You can change them if you like." They asked her.

"TIA…TAO….I do like those names." She chuckled.

Lenora told her about them being only about 5 pounds when they are fully grown.

Sofia"s eyes opened wide, "You're kidding! We can carry them in a shoulder bag!"

"Yaa… You can," Lenora nodded.

"Wow….I'm just overwhelmed. This is so fabulous!"

She kissed the two puppies.

"I love you," She said to them.

Then it hit her!

"OMG….. We go back on the ship for three weeks," She squealed, "What do we do?"

Ashton assured her they were in good hands with Lenora.

"Ohh…. Thank You! My heart jumped for a minute there. I will be missing them, though."

"I'll send lots of pictures, and we can FaceTime," Lenora said.

"Ya…. I hope so," Sofia snuggled the pups.

Sofia returned to the living room, laying on the carpet and playing with her new love.

She was ecstatic, "TIA…TAO….I love them."

Lenora got up, "Well, it's time for me to go. I'll leave you two alone with your babies. Let me know if you need anything or have any concerns. I'm very familiar with them. My husband and I have had many Yorky and Yorky Poos over the years. We were always involved with the SPCA. We fostered for years. I still donate regularly."

"Oh… that's wonderful," Sofia said, "I love hearing that. We're going to Walters Rescue tomorrow. If you'd like to come… let us know."

"That sounds good," Lenora responded, "Maybe I will, if you don't mind."

"Great… How about 10.00 AM?" She asked.

"I'll be ready," Lenora replied.

"Ok… Talk to you then."

Lenora left.

Sofia spent the rest of the day calling and texting pictures to her friends.

They all fell in love.

She told them they should have their get-together at her apartment.

She and Ashton can rearrange the furniture. They'll make it work.

That way, everyone could meet their new babies.

Maina said, "ok…I'll cancel Alexanders."

Sofia sent some beautiful pictures to Frank and Walter.

They were completely taken with the puppies.

"What adorable babies they are," Frank stated, "You must be thrilled!

"OMG, Frank…I can't believe it! I'm still in shock. All my life I wanted a puppy…. Now I have two!" She fought back the tears.

"And……From Walters Rescue! That's so great."

"My early Valentine's Day gift!…." She cried.

"Sorry," she said, "I just get so emotional about animals. Ashton is tooooooo wonderful!"

"I'll have to get him a Ferarri or Lamborgini," She laughed.

Frank laughed at her, "Yaa…. Sure, he'll love that."

"Ok, I'll let you go… we'll see you in a week," She said, "Take care."

"Ok, my dear, you just have fun with those precious fur balls," Frank replied.

They hung up.

While Sofia played and bonded with her babies, Ashton started to make plans for their get-together.

First, peruse the menu, and then commence the rearrangement of the furniture. He is determined to ensure everything falls into place.

Opting for easily manageable options, he settled on a selection of easy-to-eat items. Pizza, sliders, wings – nothing that necessitates the use of a knife and fork.

"Let's keep it casual." He said.

He checked with Sofia, who just said, "Whatever." She was too busy to care.

"You decide, Hun... I'm good with anything."

Soon, the puppies were worn out. She brought them to the big, soft, cozy bed Lenora had picked up for them.

It was only a minute or two, and they were asleep.

Sofia left them to rest.

Ashton had made some fresh coffee, and they sat discussing the party.

They thought about how they would set things up.

It was looking good. There was enough room.

Sofia asked Fred and Ricky to bring Moka and Lenora to bring Mia.

They kept a corner enclosed just for their pets. She couldn't wait to see them all together.

She sat staring at the table, sipping her coffee. Ashton asked what she was thinking about.

"Oh, I'm thinking I'm the luckiest person alive. My friends...You....and now the pets I always dreamed of. I don't know what I did to deserve this. I still can't believe this." She looked at Ashton with her teary, doe-eyes.

Ashton looked at her, "Sofia…you have no idea how special you are. You are always looking out for and taking care of everyone. You're honest, sensitive, innocent, and lovable. How can anyone not love you?"

"Awe…Thanks, Hun. I just try to be the best I can." She succinctly replied.

"Well," Ashton kissed her, "We need more like you."

"So, are we set for our get-together? Have we missed anything? Let's set up the room now! We only have two days." She said.

"Good idea," Ashton said as he jumped up, "Let's do it."

As it turned out, they had more than enough room.

"It's funny how moving things around can make such a big difference." They chuckled.

They liked the new setup even better. They'll keep it this way.

"Yaa… this is nice!" Sofia said, "I like it a lot!"

"Well… that's done. Food is decided. Now, you have one big decision to make!" He said.

Sofia looked at him surprisingly, "What big decision is that?"

"Ohh… this is important! What cute outfits you'll be debuting the puppies in!" He laughed.

Sofia broke out laughing, "Yeah... that will be the hardest!"

She giggled, "This will be fun. I love it!"

The next day, they made sure the apartment was clean and set up. They checked on their food orders and verified delivery time for the next day.

Sofia went online and searched for beautiful puppy clothes.

There were great toys as well.

There were lots to choose from. Also, she picked out cute little children's wardrobe to use as the puppy's closet. This will also keep all their supplies together.

Ashton got the biggest kick out of watching her. She was in a zone.

"He created a monster!" He laughed to himself.

The next afternoon arrived swiftly, and they were all set for their guests. The puppies were adorned in matching denim overalls, appearing incredibly adorable.

Lenora had done a great job securing a few outfits, and Sofia couldn't have been happier.

As their friends started to arrive, Maina was the first, as expected.

They exchanged hugs, and soon, Maina found herself on the floor, captivated by the charm of the puppies.

"OMG... they are beautiful! I want them," She said.

Sofia laughed, "Never going to happen," she replied.

"They are all mine! Ours!" Sofia looked at Ashton.

"I'll babysit any time," Maina threw a ball to the puppies.

Following Maina, Fred and Rick made their entrance, wearing broad smiles. Sofia greeted them with warm hugs and gave each of them a kiss.

To her surprise, they brought wine and a rose as a sweet gesture. Moka, their furry friend, also had a bag in her mouth containing a toy for the puppies. It seemed their guests never arrived empty-handed.

"Ohh... Thank you," Sofia expressed her gratitude.

Yvonne and Lenora arrived shortly after, completing the group. Just then, Angel and Kaylee appeared. Ashton took charge, collecting all the coats and placing them on their bed. With the coats safely stowed away, they released Moka to join in the playtime with the other furry companions.

The food was in the oven, and Ashton put out the appetizers. He started serving the drinks. Everyone went crazy over the puppies. Sofia was bubbling over with excitement. They were all together again.

It was a fun afternoon. Great food, great friends.

They all wanted to hear about their jobs on board the ship. They wondered if they were staying on permanently.

Ashton said he wasn't sure yet as there was so much to consider.

Fred approached Ashton, inquiring about how things were going for them. Ashton shared similar sentiments, but then he leaned in and confided, "Between you and me, Fred... I think Sofia would prefer to stay here and just vacation on the ship. Three weeks is a long time to be away, especially now with the puppies. I'm not sure what she'll decide. She's torn between the ship and Exotic." The uncertainty lingered in the air, leaving the decision hanging in the balance.

Ricky joined them, saying he was just in love with the puppies. He proceeded to show them some of the hundreds of pictures he had taken. Of course, he was in most of them.

Fred shook his head, "Maybe we should get you some matching outfits with them!"

"Ha Ha….," Ashton broke out laughing.

"Very funny," Ricky said, "But that does sound cool."

Sofia now joined them, "I miss you guys so much you know?"

Fred wrapped his arms around her, "We miss you too, my love."

Ashton went into the kitchen and brought out trays of hot food.

"Ok, everyone…. Come and get it!"

Then, he opened up more wine and offered more drinks.

Returning to Fred's side, Ashton felt a strong connection with him that had been present since they first met. They shared a notable similarity, both being intellectually inclined and passionate about educational learning.

Their camaraderie seemed to deepen as they conversed, finding common ground in their pursuits and interests.

On the other hand, Ricky presented a contrasting personality. His interests leaned more towards the arts, particularly singing, dancing, and, above all, acting. This diversity in their preferences contributed to a well-rounded dynamic in their relationship.

Ricky, with his flair for drama, was often the center of attention. Despite the differences, Sofia found their unique blend of personalities lovable and authentic, appreciating the richness each friend brought to their group.

Angel and Kaylee immersed themselves in the joy of playing with the puppies, sprawled out on the floor as the little ones climbed all over them. This interactive playtime served as a fantastic opportunity for socializing the puppies, ensuring they grew accustomed to different people.

Meanwhile, Yvonne and Lenora enjoyed a leisurely sip of wine, observing the lively activities unfolding in front of them.

The atmosphere was filled with laughter, warmth, and the delightful chaos of furry companions and friends coming together.

Sofia brought out the outfits Lenora had bought for them.

Maina ran over and started going crazy. She thought the clothes were just too adorable.

The afternoon unfolded wonderfully, providing a welcome escape for everyone as they let go of the pressures of work and life.

Together, they found solace and relaxation in each other's company.

Maina, with her demanding role as a nurse, faced long hours and a heavy workload. Kaylee, committed to overtime at Exotic, and Angel, juggling dental studies and work as a dental hygienist, had their own challenges.

Despite their individual struggles, these gatherings became therapeutic, offering a precious opportunity to forget the world's demands, especially with the lively addition of the new puppies.

Sofia couldn't help but grin from ear to ear, basking in the joy of the moment. However, the atmosphere shifted when Maina announced she had to leave.

Being on call, she had received news of some serious accidents on the highway and was needed urgently.

Though disappointed, Maina apologized to Sofia and Ashton, understanding the gravity of her responsibility.

The mood momentarily sobered as the reality of Maina's profession took precedence.

"I'll call you later, Hun!" She yelled as she ran out the door.

"Ok love you," Sofia yelled back.

"Ohh… I hope no one's hurt too bad!" Sofia frowned.

The afternoon started winding down. Soon, her friends had to call it a day.

Kaylee had an early flight the next day, and Angel had some heavy studying for an exam.

Sofia was sad to see them go. Yvonne and Lenora went back to their places. Ashton gave them a lot of leftovers for later.

Soon, only Rick and Fred were left.

Ashton put on some fresh coffee from their specialty collection.

A robust Italian blend, imported all the way from Venice, graced the gathering.

Fred found himself impressed by the quality of the coffee; it stood out as one of the best he had ever tasted. Even Ricky, with his more artistic inclinations, enjoyed the rich flavor.

As they savored their coffee, the group sat in peaceful quietude, observing the puppies who had, by now, almost lulled themselves to sleep.

Sofia, moved by the serene scene, went over and gently covered the slumbering puppies with a soft blanket.

The subject of the rescue came up. Sofia mentioned they were going back, this time with their puppies.

"I'd really like to volunteer there when we get things sorted out on where we're going to be. Either way… I should be able to find some time. There are so many things that can be done to help bring in more adoptees."

"My mind is filled with different ideas to enhance the experience. I want to talk to Walter when we get back on board."

Fred looked at Sofia, "You never stop, do you?"

"What?" She said.

"You never stop thinking of and caring for the unfortunate. Your heart is always out there." He replied.

"Yaa… I guess you're right," Sofia sighed, "It's just the way I am."

"Well," Ricky said, "We're right here with you. Anything we can do to help, just let us know."

"Thanks, Hun…. You guys are the best!" She leaned over and hugged them both.

"I'll probably take you up on that. You know that, right?"

They all laughed.

"Well, I think it's time," Ricky said to Fred, "It's been a great afternoon. These get-togethers are always the best! You only have a few more days here, but maybe we can have coffee before you leave."

"Yes," Ashton spoke up, "I hope so."

"Me too," Sofia added.

"Let's plan for Saturday! Just the four of us. We can have it here, and you can bring Moka. I want the puppies to become best friends." He said.

"Done!" Said Ricky, "We'll bring some Chinese food for dinner! How's that?"

"Perfect," Sofia said.

They said their goodbyes, and the guys left.

The next couple of days, Ashton and Sofia spent getting close to the pups, and enjoying long drives. They took the pups with them.

They let them out in the park for brief fresh air and exercise.

Of course, they had little snowsuits to keep warm.

To Sofia, this was now her first family. The family she always wanted.

It was going to be a very hard time leaving them for another three weeks.

She was starting to become sad.

One more day, then they would hop on a plane for the ship.

At least she knew Lenora would take good care of them. Still, it didn't change her feelings.

Ashton didn't bring the subject up. He let her work through her feelings and emotions.

They woke up on the final day without excitement.

Sofia went straight for the babies. She was rocking them in her arms.

Tears were slowly rolling down her face. She dreaded leaving.

Ashton became very upset as well.

In the bedroom, Ashton slipped away to send a text to Robin, updating her on the events unfolding. He detailed the tiny newcomers to the family, sparking curiosity and concern.

Robin, taking some time to ponder the situation, had a thought that prompted her to speak with someone in a position to make a significant decision.

After deliberation, Robin decided to take a more personal approach and called Sofia to discuss the matter in person. The call would provide an opportunity for a direct and heartfelt conversation, ensuring that the decision-making process was thoughtful and considerate.

Sofia's phone chimed. She saw it was Robin. She just stared at it.

Ashton said, "Answer it, Hun."

"Who is it?" Sofia sighed.

"Robin," she said.

"Well… answer it!"

"Hello?" Sofia reluctantly answered, "Hi! Sofia? Oh… Hi Robin. What's up?"

"Oh, I heard you had a little surprise when you got home!" She giggled.

"Yaa….," Sofia responded.

"My two puppies! I love them to pieces." Sofia chuckled.

"That's wonderful! What are you going to do with them while you're here?" Robin asked.

Sofia mentioned the neighbor. Robin heard the sadness in her voice.

"Ohh, that sounds great! But… would you consider bringing them with you?" She asked.

There was silence on the phone

"What?" Sofia squealed, "Really? You're kidding, right?"

"No! I've had it cleared already!" Robin informed.

"You guys are in a suite, plus you're helping us out! You are nowhere around the other passengers. No one will even know they're there. Plus, you do own the suite, so that classifies as a home." She further explained.

Sofia lit up like a firecracker, "OMG, thank You so much!"

"I love You!!!!!! …. Thank You …...Thank You! See you tomorrow! Come and see them!!!" Robin said.

"I will," Robin promised.

"Ok…... See you then."

They hung up.

Ashton stood in the doorway, a sneaky grin on his face.

Sofia looked at him.

"You know, don't you," she stated, "You did this, didn't you?"

Ashton shrugged.

"What?" He said.

Sofia ran and almost knocked him down, giving him the biggest hug and kiss.

"Omg…. I Love You, Ashton Davis!"

"I love you too, Sofia De Carlo."

Ashton took her hand, leading her into their bedroom.

After sharing a passionate moment of love, their connection deepening, the sound of the puppies' cries interrupted the post-bliss atmosphere.

With laughter, they both jumped up, quickly tending to the hungry little ones.

Sofia headed into the kitchen, preparing separate bowls for each puppy.

The tiny furballs eagerly dove headfirst into their breakfast, occasionally switching between dishes. Sofia made sure to refresh their water bowls as well.

The playful energy of the puppies seemed to uplift Sofia and Ashton's spirits.

They, too, had a change of mood, sharing a warm moment as they prepared their own breakfast.

With the puppies contentedly fed and watered, the couple turned their attention to the upcoming departure, starting to get their luggage ready for the afternoon journey.

Sofia took out an extra suitcase that she would use for the puppies. Because of their tiny sizes, they were able to go right on board with them. Their carriers fit under the seats.

That was a major bonus. Sofia wouldn't have rested with her babies in some cold storage area.

The anticipation built as the evening approached, with the four of them setting sail at sea.

Frank and Walter, eager to meet the puppies, would be greeted by the adorable sight of the little ones dressed in matching outfits.

Sofia's excitement bubbled over as she looked forward to their time on the ship.

The thought of sharing the experience with the puppies and their friends filled her with joy.

Meanwhile, Ashton sent a text to Paul, confirming the time for pick up. In his message, he hinted at two additional companions joining them, keeping their identities a mystery.

This piqued Paul's curiosity, leaving him intrigued about the surprise guests who would be part of the evening's adventure.

Lenora, anticipating the needs of the pups, made a thoughtful choice when gathering the main supplies. Among them, she included a couple of reusable pee pads—a practical solution for the ship's limited space.

Carrying a large box of disposable pads for three weeks would have been impractical, making the reusable option a godsend.

As for the pups' diet, the crew decided to simplify things by providing a mix of chopped vegetables with either beef or chicken from their own food supplies.

This practical approach allowed them to meet the nutritional needs of the pups without the complications of carrying specialized pet food for an extended period.

They acknowledged that they could revisit and refine the pups' diet as the journey progressed, confident in their ability to adapt and find suitable solutions along the way.

Sofia also thought she could hand wash their clothes in the sink and lay them on a chair to dry. Same with giving them a bath.

With each challenge solved, Sofia grew more excited, and that made Ashton even more excited.

Once everyone was ready and packed. Ashton thought it would be good to play with the puppies until they were all worn out.

This way, they would almost be asleep while on the plane.

They tossed the balls back and forth, having them run in circles repeatedly.

It was time to meet Paul. Just as predicted, the two babies were sound asleep.

They carefully carried them out to the limo.

Paul was standing there and couldn't believe what he saw.

Sofia put her finger on her lips to tell Paul to keep it quiet.

It had to be a minimal conversation as he passed a mile-long smile and then got into the car.

The flight went smoothly. The puppies slept through. Babies do need more sleep than the older ones.

Yes, balancing everything was a bit of a struggle, but they managed.

Ashton just got a porter to help.

Boarding proved to be a smooth process, and before long, they found themselves back in the comfort of their suite. Silently, they set about creating the ideal space to contain the pups.

Once everything was in order, they took a moment to prepare a cup of coffee.

With warm mugs in hand, they settled outside. The air was filled with a peaceful quiet, and as they both exhaled, a sense of relaxation and contentment enveloped them.

"We did it! Cheers!" They chuckled.

They leaned back and closed their eyes, letting the breezes flow around them.

That was one big whirlwind. The evening was theirs to enjoy.

The pups were still sleeping. Ashton and Sofia dozed off for about 30 minutes.

Then, Ashton got a text from Robin.

She was bringing a light dinner for them if they hadn't eaten yet.

"Oh, perfect," He said, "We haven't even thought about food."

"Great… I'll be there in half an hour." She replied.

Ashton woke up Sofia and they hit the shower. It brought them back to life.

The babies were still asleep.

Ashton got out a bottle of wine to serve when Robin came.

He set the table.

Soon, Robin was at the door. She had three trays containing Spaghetti and meatballs.

"Ohhh…. Awesome!" Sofia said, "I'm starving!"

On top was a basket of fresh Italian rolls with butter.

Ashton poured the wine.

In a soft, hushed tone, Sofia expressed her anticipation, mentioning that she would check on the puppies after they had finished their dinner. Perhaps, she mused, by then, they would be awake and ready for her attention.

"Ok, can't wait." She replied.

They enjoyed their meal.

"Wow, thank You so much, Robin! That was delicious. I'm stuffed now." Ashton got up and put on the coffee.

They chatted about the week's events. Robin was thrilled about the surprise. She also gave them their work schedule.

"Oh yes. Thanks."

"We set to go," Sofia said, "We have it all worked out. And we promise the puppies won't be any trouble."

"Thank you for allowing them," Sofia said, "It means a lot to me."

"No problem. Besides, you're putting yourselves out for us. It's the least we can do. Plus, your dad owns a ton of stock in this ship! And… you own this suite!" Robin said.

"Well…. We still appreciate this," Ashton gave her a hug.

Just then, Sofia heard the puppies. She gave them some food, then brought them both outside to meet Robin.

"OMG! They are beautiful!" Robin gasped, "They're twins!"

She took one from Sofia.

"OMG, How sweet!" She hugged and kissed the baby.

"You have TIA, and the other one is a boy. His name is TAO." Sofia told her.

"Awe, that's so cute!" Robin thought the babies were adorable.

Then she put the puppy down, and they watched the two of them run, exploring every inch of the deck.

"It's so entertaining," Ashton commented.

"Yes! I see that," Robin laughed.

"So," Robin spoke up, "How did you like working on the ship? I know it's only been 3 weeks, but what are your thoughts? So far."

Sofia kind of tilted her head, "I really enjoyed it; It's just the time away for someone just starting out. It's perfect. I wouldn't mind doing this on occasion, but maybe not full-time.

"Don't worry, though; we are still staying on to help out." She continued.

Robin listened and nodded, "I know what you mean. I planned on this from the beginning. You guys didn't. This is what I chose to do and wanted to be."

Ashton spoke up, "The cruise ship has always been a vacation for me. So, It's a bit strange to be working on it. But it has been fun. I don't mind. I wouldn't mind doing this part-time. That would be cool. So, don't worry, Robin, we're here whenever you need us. We'd never leave you stuck! Trust us."

Robin smiled, "Thanks, guys. We've got some good trainees in the works now. OK, I should be going. I'll let you get settled, then see you in the morning. We'll be busy with being at sea. You know how it goes. Get some rest."

With that, Robin left the two for the night.

Efficiently, they unpacked, laying out their uniforms for the upcoming tasks. Simultaneously, they ensured the puppies were comfortably settled for the night, hopeful that they would sleep undisturbed until morning. With everything in order, it was time to retire for the night.

Over the next few evenings, they joined Frank and Walter for dinner.

Twice, they had them up in their Suite. The two men fell head over heels with their puppies.

Sofia finally got to spend enough time talking to Walter about the Rescue.

He opened her eyes to what was really happening out in the world.

She was just heartbroken. Everyone felt her sorrow and devastation.

She couldn't get those poor animals out of her head.

She would wake up in the night with all kinds of ideas. She wanted to mention them all to Walter, and she did.

He was amazed at her train of thought. She impressed and surprised him over and over.

Frank sat and listened to all her thoughts as well.

He looked at Ashton with total surprise.

"You really are a dreamer, Sofia! That's a great asset. Without dreams.... What do we have? I really admire you!"

Frank went on to say, "You had such a sad start to life. But instead of dwelling on that and letting it bring you down, you turned it into a stepping stone. You are a very caring, loving, and positive young lady. I regard you highly for that. Never give up your dreams!"

Ashton sat listening to the two men. He never felt so proud of Sofia as he did at that moment. He fell even more in love with her. He realized how much she cared for abused animals and homeless people.

But how deep it went was more than he thought.

The following weeks went by fairly quickly. Between work, the puppies, and long conversations with Frank and Walter, time just disappeared.

The next thing they knew, they were on their way back home again.

They were both getting the hang of traveling with the puppies.

They had a real routine now with feeding, dressing, and how to get them to sleep for the night.

It was rather gratifying.

Sofia was a real natural at playing the mommy.

Ashton could sense that she was treating them the way she never was as a child.

He pictured the two of them being married and building a life with their own children.

After swiftly unpacking and settling back in, they immediately began preparations for their next departure in a week.

Knowing their uniforms were already on the ship lightened their packing load.

With the clock displaying only 8:00 PM, they opted to unwind and savor the evening. Pouring a glass of wine, they decided to relish the moment.

Sofia, seemingly in a contemplative mood, sipped her wine as they snuggled up together on the couch, observing the playful antics of the pups.

Ashton asked her what she was thinking about. She just shrugged.

Then, she turned and looked at him, "You know, I had no idea how much I had buried inside. I always had secret prayers that the next foster home would have a pet, but I thought maybe I was just lonely. I remember how I couldn't, and still can't, watch those commercials about the animals in the SPCA or shelters are abandoned or abused. The sadness in their eyes, longing for someone to bring them home and love them. I would have to look away because I would literally break out in tears. I could relate to them."

"One day, it happened. My foster dad saw me crying and got mad at me, calling me stupid. I ran to my bedroom and cried even harder. After that, I would just leave the room. I will never let that happen again. Anyway, I've never told anyone about that before." Sofia wiped tears from her eyes.

Ashton held Sofia tight. He bent down and kissed her passionately, "Don't ever be afraid to be yourself. The way you feel is the way you feel. Like my father told you, follow your dreams. Well, I'm calling the rescue tomorrow. I'm setting up an appointment to have them train me for part-time volunteering. I want to help out. I think that's a great idea, Hun! I'll go with you."

"Really?" Sofia perked up, "You'd want to volunteer too?"

"Of course! We're a team! Awesome!" Sofia poured them another wine.

The atmosphere lightened as they clinked glasses, toasting to their decisions and the exciting journey ahead. Following the toast, they spent the remainder of the evening playing with the puppies until it was time to retire for the night.

The next morning, Sofia sent a text to Maina. She told her what they were going to do.

Maina was working for a while before she got the message.

Her reply was, "That's great! I think you'll love it! I'll call you when I get home. Xoxo."

Sofia and Ashton took the tour again, this time with a new perspective.

Sofia took mental notes of everything. Ideas were coming to her from every angle.

She went there with more of a business attitude rather than a visit.

When her emotions started to flow, she told herself she was there to help make things even better. That attitude really made it possible for her to stay and carry on. They made several visits throughout the week. She felt good inside.

They also enjoyed a dinner with Rick and Fred, plus a shopping afternoon with Maina and Angel.

Kaylee was off on a trip with Exotic.

"She was in Fiji. Lucky girl!"

Sofia thought about all her trips. She really missed them.

She got a taste of the places she had always heard about.

Those trips are shorter but very intriguing.

That's how she and Ashton started to get close. And with that, those butterflies came flying back!

The week had been incredibly busy yet undeniably satisfying. Sofia eagerly anticipated sharing the details of her visits to Walter's Rescue with him. As they embarked on another journey to the ship, the puppies peacefully slept, allowing Sofia a moment of contemplation as she gazed out the window, watching the world pass by through the clouds.

Sensing her introspective mood, Ashton held her hand, providing silent support and understanding. He knew that her mind was swirling with a myriad of details and decisions, and in that quiet moment, he allowed her the space to navigate through her thoughts.

Ashton bent down and brought one of the puppies out. He put it on her lap.

Within seconds, there was a huge smile on her face.

"I thought you might need a distraction," he told her, "I know you are torn on what path to take.

Whatever you decide, I'll be there with you."

Sofia leaned over and gave him a warm kiss.

"I know you will," she whispered, "I love you for that.

She snuggled with little Tia, then put her back before she woke up completely.

They soon were back in their suite on the ship. They got the puppies settled in.

It was early, so they made some coffee and sat out on the deck.

Ashton ordered some fresh fruit and pastries. That would hold them till dinner. They were meeting with Frank and Walter.

There was a little sprinkle of rain, but not enough to drive them inside.

They had a large overhang for covering, so they were dry.

Sofia started throwing out a whole lot of ideas and thoughts for the Rescue.

She had quite the list of possibilities in that head of hers.

Ashton was amazed at what she was thinking about.

They did sound fascinating, though.

He kept on listening and picturing in his mind what she was describing.

"I think…," he said slowly, " we should run these by Walter. See what he says. I think your ideas are great. However, we will have to find funding somewhere. Perhaps put on some events and maybe some 50/50 draws. Maybe a funding drive! I know your ideas are going to be extremely expensive."

Sofia looked at him, "Yaa, I know. That's the hard part. I'll figure something out. Perhaps Walter will have some ideas."

They put their feet up and closed their eyes. The breezes were warm and soothing.

They needed a break before starting another busy week.

It was good to clear their minds.

They were lucky to get about an hour's rest before the little ones started stirring.

That was ok, as it was almost time to get ready for dinner.

Sofia and Ashton got down on the floor, playing and throwing a ball back and forth. The puppies were running like crazy.

They spent about 20 minutes, then showered and changed.

Frank and Walter would be meeting them in the private dining room.

The showers helped to refresh them. They were set to go.

First, they fed the babies. They were acting hungry.

Then they left on some calming music. Sofia always did that when she had to leave them.

The soft noise provided a comforting company in their absence.

They joined the men.

"Well," Frank said with a big smile, "Welcome back aboard!"

"How was your week at home?" Walter added.

Sofia looked at Ashton, then paused, "It was very interesting! So much went on, and I really came to see things a lot more clearly. We spent a lot of time at the rescue. I think that unleashed a monster," She gave a half laugh.

"Now," she continued, "There are ideas swirling around in my head that I just can't seem to let go of. And I don't think I want to let go of them Either."

"Well, tell us, my dear! Sounds intriguing! What's on your mind?"

"Wait, let's order first. I'm getting hungry," Frank stated.

They preceded to give their orders, along with more wine.

"OK," Walter said, "Let's hear your ideas."

Sofia glanced at Ashton, "I'm afraid you'll think I'm crazy or off the wall."

"Just spill it, sweety; let me decide!" Walter laughed.

"Ok.....Here it goes! So................,"

Sofia began by sharing additional details about their visits to see the animals.

She then proceeded to discuss numerous ideas she had to attract more people and increase the likelihood of adoptions.

She emphasized the vastness of his property, highlighting the numerous possibilities for utilization.

There dinners arrived, and Sofia paused there to enjoy her meal.

Walter kept looking up at Sofia while he ate. He appeared to be in deep thought.

Sofia was feeling self-conscious and nervous.

Maybe she should have just kept it all to herself.

Ashton broke the quiet atmosphere, "So I hope you guys behaved yourselves while we were gone?"

Everyone laughed.

"Yes, we did. We played cards and went to shows." Frank smiled.

"We have our hangouts, you know." He chuckled.

Walter didn't comment. He was staring off into the air. His mind was working overtime.

Suddenly, Walter slapped the table, "You know, I think you have some great ideas there! I do have a lot of unused land. We just cut the grass, and that's it."

Sofia looked up in surprise, "Really?"

"Yes, I'm sure we can make much better use of my property. You'd have to let me check into what it would take for permits and such. I'll need more information on what you have in mind." Walter said.

"Yes, if you come up with some kind of plans, I may be able to call in a few favors," Frank added.

Sofia let out a major sigh. She took a drink of wine, "Are you guys serious? I can't believe it!"

"Sofia? I am not a young man anymore. I live alone, and I have no family. I could use some life around that giant property. If these ideas of yours will help my Rescue… I'm all in! How about we get together in your suite for dinner tomorrow night? You come up with a bit of a rough sketch of what you are thinking about. Later, we'll have to have an architectural design." Walter suggested.

"OMG……….. This is unreal! Ashton? They love my idea!" Sofia jumped in excitement.

"How about that Sofia…. see?... You are great at ideas. Why do you doubt yourself all the time?" Ashton replied.

"I just thought it was way too much to hope for. It would be a major undertaking." Sofia said.

"Yes," Walter added, "But a purposeful one. I'm sure we can make it happen."

"OK, let's end this dinner now. I'm too excited! I'll get some paper, pencils, and pens from the front desk. I'll do the best I can. I'm not good at drawing, but we'll see. Maybe Ashton can help." Sofia asked.

"Sure," he said, "I think I know what will work. We'll keep it simple."

They all stood up and headed out.

"Good night, everyone," Sofia yelled back as she almost ran down the hallway.

It was still early. That was a great thing.

"Put the coffee on, my love! I'll order some supplies." She said to Ashton.

Sofia changed into something comfortable, then awaited the things she ordered.

She poured a coffee and sat at the table.

"I still can't believe it," she said to Ashton, "It's such a big project."

"You forget who you're talking to," He reminded her, "These things are everyday business for my dad. Walter, too, has had his share of important projects."

"I guess you're right. They both are businessmen I'm just a dreamer!" She laughed.

The supplies arrived promptly, and Sofia immediately immersed herself in sketching out her ideas.

Ashton proposed the idea of using square boxes to represent the buildings, simplifying the process.

Her vision was straightforward and clear, offering multiple possibilities for construction, including the option of movable units if necessary.

The hope was that no unforeseen problems would arise during the implementation.

Sofia sat quietly, picturing all the details she had thought of. Her drawing wasn't too bad. It did look like what she wanted.

While she was touching up some lines, here and there, a couple of new additions came to light.

Taking a moment to reflect on the new ideas, she leaned back, contemplating them further.

She aimed to be well-prepared in case anyone had questions about her plans.

The feasibility of her setup was crucial to her, and she harbored hope that it would be deemed achievable.

With confidence in her concept, she anticipated its approval and warm reception.

Ashton took her work when she thought she was done.

He thought about it and loved her ideas.

"This would help out in so many ways," he stated, "I really like it! I can't see any reason for the City not to approve this. The zoning may be an obstacle, but that can be handled."

"Wow, I'm excited about this!" Ashton chuckled.

"Now…. Time!…. How are we to do this when we're never here for long? We would have to be overseeing every step." He added.

"Well," Sofia said, "Let's find out if Walters is with us on this first. Then, let's see if we can pull it off, as far as the city and building permits go."

"Yaa, we'll show this to Frank and Walter tomorrow night and see what they think. They'll know better than us." He replied.

"Ok, I'm off to bed. We both have early and hectic days ahead. Let's check on the puppies. I just love those babies! They are so well-behaved, too. I'm glad they adapt to just about anywhere." Sofia said.

The Puppies were asleep. Sofia and Ashton soon were as well.

Sofia's prediction proved accurate; the next day unfolded in a whirlwind of activity.

The ship was brimming with people, each with their own demands, and she and Robin found themselves darting around tirelessly.

By the time she returned to the suite, Sofia was utterly exhausted. However, her weariness didn't deter her from meeting with the two gentlemen.

Upon Ashton's invitation, they were welcomed for dinner in the suite, allowing Sofia to dress casually, a relief she expressed with a grateful, "Thanks, Hun... That helps."

After a rejuvenating shower, she spent some quality time playing with the pups until Frank and Walter arrived.

Ashton had prepared the table, and a delightful pasta night awaited them.

Sofia, expressing her hunger, declared, "Yum... I'm hungry!"

They ventured out onto the calm deck, where the lingering daylight provided a serene atmosphere.

The meals arrived, and they hastily finished their dinner, eager to delve into business.

Sofia eagerly presented her drawings to Walter, who scrutinized them intently.

He eventually laid the papers on the table, folded his arms, and sat in contemplative silence.

A nervous frown crept across Sofia's face, prompting her to glance at Ashton, who simply shrugged.

Ashton, recognizing the need to ease the tension, rose and fetched the wine, pouring glasses for everyone.

Frank patiently awaited Walter's thoughts as he picked up Sofia's designs, studying them carefully.

With raised eyebrows, he nodded in approval. He gave a thumbs up to Sofia.

She smiled nervously.

"Finally....," Walter spoke up.

"Sofia, where do you get your fantastic ideas? This is absolutely wonderful!" Walter appreciated her work.

Sofia let out a huge sigh of relief.

"This could work!" He spoke.

"I love it! You cover a few different needed situations here. You really thought this through!" He said while looking at the design.

"I'm In!" He said.

"OMG," Sofia blurted out, "You really think we could do this?"

"I don't see why not!" He responded.

Ashton raised his glass.

Cheers Everyone!

Yes…..Cheers!

Sofia, sensing the need to break the tension, went over and picked up the puppies, offering one to each man.

Their eyes lit up, and soon, they found themselves acting like kids, playing and cuddling with their furry companions.

Amidst the joyous atmosphere, Frank turned to Walter, expressing his enthusiasm for the concept. "Let me know what I can do to help make this happen. I really love this idea. I think it will attract more people to adopt these pets. I'll make a few calls tomorrow, starting with finding an architect."

Walter, placing the puppy down, stood up.

"Come on, Frank. We should let these two enjoy their evening. We can go down to our favorite hangout and go over this some more."

Frank followed suit, and they bid their good nights, leaving Sofia and Ashton to savor the rest of their evening.

Ashton and Sofia played awhile, the put the pups to bed.

They made themselves a coffee and sat out in the evening moonlight

Both were more relaxed and unwinding.

"Wow... First phase... Accomplished! I'm so happy!" Sofia exclaimed.

"It means a lot to me that they like my ideas. Can you imagine? Having a complex like that? It would be very useful all around! This would be a godsend on many levels!"

Ashton leaned over and kissed Sofia, "Like Walter and Frank both have said, never give up your dreams! Now, things are in motion. Let's cross our fingers and hope others will be on board. Time will tell."

"Ohhh..." Sofia broke in. "We'll have some decisions to make, as far as where we'll be working and how we can work this project in if it happens."

"Yeah, that's going to be quite a feat," Ashton replied, "We'll have to discuss it with my dad."

"I do have a couple of ideas about that," Sofia said. "I have thought about it too."

"Wow... Every time I blink, something is changing! First, the ship, now the rescue! Thank God we're still young," she laughed.

"We still have a lot of energy!" They both laughed.

"Okay, let's get some sleep. Another busy day at sea tomorrow! I'm mentally tired now." They got up and went to their room.

Sofia fell sound asleep in Ashton's arms in just a minute or so.

Ashton brushed his fingers through her long blonde hair, feeling content. He too was off in dreamland in no time.

No surprise, the morning came in a flash! With the light came a sprinkling of rain. That made their morning coffee taste even better.

The air was warm and fresh.

Sofia was in a very energetic mood. She wanted the day to go by just as fast as the night did.

They enjoyed a breakfast of fine pastries. As they poured another coffee, there was a knock at the door.

Ashton opened it to find Robin.

"Sorry to bother you. I was just passing by and thought I'd take a chance you'd be free." Robin said.

"Sure, come on in… I'll get you a coffee." He said.

"Great," she said.

"Good morning, Sofia!" She said.

"Hey, have a seat." Ashton brought coffee and a plate of pastries.

"Ohhh.... Looks and smells wonderful!" Robin stated.

"What brings you by, Hun?" Sofia looked at Robin.

"Well, I thought I'd let you know. We'll be doing heavy training this week. Admin has arranged for a group to board on Thursday. Tomorrow, we dock in Curacao, then Thursday in St. Lucia. You can get off there and have another week at home if you would like." Robin said.

"It looks like things are getting back to normal as far as staffing goes. We've been getting a lot of responses for applications. Have you decided at all on what you'd like to do?"

Robin sipped her coffee and took a bite of pastry.

Sofia glanced at Ashton, "Well, we were going to talk to you about that."

She went on to tell her what was in the works, "I think, with these new plans, maybe we'd be better off staying with Exotic. As much as we love the ship, it would be best to keep it for our vacations."

Robin agreed, "Yaa, it would be very difficult going back and forth from here. I will be sad to see you go, that's for sure. It's been great having you here, and you've been a great help. But.... I understand. So, should we call Wednesday your last day?"

Ashton spoke up, "Sure, that sounds great." Sofia agreed.

"Ok, I'll take that to admin, and they can take it from there. Oh, I'll miss you guys! Now I'm sad." Robin became emotional.

"Ohh, you know we'll be back lots of times. We have this beautiful suite! Look! Even the puppies are content here." They tried to soothe her.

"OMG…I'll miss them!" She went over and started mauling them.

Ashton and Sofia laughed.

"So I guess I'll see you shortly. We have a busy day. There are a ton of events going on." They said.

"That's ok, the day will go fast. Thanks for breakfast, guys!" Robin replied.

"Any time, Robin, see you in 15 minutes," Sofia responded.

"Yaa, I guess I should get ready, too. I'm sure we'll be busy as well." Ashton said.

They both rushed to get going.

They ensured the pups were taken care of—fed and provided with plenty of water. After a hug and a kiss, they were off.

As predicted, the day unfolded as a whirlwind of activity. Sofia and Robin remained tirelessly engaged for hours.

Sofia, sensing the busyness, asked Robin if she was sure about letting them go on Thursday.

She offered to stay on if needed.

Robin reassured Sofia, saying no, they would have lots of help.

"Well, if you change your mind, just let me know," Sofia replied.

"Thanks, Sofia. I think it's time we fend for ourselves now," Robin said with gratitude.

They navigated through each event and attended to each guest's request one at a time. As the day came to an end, Sofia said, "Whew... That was hectic! We may need new shoes!" She laughed, and Robin agreed.

"Okay, I'm going to put my feet up now," Sofia announced, "Maybe I can get a foot massage out of Ashton!"

"Ohhhh... I wish! Lucky you!" Robin replied.

"Okay, I'll see you in the morning. Good night." Sofia replied.

"Night, Sofia," Robin waved.

Ashton was already there when Sofia came in.

He had wine on the table, along with a variety of petite sandwiches, shrimp cocktails, and salad.

Sofia entered the deck area and dropped into her chair.

"I'm done!" she said as she sipped her wine. "That was a brutal day."

"Well we don't run around like you two. You must be exhausted." He replied.

"How about a hot tub and foot massage?" Sofia asked.

"Ohh, I think that could be arranged. I'll see what I can do." Ashton replied.

Sofia closed her eyes for a moment. Then, they picked up the sandwiches and had some salad.

Ashton put the Shrimp in the fridge for later. They both changed for the hot tub.

They brought their wine and slowly climbed into the soothing water.

"Ahhhhh.... I needed this," Sofia stated, "My body is sore and tired."

"Two more days! I think that's great. Then back home. I'm so anxious about what Walter will find out. I hope there are no problems with our Idea." She said nervously.

Ashton nodded, "I think, one way or another. We can make it happen."

Sofia sat up and turned to Ashton.

"I think maybe we should have a serious talk here. We are going to need a lot of time for this project. We should think about what we're doing as far as Exotic Airlines is concerned. Are we going back... Are we going to just concentrate on the rescue?" Sofia suggested, bringing up the need to discuss their future plans and priorities.

"Yaa... There are so many changes again! We've got to be crazy!" He said.

They laughed.

"I thought I would be staying at Exotic for the rest of my career!" Sofia stated, "I loved the short travel experiences. Now, I'm just torn."

Ashton took a thoughtful sip of his wine. "Let me see what I can do about that. Maybe I'll give Kyle a call. He may have some suggestions. After all, he's the one who makes up the schedules."

"Yaa, that's a good idea," Sofia agreed. "When we get home. He's gone now for the day. I'll also talk to my dad. He seems to like our ideas. Maybe he could come up with a game plan also. He's very easy." They considered seeking advice from those around them to navigate the complexities of their future plans.

"OMG Ashton. Do you realize how much life has been changing? Almost every week or month, something comes along, and we're going for a different ride! First... Exotic happened. I thought I'd be there forever." Sofia contemplated on her thoughts.

"Then... now... the cruise ship... And, I really do enjoy it here. I had thoughts of living on this ship for a long time! But... then the Rescue. It would be very hard to be in both places. The travel would be crazy! The ship is hard to plan, as far as timing goes. Not all the islands are guaranteed to have flights out when we dock there." She added.

"So, my thoughts go back to exotic. They are only short trips away. We would still be able to oversee the expansion and still be able to work. I don't know. This all came about so fast! What are your thoughts, Hun?" She asked.

"Well, I'm pretty sure I know what we're going to do. But there are a lot of obstacles to conquer first. I think we should go back on Thursday, as planned, and then see what happens. Maybe Walter and Frank will have something for us. Maybe not. We're not yet sure 100% we can do this." Ashton replied.

"Ohhh, I hope so," Sofia stated, "It would be such a good thing for the City and for the animals. I'm on pins and needles here."

"Wow, wouldn't it be great to see it happen? It doesn't seem real! Just picture it, Ashton. The people coming and going and wanting to rescue those poor pets? I don't think I ever wanted anything more in my life! Something is telling me not to give up hope. The suspense is killing me now, though." Sofia jumped in excitement.

Ashton hugged her and kissed her passionately. Then, he reached for his wine.

Sofia took her glass of wine.

"Where will we be a month from now?" Sofia anticipated.

"We'll need to have patience! Time will tell." Ashton pondered, acknowledging the uncertainty of their future and the importance of allowing events to unfold in due course.

CHEERS!

Could Sofia and Ashton be able to build their empire?

Cross your fingers!

Printed in the USA
CPSIA information can be obtained
at www.ICGtesting.com
LVHW012306010424
776112LV00045B/344